For Freedom's Cause

Books by Barry Smith

The Kimberley Trilogy
For Freedom's Cause
Battle for the North
Kimberley Kill

For Freedom's Cause

Barry Smith

For Freedom's Cause

Published by Barry Smith

First published 2011
This edition published 2016

© 2011 Barry Smith

All rights reserved. Without limiting the rights under copyright above, no part of this publication shall be reproduced, stored in or introduced into a retrieval system or transmitted in any form or by any means (electronic, mechanical, photocopying, recording or otherwise) without the prior permission of both the copyright owner and the publisher of this book

This is a work of historical fiction. Please be aware that this novel is set in the Australia of the 1920s when times were different regarding attitudes towards the treatment of the Indigenous people of Australia. This book seeks to reflect the lives and treatment of Aboriginal people in the Kimberley outback and on cattle stations at that time. It does not represent 21st Century views nor the opinions of the author.

Cover photographs reproduced courtesy of the Manchester Regiment Museum and Archive, Tameside Metropolitan Borough Council and The Victorian Pictorial Roll of Honour.

A Cataloguing-in-Publication record is available from the National Library of Australia.

ISBN:
978 0 9871779 6 4 (pbk)
978 0 9871779 7 1 (ebk)

www.faceboook.com/BarrySmithWordSpinner

Dedication

This book is dedicated to my grandfathers who fought in the First World War and whose memory inspired me to write it.

Charles Henry Bevan – Corporal in the Green Howards, who saw action on the Somme and at Ypres, finished the war as a prisoner of the Germans and survived to sing nursery rhymes as he dandled me on his knee.

A copy of the letter that King George wrote and signed, welcoming him home from captivity, is printed on the following page.

Daniel Smith – Private in the 11th Battalion of the Manchester Regiment who died in fighting near Cape Helles on the Gallipoli Peninsula on 22nd August 1915. Although I never knew him I am proud to have visited his memorial in Turkey and left a commemoration on behalf of myself and my brother, Charles.

Age shall never weary them.

Cpl. Bevan
38806

BUCKINGHAM PALACE

1918.

The Queen joins me in welcoming you on your release from the miseries & hardships, which you have endured with so much patience & courage.

During these many months of trial, the early rescue of our gallant Officers & Men from the cruelties of their captivity has been uppermost in our thoughts.

We are thankful that this longed for day has arrived, & that back in the old Country you will be able once more to enjoy the happiness of a home & to see good days among those who anxiously look for your return.

George R.I.

Acknowledgements

My grateful thanks to

Rae – My constant muse.
Coral and Maritsa – For perceptively sharp but kindly observations.
Jennifer – For so much know-how and assertive encouragement.
Sandra – My dearest friend.
For always being there for me and believing in me over so many years.

Contents

1.	Alexandria, Egypt, 1916	1
2.	Manchester, England, 1913/14	4
3.	Melbourne, Australia, 1914	14
4.	Manchester, England, 1914/15	21
5.	Near Mansfield, Victoria, Australia, 1914	30
6.	Manchester, England, 1915	34
7.	Anzac Cove, Turkey, 1915	38
8.	Melbourne, Australia, 1915/16	44
9.	Western Front, Belgium/France, 1917/18	52
10.	Western Front, France, 1917	58
11.	A Home Fit For Heroes	63
12.	Taking to the Dream Road	66
13.	Back Down-Under	72
14.	Law Without Order	75
15.	Irish Troubles	80
16.	Manchester Once More	88
17.	Melbourne Unrest	95
18.	Dan Down-Under	100
19.	Liza, Elspeth and Bill	104
20.	Down, Up and Out of the Mine	108
21.	Elspeth Plays Her Hand	112
22.	The Secret Army	114
23.	Brothers in Arms	118
24.	Going West	123
25.	No Peace in Perth	129
26.	Heading North	142
27.	At the Kimberley Station	151
28.	Together at Last	155
29.	Duty Calls, Once More	168
30.	The Peace of Home	181
31.	No More War	186

1
Alexandria, Egypt
1916

Through the shimmering haze of an Alexandrian afternoon, Dan Bevan's attention was drawn to a group of men playing a strange game. Whilst his own passion was soccer, being born and bred in the home of Manchester United, he had seen Wigan miners, back at the barracks, playing rugby league with a similar oval shaped ball. But these men were playing a game he had neither seen nor heard of before. He wondered what sort of white men would exert themselves like this at the hottest time of a North African day.

They were booting the ball to each other over distances in excess of thirty to forty yards and the would-be receivers leaped high in the air, jostling and grappling with each other to take it cleanly, before crashing to earth with bone jarring thuds on the sun-baked, iron-hard surface of the parade ground. But even more bizarre was the way they hand-passed over their opponents' heads in high looping arcs, by giving the ball a prodigious one handed punch. Clearly there was no offside rule as teammates stood, seemingly unpenalised, in all parts of the field, both in front of and behind the play.

He had barely stopped to watch when, suddenly, high to his left the ball plummeted towards him full out of the blinding sun. He just had time to pull down the brim of his solar tope, to limit the glare, when he found himself running forward and instinctively, leaping to catch it before it hit the ground.

This was the last thing he remembered, until he awoke later that afternoon in the casualty centre of the British military hospital. As consciousness returned and before his vision came back into focus, he heard a male voice exclaim.

"*Look! He's coming round. Thank Christ for that. Thought for a minute Charlie you'd done 'im in.*" Close on the heels of this strange exclamation came another slightly smoother, but no less nasal voice, saying,

"G'day mate, how are you going? Sorry about the shirtfront. Mistook you for one of our blokes. Still, wasn't a bad mark for a new chum."

Slowly it dawned on Dan that the voice was addressing him.

Standing on either side of the bed were two soldiers in khaki uniforms of a much finer grade and trim than the shoddy British army issue that he was forced to endure. The one, with a voice like a rusty cement mixer, was a lean rangy Sergeant of a dark and dusky complexion and the other, who had spoken directly to him, was a giant of a man, well over six feet tall, whose uniform sported an army Captain's insignia. He must have tipped the scales at sixteen stone or more. Presumably this was the one called Charlie.

The Sergeant departed with a cheery wave to Dan and a nod to his boss and before Dan could recover from his daze and muster a passable salute, he felt the firm but considerate restraint of the officer's hand, pushing him back onto his pillow and absolving him from his discomfort with an off-hand, *"Don't even think of it, mate, we're not too big on that bull dust in our lot."*

This gave Dan pause to take a more considered look at his visitor, whose tanned complexion almost matched the burnished hue of his Sam Browne belt. His hair was jet black with faint touches of gray and he sported a luxuriant walrus moustache, which, along with the feather in his bush hat and rising sun badge, tagged him as an officer in the Australian Light Horse.

"So, what happened?" said Dan, conscious of his own, sun-blotched, freckled face and flat Mancunian vowels, *"and what am I doing here?"*

"Well, you tried your hand at Aussie rules football and mistaking you for one of our players I put a strong tackle on you, which caught you unprepared. Sorry about that mate, no harm intended. As a matter of fact the blokes were pretty impressed with the way you went for the ball, with me bearing down. I've got a bit of a reputation for taking no prisoners on the footy field."

"No offence taken." replied Dan, reaching out to shake Charlie's outstretched hand, *"I take it your name's Charlie, mine's Dan."*

"Glad to make your acquaintance." The Australian replied and added with a wry smile. *"Could have been under better circumstances, but looks as though there's no permanent harm done."*

"Well, at least nothing the Turks haven't tried on me already." Dan replied with a rueful grin.

For the next hour, they got down to becoming better acquainted, with the usual enquiries about where they came from, what they did before the war and where they had fought. It seemed they had just got into their stride and were deep in comparing their roles in the recent failure in the Dardanelles when the ward sister burst in and having chided Captain Elliott for smoking his extremely pungent pipe near a patient, brought an end to their meeting and drove Dan's visitor away.

He was discharged from hospital the next day and within the week was away with his regiment to Mesopotamia where he was to join Maude's force in the attempt to revenge the defeat at Al-Kut and open up the road to Baghdad. The Light Horse was off to Palestine and he wondered how and where Charlie's war would end. They had exchanged addresses but neither had any real expectation of meeting up again.

2

Manchester, England
1913/14

A large crowd had gathered around the gas lamp on the street corner. Under a sea of cloth caps, the men snugged mufflers tighter under their chins and shrank deeper into their coats, in a vain attempt to keep out the relentless drizzle, whilst a few women clutched their shawls tighter around their heads and shoulders, some sheltering kids from the cold and wet of a Manchester winter's night. They had come to hear the German speak.

It was a rotten night and a street in Ancoats in mid winter, was a rotten place to attend a public meeting. But it wasn't every day you got the chance to see and hear the nephew of Friedrich Engels talking about the sorry condition of the English working class, in the very place where his uncle researched and wrote his famous revolutionary book.

Dan Bevan had never been of a socialist inclination, even though he had started in Bradford pit at the age of fourteen, tending the pit ponies under ground. Nor was he more than a compliant union member during his five years as a collier, working twelve-hour shifts, hacking and shoveling to meet his daily tally of Lancashire coal. Now that he had been promoted to Deputy and was studying at night for his mining engineer's ticket, he was considered to be a management man and his ambitions rose far beyond these grimy, treeless streets. To him, Communism was no more than an interesting foreign philosophy, to be debated with his mates over a pint in the vault, after classes were done.

But this area was his home, where he had been born and raised and though the fortunate possession of a good head for figures and the rare chance to study were pushing him up and out of this place, they were still his people and he was curious to hear what this man could say that could make one jot of difference to the opinions and condition of such folk.

It was hard to make out the speaker's features under the umbrella that warded off the rain and shielded him from the light of the lamp.

But the voice was strong and despite his guttural and heavily accented English, it carried clearly and was easily heard even through the steamy damp cloud hovering above the drenched, but attentive gathering.

"Comrades! You may have heard of my uncle, Friedrich Engels and some of you might even have worked at his mill. He never forgot you. He always spoke of you fondly and your coming out to hear me on such a night proves him right when he said Mancunians are an honest, hardworking people who will always stand up for a righteous cause.

Well, what more righteous cause could there be than your right to a roof over your head, bread on your table and a decent well paid job to pay for these necessities. My enemies claim that I speak theoretical twaddle, but I am here to speak of your real needs and rights and to show you they can become a reality, here on earth, not in some distant heaven of the parsons dreaming and the mill owners promising."

It was clear that he had done this before and knew how to grab the attention of people like these and hold it until he had done. This was not the place for Hegel, the Dialectic or the withering away of the state. They wanted to hear about better housing, permanent jobs, schooling for their kids and the prospect of higher pay. He knew it and gave it to them straight from the heart, constantly referring to his uncle's time spent working in the mill at Ermond and Engels and his understanding and care for the working men and women of the North, which had inspired him and Marx to design a new society in which the worker was king.

Dan admired his oratory but found the content too thin to risk a further drenching and was about to be on his way, when the speaker made the fatal error of suggesting complicity between the Kaiser and their King;

"If Britain and Germany should go to war, you will be the losers, not the almighty Kaiser Bill and his cousin, your King George. They will be safely behind the lines, drinking champagne in their palaces whilst you fight, bleed and die in some European field."

A sea-change came over the crowd. Tolerant silence was broken by loud interjections, which soon gave way to the growing rumble of an angry mob. He had been on safe ground denouncing the accelerating naval arms race and greed of those who stood to grow even richer from the bloodshed and sacrifice of workers, if England were drawn into war. But then, happy as they were to laugh at the strutting antics of Kaiser Bill, his cousin George was another matter and above all, he was both their King and head of the Empire, under whose flag many of them had fought and served. The rumble rose to a roar and then, as soon as he had been spirited away and a squad of constables had taken up position across the street, they sang the national anthem and dispersed good naturedly, in search of hot fish and chips and the last round of beer.

Dan was relieved that a riot had been averted and drifted along with the cheerful, homeward throng. But, he was troubled by the contradiction between their poverty of living, their veneration for royalty and the miseries armed conflict with Germany would surely bring. He spotted the Guardian's man talking with a police sergeant and looked forward to seeing what Scott's editorial in the morning paper, would say.

The warmth of the public bar at the Church inn, fueled by two roaring coal fires, soon thawed his bones and a pint of Chester's and the cheerful exchanges of some of his miners soon restored his good humour. He was greeted by a man who was selling his wares from a wicker basket, balanced on his head.

"Ow do Dan." He said, tossing him a paper bag of cockles and whelks. "Ere, get these inside yer."

Catching the treat and supping at his first pint, he slipped into the nearest settle, all set for some banter and chat.

Whilst at first, the talk was focused on United's chances on Saturday, against Stoke, it soon turned to the meeting, which most occupants of the bar had attended. Again, he was struck by the distinction the men made between toffs and mine owners, for whom they had little regard and the Royal family, on the other hand, who still seemed to merit the afterglow of esteem, if not adulation that had been Victoria's due until her death, earlier in this new century. The old men, playing dominoes and cribbage on the fringe of the discussion group, some of them, having fought with Roberts in Afghanistan and on the South African veldt, were still staunchly for king and country, but had their doubts about fighting the Krauts.

"They won't cut and run like the Pathans, yer know," said one veteran. "They're like us, only there's a lot more of 'em."

"King George ought to have a word with Kaiser Bill and tell 'im to stop this bloody daft battleship race," said another.

He let himself into his digs quietly, so as not to disturb his landlady and before going upstairs, banked up the fire, piling coke on top of precious coal to damp it down and saving having to relight it at the ungodly hour when he would rise and ride his bike to the pit. He smiled thankfully at sight of his brew can and snap tin on the table, which contained thick cheese and onion sandwiches and tea and sugar in twists of newspaper. That was one less job for him to do, in the freezing dawn.

The hot water bottle had taken the worst of the damp and chill off the sheets and before he drifted off to sleep, Dan recalled the conversations in the pub and he agreed that the old boys had made a good point. But, if war came, it couldn't last long and until it ended, coal would be in even greater demand and he and his men would be considered far more useful at the mine than getting involved in any fighting.

The persistent rat a tat of the knocker-up's cane on his bedroom window brought him surging to wakefulness from the deepest of sleeps. It was pitch-black outside and there was ice on the inside of the window. He groped for his matches and lit the gas mantle to signal he was up and send the knocker-up on the way to his next victim. As he groped under the blankets for his clothes, which were still warm from the bed, he could hear the cheeky chatter of lasses and the clatter of their clog irons on the cobblestones, as they set off to start the early shift, down at the mill. It was high time he was on his way.

Coasting down the brew past the cemetery, he felt his hands almost freeze to the handlebars of his bike, but then the inevitable up stretch from the gasworks set his blood racing and brought him puffing and panting to the gate of Johnson's wire works, just as the first opening of the furnace door bathed everything in its fiery orange glow. Not such a bad job, he thought, on a morning like this. Waving to Alf, the colliery gateman, Dan sped across the yard and secured his steed in the shed.

The pit was a hive of action. Steam belched from the winding house as cage loads of pitmen began the gut-wrenching plunge to their day's work far below. Soon he was with them, he and the safetyman, checking the underground road ahead for gas and testing the props that shored up the roof, before giving them the all clear for the shift to begin.

Dan's was a family of miners. His dad had come up from the Rhonda valley in South Wales in the late 1880's and continued his career underground. He met and married Dan's mam, a year later, at the Moravian chapel in Wheeler Street and barely a year after, they returned to christen their son. He had idolised his dad and although Dan's grasp of the three 'Rs' greatly exceeded his old man's, there was a kindly wisdom and tenderness beneath the rock hard veneer of stubbornness that his dad presented to the world and all, but a chosen few, who were dear to him or who had succeeded in living up to his exacting standards and winning his trust.

It was thanks to the company rule that relatives must work on different shifts that he was not down with his father's crew when a methane gas explosion brought the gallery roof down on top of them, killing him instantly with all of his mates. His mother never got over the shock and two years later, she fell victim to a deadly strain of the flu and died in Ancoats hospital of pneumonia and a broken heart.

The light had gone out of Dan's world and at the age of eighteen he thought it would never come back again. But, despite his sorrow and shock at this double loss, he was not as alone as he thought. The pit's chief engineer, Arthur Evans, had always had a soft spot for young Dan, especially as he had no kids of his own and he quickly took the grieving youth under his wing and together with his widowed sister, Beatrice, offered him a place in their home and their hearts.

The tragedy had closed off one life and had opened up another, which would surprise, challenge and puzzle him in so many previously inconceivable ways. From this moment Dan was steeped in the Manchester school of hard work and self-help liberalism, that had motivated its citizens to fight for the franchise, free trade, the repeal of the combination acts, which had made modern industrial trade unions possible and the founding of friendly societies and cooperatives that would outlive his generation and the one after.

'Beattie' Brown, as everyone called Beatrice, had been married to a struggling parson who had sacrificed his youth and ultimately his health, to missionary work in India. Never was he to know anyone so thrifty by nature. She was so afraid of the stigma of a pauper's grave that she even contributed sixpence a week to a burial fund to ensure she went out in appropriate style and was not beholden to anyone in the hereafter, even to her prosperous brother. She taught Dan that you should look after your money very carefully and other-people's twice as well. This was to be advice that would serve him well all of his life and though she was close with money and sparing with her emotional self, nonetheless, he learned from her the difference between meanness and financial prudence and that both discipline and kindness could go together, hand in hand.

Arthur, on the other hand, was his mentor and inspiration and opened up to Dan whole worlds of possibility that he had never known before. Not only was he a fine engineer and well read, but also a man of the world, having marched up the Khyber Pass to Kabul with the colours and lived to tell the tale, mined for gold in Kalgoorlie and diamonds on the Rand. At weekends he walked Dan along canals, under railway bridges, through stations and shunting yards, extolling the engineering feats of the men who had made the industrial revolution possible and who, along with the muck, had brought money and jobs to the north.

Also, from Arthur, he learned to appreciate the classical repertoire of the Hallé orchestra and after attending political rallies at the Free Trade Hall and challenging lectures at the philosophical society, Dan was schooled to argue both sides of each proposition and persuasion, not to accept things on face value and never to close off his mind. He was encouraged to explore the origins of English liberalism, by delving into the works of Locke, Bentham and Mill and to learn from the examples of the mill owner philanthropists, that men and women could be employed, both productively and humanely, to the mutual satisfaction of owners as well as those who managed and made.

It was at Arthur's instigation and through his recommendation that Dan was enrolled in night school studies that led to his gaining licensed membership of the Institute of Engineers. But it was through his own hard work and character that he earned the right to exchange his pick for the Deputy's helmet and badge of office. His father would have wondered at this crossing the line between worker and boss but there is no doubt he would have been mightily proud. Although it was Arthur's influence that had encouraged him to practise individual liberalism in the way that he approached life, work and the management of his men, it was from his father that Dan had learned to present a front of stubborn, flint-hard resolve to those who dared resist him or could not meet his exacting demands. Only the most trusted of his male companions and the few women to whom he was close, both dared and were allowed, to tell him how sad it was that others could not experience the sensitivity, fun and compassion he hid so well behind the inscrutable mask of his enigmatic smile.

The strident blast of the pithead steam whistle announced the end of the shift. Cage loads of tired but thankful men, cheered by the prospect of a bath by the fire, some slap and tickle before tea and a night of darts or billiards down at the club, were happy to be plucked whole and alive back out into the premature dark of the winter's afternoon.

Dan enjoyed the privilege of the management bathhouse and although the telltale blue-black miner's eye-shadow gave away his profession, he cycled home more comfortable and cleaner clad than the men who trudged beside him or rattled by on the brightly lit double deck trams. His thoughts were of tea and after that, some good fireside chat. It was

Sunday tomorrow and Beattie had promised steak and kidney pudding, his favourite treat.

The summer of 1914 arrived in its usually hesitant fashion but, despite the frequent showers and less than warming sun, Dan planned to seize the opportunity of a bright dry Sunday morning to get out of town, stretch his legs and treat his lungs to a dose of fresh upland air. The early Sunday special was so packed with hikers, ramblers and picnickers heading for Lime Park, that Dan was hard pressed to find a clear space amongst the piles of rucksacks, hampers and brollies, in a crowded carriage. With a jerk and a shudder the train started on its way and was soon clickety-clacketing through the southern suburbs to the accompaniment of a cheerful young chorus, singing with more gusto than tone, *"I'm a rambler, I'm a rambler from Manchester way and I tek all me pleasure the 'ard moorland way…"*

At Edale railway station, a stream of walkers flowed onto the platform and poured through the ticket barrier, before breaking into club groups and private parties, which set off vigorously to all points of the compass intent on either hard High Peak tracks or gentle meanders down soft limestone dales.

Dan held back to let them get a head start so that he would have the way to himself and then, just as he was getting started an energetic young couple called out to him.

"Hello Dan. Fancy meeting you here? Where are you off to?"

"I'm off over the top and down to Castleton."

"That's where we are going too. Let's team up and go together."

Arm in arm with his good friends Ted and Eliza Miller, he set off to walk over the top to Mam Tor and on down to Castleton, passing the Blue John mine along the way. His intention to enjoy the quiet of his own company rapidly gave way to the pleasurable anticipation of their cheerful companionship.

Edward Miller, who taught French and German at Manchester Grammar School and Elizabeth Smith, who supervised the girls at a Chadderton Mill, had befriended Dan after he shared a table with them at a meat and potato pie supper they had organised, to raise money for the local Ragged School. Whilst Ted came from a comfortable middle class home in the smart suburb of Didsbury, Elizabeth hailed from the back streets of Oldham but, both Ted and Liza, as they preferred to be called by those who were familiar with them, were equally committed to helping people less fortunate than themselves. They devoted their spare time to helping feed the needy, using their talents in teaching poor girls to read, write, cook and sew and they organised an annual outing to the seaside, for those who were disabled or could not afford to go.

Their initial chatter subsided and lapsed into the complicit silence of fellow sufferers, as they crossed the style over the dry-stone wall at the edge of the village, broke into single file and began the long steep trek up through the scattered and unperturbed black-faced sheep, intent on ascending to the distant head of the dale. Soon, they were shedding their woolen jackets as the heat of their exertion began to tell and both men, despite feigning chivalrous tolerance in response to Liza's appeal for a rest, were secretly relieved to take a breather and slake their thirsts with refreshing gulps of fresh icy water from the beck that coursed down beside them, replenished and swollen by overnight rain.

When they had drained their enamel mugs, they began to share news of their homes and their work, until a wisp of black cloud shadowed the sun and a chill spatter of rain sent them scrambling onward and upward to the top of the ridge. Dan was pleased to see them so at ease with each other. They had been wed for two years now but friends had feared they were too socially mismatched for the marriage to last. Ted was a charmer and a dreamer who saw nothing but good in everyone he met. He had spent a year teaching English at a Berlin Gymnasium and had returned full of enthusiasm for the diligence and discipline of his pupils and a head full of theories about workers rights and social equality that had flourished for a short time in many German industrial centres, until the Prussian Aristocracy and military classes had checked them with a more than firm restraining hand. He would have applauded that winter's night speech in Ancoats, a few months ago.

Liza, on the other hand, had grown up in a family of six children, which had survived on the sole earnings of her loom hand mother, after her father had died prematurely, by slipping on ice and falling under a speeding tram on Oldham Road. She had known the pinch of poverty and whilst she shared Ted's concern for the growing inequalities in wealth between those who owned and invested and those who toiled in mines, factories and mills, Liza was a hard headed pragmatist, who believed that a remedy had to be based more on education and merit than through state sponsored charity and political unrest. But despite these differences in outlook, they were devoted to each other and very much in love.

It was Liza who broke the silence as, with relief and satisfaction, they reached the top.

"What do you make of that business in Bosnia Dan and is it likely to affect us?"

Before he could reply, Ted jumped in, eager to air his knowledge of central European diplomacy and what the Germans were likely to do.

"There's a Germanic kinship between Vienna and Berlin and likewise a common Slavic origin has made the Russians the protectors of the Serbs. So the Germans and Russians are bound to take opposite sides in any dispute between Vienna and Belgrade."

"But could it lead to war?" Dan asked.

"I doubt it. It will probably lead to a lot of Great Power threats and sabre rattling that will subside after a brief and not too serious chastisement of Belgrade by the Austrians, with Germany and Russia looking on to ensure honours are even and that things do not get out of hand. After all," he reasoned, "It can't be all that serious if the Kaiser is going on his annual cruise up to the north cape of Norway and anyway, aren't the royal houses of Britain, Germany and Russia too closely related to ever go to war against each other?"

Dan remembered the fickle Ancoats' crowd and said, "I'm not so certain. But I can see no reason for us getting involved, even if France backs Russia. We have no treaty obligation to go to the aid of the French."

Liza stopped at the end of the ridge and pictured the expanse of the Lancashire and Cheshire plain, just beyond her view, with its dwindling corridors of trees and fields squeezed between the expanding industrial cities and the tangled arteries of railways roads and canals. She summed up their collective thoughts and feelings by expressing the devout wish that he was right.

"I hope so, for the sake of all the young men down there and the women who depend on them."

After this somber reflection, they went on, merrily, casting their cares away on the gusting Pennine wind and no more serious thought or word crossed their minds or left their lips throughout the length of the day's hike. Just before dusk, tired and happy, they dropped down from the darkening moor into the lighted streets of Castleton and by bus and then train they were soon conveyed and deposited back into the centre of Manchester.

Manchester | England | 1913/14

Coming out of the station and walking across town, they soon realised that this was no ordinary Sunday night. The usually empty streets were full of people, some with union jacks, some singing land of hope and glory and all heading towards the Town Hall in Albert Square. Ted approached a policeman and asked him what all the to-do was about. When he came back to them his face was ashen and grasping his arm in support, Liza said,

"What's up Love?" and after a deep sigh he gasped, *"Germany's marching on France straight through poor little Belgium and now we are in it too."*

"Bloody hell!" Dan swore. *"Who would have thought it?*

I'd better be going. There'll be lots to do at the pit tomorrow and I must get home to see what Arthur wants me to do."

After thanking them for a lovely day and each urging the other to take care, they parted in true Lancashire fashion, wishing each other, *"God bless!"*

Dan strode away, up Market Street and across Piccadilly, heading for home with pain in his heart and much to trouble his mind.

3

Melbourne, Australia
1914

A world away in Australia, Charles Elliott stood in the bedroom bay window of his elegant, East Melbourne house, holding on to Alice's hand, as they gazed out across the rooftops on a chilly August morning. They had just got the news of Britain's declaration of war on Germany and were contemplating the inevitability of Australia's joining in.

"I'm sure we'll be in it Alice. *The old country's really going to be up against it fighting the Central Powers. If it wasn't for the navy, they might be in danger of invasion."*

"I fear you are right Charles, but if our men enlist it will be voluntary and surely your work at the bar is too important for you to be expected to go?"

His response evaded her question, *"Volunteers, from each of our colonies, went to fight in South Africa, but this will be the first time that Australia will be sending our men to war."*

The morning sun lit up the eastern face of the tower of St Patrick's Cathedral and Charles wondered, *"How will our Roman Catholic prelate react to the news?"*

Daniel Mannix had only arrived in Australia last year but the pro-Irish independence stance he espoused would suggest that he would be less than supportive of any Australian contribution to Britain's cause.

It was time Charlie was off to his chambers, as there was much to prepare before his appearance in the Supreme Court later that day. He turned and after tenderly embracing his wife of six months, he kissed her farewell and taking his coat and hat from the maid, strode out towards the Fitzroy Gardens and the southern end of Spring Street, where he would just have time to duck into the Windsor Hotel and see what was on the go.

Even before he entered the hotel's dining room he could hear the bass rumble of many male voices coming from that usual oasis of considered calm. Inside it was bedlam. Not since the day when the Prince of Wales called in, after the Federation ceremony at the Exhibition Building, had there been such a turn-out of leading Melburnians and so early in the morning. All the tables were occupied by the usual cliques and, exchanging greetings and shaking hands with professional contacts and friends as he went, Charles navigated his way across the crowded room to a table close to the fire where a group of his former Geelong Grammar school mates were gathered in unprecedented numbers.

"*G'day Charlie!*" they chorused and invited him to *"Pull up a pew and have some tea and toast. Afraid they've run out of kippers but, there are still some boiled eggs and plenty of toast."*

At school Charles had been a good if not spectacular scholar. Good enough to take honours in law at Melbourne University and proceed to the bar, where he specialised in both matters commercial and constitutional. But to the old boys of his generation he was affectionately known as 'crusher Elliott' because of his fearless tackling prowess on the footy field and to his familiars just plain Charlie. But, to his mother, wife and immediate family, he was always a much more dignified Charles.

"What do you think Charlie? Surely we'll be in it and can we get there in time before the Poms and Frogs have all the fun?" asked Fred Jones, one of the more headstrong and thoughtless members of the Geelong push.

"You had better ask those blokes over there Fred," Charlie flung back, pointing to a table in a far corner, set at a discreet distance from those in its vicinity, where the Prime Minister and Labor leader, Andrew Fisher, were deep in discussion with the Attorney General, Billy Hughes, and of all people, the editors of the Argus and Age.

"That's a devil's crew if ever there was one." He added.

Parliament had sat late on the previous night debating the crisis and no doubt, after that the Cabinet had convened to confirm Australia's stance. This meeting must have been in preparation for a public announcement. Not that there could be much doubt about the decision especially as Labor was likely to win the upcoming election and given Fisher's recent pledge to support Great Britain, 'to the last man and the last shilling.' Nonetheless, Charlie would have loved to be within earshot of their deliberations.

On another table he spotted the ageing Edmond Barton, who still sat on the High Court bench, conferring with the chairman of the Commonwealth Bank and that reminded him that he must contact his broker for advice on how the market would react to a probable declaration of war. Finishing his toast, he bade his companions cheerio and left the table, heading for the cloakroom. In the passage he passed Andrew (Banjo) Paterson, who had been a war correspondent during the South African campaign and was back working as a journalist with the Sydney Morning Herald.

"*This will be a bad one.*" Paterson confided, with a reflective sigh.

"Yes," said Charlie, "*The Germans will be a far tougher nut to crack than those Boer farmers, not that they were easy, according to my old man.*"

"*He is absolutely right.*" Banjo agreed, continuing on his way. Collecting his hat and coat from the attendant, Charlie sped out the door down Spring street into a Collins street, bustling with clerks heading for their offices and echoing to the clatter of cable trams crossing the junction points and the raucous cries of newsboys yelling,

"*Read all about it, Diggers going to war!*"

The morning passed quickly and just before the lunch recess, the presiding Supreme Court judge took the unprecedented step of halting the case before him to announce to a hushed courtroom,

"*It is my sad duty to advise you that the Prime Minister has announced that Australia has declared war on Germany and her allies. I am sure you will all join me in praying for a speedy victory and the safe return of our men who will soon join the war in Europe.*"

It was unlikely that he would ever again pronounce such a heavy judgement. Charlie shared the grave external demeanour of his gowned and bewigged colleagues but inside, he felt a sudden tremor of excitement, at the prospect of foreign adventure and the chance for the newborn Australia to prove its loyalty and show those puffed up 'pommies', what its men could do. There was much to consider, discuss and plan for and as soon as the court had risen for the day, he returned home to share his thoughts and feelings with Alice.

Over dinner, they agreed that, as Charlie would not be required to put in an appearance at the court again for several days, they should spend an extended weekend with his parents on the family sheep and dairy property, high in the Strzelecki Ranges, in South Gippsland, just a hundred miles or so to the South East. It would be good to confer with Charlie's father, who had served with the Victorian Volunteers against the Boers and a break in the bush would do them both a power of good.

He badly needed some time in the saddle to work off the too indulgent city living that was padding his powerful frame, although it would be hard to resist his mother's hearty farmhouse food.

Charlie Elliott had grown up as a true country boy, running wild without shoes in the bush, swimming in dams and vainly chasing possums up trees. Later, on leave from school and University he worked as station hand and then jackaroo, holding his own at the back breaking work with the toughest of the local men. He rode the steep Strzelecki slopes without caution or fear and could shoot a reckless fox or rabbit dead through the eye at a hundred paces. The local footy team prospered by his inclusion and he was called frequently to prop up the local pub's less than sober bar.

His father was waiting with the trap to collect them from the station and they were soon spinning along the lanes whilst exchanging city news for enquiries about mother, milk and wool prices and the chance of more much needed rain. The glory of the bright winter's day and the joy of city-country reunion cast aside all cares and forbade any mention of war. As they gained the crest of the Grand Ridge road, to the north, lush green slopes fell away down below them and through occasional breaks in the dense stands of blue-green, gums they caught tantalising glimpses of Bass Strait's Southern seaway and the foaming white froth of its collar of surf. Charlie inhaled the aromatic scent of the bush in heady delight and knew that this was truly his home.

As they bowled down the drive to the house, they were met by a canine charge of working collies, kelpies and housedogs, barking and yapping their familiar greeting and saluting the return of their old friend the horse. From the wide encircling verandah, Mrs. Elliott senior waved a greeting and confirmed Charlie's hope that they were to be treated to his favourite home cooked roast.

The food was excellent, as only a home cooked meal could be and free flowing conversation and good digestion were aided and abetted by a bottle of Shiraz, the fruit of Phylloxera-free vines that George Elliott had acquired and brought back from vineyards near Stellenbosch in the Western Cape, on his way back from the war.

After a more than ample lunch of roast leg of lamb with all the trimmings followed by the coup de grace, in the shape of a steamed apple pudding with thick custard cream, Charlie's mother took Alice into the lounge to hear about the progress in setting up their East Melbourne house and to catch up on the city news. Before making an afternoon check on the stock, Charlie and his father retreated to the library to indulge their mutual taste for strong pipe tobacco and a dram or two of single malt whisky.

Despite this taste, the Elliotts did not share a common Highland heritage with the many squatters who had established sheep runs in Victoria's Western District. In fact they were not of pure Scottish origin, being descendants of border raiding families who, for five hundred years, had conducted an endless practice of tribal cattle raiding, village burning and brutal rapine and murder.

As a boy Charlie had thrilled to his father's and uncle's stories of the legendary feats of the Border Reivers. He often revisited an old and worn history of the border struggles that had pride of place in the library of his Melbourne home. Its account of the contestants was harsh and unforgiving but still a little tinged with respect.

'...their hallmark was treachery, cruelty and disdain for the respective monarchies, on both sides of the Anglo Scottish frontier. Their skills consisted of mounting surprise horse back raids on unsuspecting neighbours and having stolen their cattle, melting away into trackless mountain wastes of peat bogs, high moors and rainy, misty dales which pursuing strangers entered at their peril and from which, few returned whole or alive. The complexity of the changing family allegiances made labels such as English or Scottish redundant but what was certain was that their ability to fight on horseback made them the most deadly light cavalry since the Mongol hordes swept out of the Asian steppes onto the unprotected plains of Europe...'

At first Charlie and his father spoke of stock and fencing and the rising prices for mutton, beef and military wool that the conflict would bring. The brokers, Michells and Elders, were active in the markets and they agreed that now was the time to put on more sheep.

Between them there were few of the barriers that divide generations and he had no fear of raising his dilemmas about following the flag, wherever it might go, or staying to nurture his newly consummated marriage and seek to serve his country by putting his respected legal skills at the service of the wartime government. George Elliott was too wise to offer his son advice that would sway him one way or the other and he chose rather to talk about his own reasons for going to war and what the experience had meant for him.

Putting aside the sense of adventure and blood lust that seem to be the natural motivators of male warriors down the ages, he reflected that,

Melbourne | Australia | 1914

"At the time many of us felt obliged to go as members of an Imperial family, which had ensured the security of this colony far away at the end of the earth. It had nurtured our prosperity and granted us a peaceful and bloodless transition to self-rule with the gift of a system of government, law and language for which the mother country had paid dearly."

Having poured them both another glass of Laphroaig and drawing deeply on his pipe, he turned to his own personal experience of war. He believed that soldiers from the Australian colonies had conducted themselves in the main with courage, honour and fortitude, as had many of their enemy but, he stressed that,

"War is a great leveler son and it is the most terrible thing to contemplate killing another human being in cold blood, especially in hand to hand fighting, when the only justification is, at best, an abstract cause, remote from your daily personal life and interests. I saw ordinary men perform extraordinary deeds of bravery, compassion and self-sacrifice and also, I saw terrible injustice, inhumanity and the doubtful behaviour of otherwise brave men, such as Breaker Morant and his compatriots, all in the name of a so-called higher cause or just base revenge. As you know, my souvenir was the personal inconvenience of a leg crippled by the Mauser bullet that passed through my thigh."

"So what would you do, Dad, knowing what you know now and if you were in my place?" Charlie asked.

"I would want to be sure that my cause was just and my motivation more than an understandable youthful thirst for adventure and such, that it justified exposing a young and beautiful wife to the possibility that she may have to live the rest of her life without my love and protection."

There was no easy response to that answer and they both lapsed into a tacit and seemingly companionable silence that, in truth, masked the turmoil of mutual emotion and shared doubt. After what seemed an eternity to Charlie, his father invited him to take a ride over the property and see the improvements to the shearing shed.

The weekend flew by and on the last morning of their stay, Charlie's program of exercises, designed to sooth the aches and strains of a hard few days of unaccustomed hard yakka, was interrupted by his father's request to join him in his study where he had something he wanted to show him. When he entered the room Charlie saw that his father was reaching into a large cabin trunk from which he withdrew a magnificent military saddle, a well worn Sam Browne belt and holster, containing a large and lethal looking Colt revolver.

"*Son,*" he said, "*I don't know what you will decide but if you do go, I would like you to take these things, which served me so well in my time. Especially the Colt, because it's so reliable in all the conditions of rain, dust, mud and even snow, that you are likely to face wherever you might go.*"

With that, they said no more about it and having kissed his mother farewell and shaken his father's hand firmly, whilst they looked into each other's eyes with a rare intensity of understanding, Charlie joined Alice at the carriage window of the departing Melbourne train. In his pocket was a letter of introduction to a Boer war comrade of his father's whom it was rumoured, was putting together a squadron of light horse. His name was Pompey Elliott.

4

Manchester, England
1914/1915

The war was going badly. The illusion of early victory had evaporated. The German armies, after early success, had fallen back and dug in on the Aisne and the core of Britain's old professional army had been decimated whilst frustrating their enemy's advance on the Marne. Politicians were beginning to temper their earlier jingoistic bombast. Headlines in the Manchester Guardian and Evening News spoke of 'Setbacks', 'Stalemate' and only reassured to the cautious extent that there would be a 'Big Push Next year.'

The music halls still had Cockney 'sparrers' like the great Marie Lloyd, leading the audiences in cheerful renditions of 'It's a long way to Tipperary' and the old favourite 'Goodbye Dolly I must leave you', but in the clubs and pubs and around the piano at home, the mood was becoming more sober if not somber as optimistic fortitude gave way to the more wistful, 'Keep the home fires burning' and 'There's a long, long trail a winding to the land of my dreams.'

Red Cross ambulance trains had begun arriving at London Road Station during the night to unload their tragic complement of maimed and dying men, out of sight of those employed in the day, working to make the city run. Dan noticed the gradual increase of men in uniform in the pubs, some with one empty sleeve pinned up, or with patches over sightless or missing eyes and others minus a leg or even both. They had nothing to cheer about other than that they were home and alive.

Kitchener's face was on every hoarding demanding that 'your country needs you' and it seemed that his pre-war prediction, that it would be won by the last million men Britain could throw into battle, was starting to come true. So many men had gone or were going to those ill-defined places known as 'over there' or 'the front' that women, in increasing numbers, were starting to take up jobs that had previously been the sole preserve of men.

The trams had been taken over by women drivers and clippies and Lloyd George's ruthless expansion of munitions works had brought more women onto the shop floor than men. They delivered the milk and post, joined the police and Dan even saw one Amazon delivering sacks of coal. They'd be down the mines next, he thought if this carried on.

It bothered him being out of it and especially as all his mates had joined up, but coal was the power behind production and so he was sure he was doing more than his bit.

On a bright but crisp Sunday afternoon, Dan set off for an outing to Delph, a little village on the edge of the moors just out of Oldham. There was to be a brass band contest and he was in the mood for a change of scene, some fresh air and fun. The charabanc had to drop its passengers at the edge of the village because it was closed to motor vehicles and even horse drawn traffic, for the rest of the day. Bunting was stretched across the street between the upper stories of the buildings and people leaned out of their upstairs windows to cheer and to shout. Stallholders sold brandy snaps and steaming black puddings and the UCP café was open, offering mugs of tea to wash down the faggots, pickled pig's trotters and steaming plates of tripe and cow'eel pie. The crowd was so dense he could only proceed at a shuffle, pressed up against the backs of those in front of him, who were mostly elderly people, toddlers and mill girls, making their way to the park and the competing bands.

At that moment a band struck up and the sprightly march made him straighten up, step out and he felt a lift in his spirits for the first time in a while. But for being hemmed in by the crowd, he would have swung his arms and marched as though on parade. Although it was a cool November day, people were gathered around glowing coke braziers outside the main street pubs warming their hands and supping Mackeson's Stout and mild ale. It was obvious who was on wartime piecework by the rate some were guzzling their way through their brass.

He stopped for a pint at the Red Lion and taking it out to stand in a patch of weak, but very welcome sunshine, he began tapping his foot in time with the band.

Just then, he heard a shout that sounded like his name and turning he saw Liza's brother, Seth, weaving his way through the throng towards him, waving his arms wildly to make sure that he'd been seen. That brought back to him the night on London Road station when he and Liza had seen Ted off to London, where he was to join a regiment of writers, painters, poets and actors, they called the Artists Rifles and who had all volunteered to go.

In a way it was not so surprising that decent, honest, impressionable Ted had succumbed to the influence of his idealistic colleagues and was soon speaking of fighting to defend the rights and freedoms of the common man from the Prussian despot and his Junker overlords.

Since then, Liza had been swept up in war work and Dan had been too pressed in keeping up with managing continuous shifts to find time to keep in touch.

"Eh up Dan" greeted Seth in his broad Oldham dialect. *"A'm real glad ter meet yeh, but you'll not like me news."*

"Likewise Seth" Dan said, welcomingly, *"But what's this bad news all about?"*

"Oh Dan you'll never believe it, Ted's been killed and our Liza's gone right off 'er 'ead."

Dan was stunned. It felt as if as if he'd been struck a heavy blow and when he'd recovered his senses and his voice, he gasped out,

"When did it happen and how do you know?"

"E were killed a week ago according t' the war office telegram and "is name were in yesterday's casualty list."

"Oh God!" cried Dan, still finding it hard to take it in. *"Why? Oh Why? Not poor sweet Ted! And Liza, I must go and see her right away."*

"'Old on mate, there's more to come," her brother cautioned, taking Dan's arm and drawing him aside away from the crowd, so as not to be overheard. "A letter from 'is officer said 'e 'ad refused t'go over the top and were taken fer a coward, court-martialed and shot!"

Dan reeled away from Seth. The words rang in his ears, but his mind could not accept their meaning.

"It can't be true. There must be some other explanation. Ted was no coward. He'd never do that!"

Later that night he left Liza's house in Chadderton, so heartsick with grief and still suffering from shock at seeing her in such a demented state, it was all he could do to walk down her street and find his way back to the tram. The double blow of losing her husband and hearing of his execution had all but driven her mad. She had rolled on her bed, sobbing, screaming and tearing out her hair, and crying that she too, *"Would be better off, dead."*

All he had been able do was to hold her, as neither of them was able to speak. When he could bear it no more he had left her, in the tender care of her mother and sisters and slipped out silently with Seth to drown his sorrows over a much needed drink in the pub down the street.

The letter she had received was short and brutally to the point;

I am directed to inform you that a report has been received from the war office to the effect that 23892 Corporal Edward Miller, 1st Battalion, Artists Rifles was sentenced after being tried by a Court Martial to suffer death by being shot and his sentence was duly executed on 30th October 1914.

All through that night he couldn't shake away the sight of the bronze death plaque in its cardboard box on the table, bearing on one side Britannia and an inscription on the other saying he had 'died for freedom and honour.'

"Fuck the King and his freedom!" Dan screamed, as he kicked in a dustbin and scraped all his knuckles by punching a wall. *"If that's all they mean by freedom, a life to them's worth sweet bugger all!"*

He had barely recovered from the tragic loss of such a fine dear friend when another hammer blow struck closer to home. The pit was losing its best men to the army recruiters and even veterans and management were required to go down to the coalface, including the Chief Engineer of the mine. It was the carelessness of a new, inexperienced, rail man that caused the accident by neglecting to securely engage the wheel brakes on a set of trucks that were fully laden with coal. The careering trucks shot out of the steep side gallery on to the main road line, just as Arthur chose to cross the track. He didn't have a chance and his trailing leg was caught by the runaway wagons, as he tried to scramble to safety across the farthest rail.

Dan went with him in the ambulance and right to the operating room door. When several hours later he awoke from the anesthetic, Dan was by his bed to reassure Arthur that he would live, but his right leg had had to come off below the knee. Back home in the kitchen he tried to console Beattie, without sensing that she was made of much sterner stuff than her tears suggested.

"I suppose there's no sense in skriking about it luv." She sniffled, wiping her eyes on her pinnie, *"and at least we've not lost him, like some."*

It was hard to know who was comforter or comforted, as they clung together tightly under the kitchen's sputtering gas mantle. Dan struggled to make sense of it. He was beginning to wonder whether it was better to take his chance fighting rather than suffering the futile risk of being maimed or killed for filling someone else's scuttle with coal.

Late in November, Arthur came home on a crutch and it wasn't long before he was stumping around the mine office swapping banter with much younger men whose disabilities had occurred much further a field. Beattie's cooking and mollycoddling was restoring Arthur's spirit and strength to such an extent that Dan felt able to take a short break. He had continued to see Liza when he could and on most Sundays, he would call in on her and her mother for afternoon tea. She had shaken off the worst debilitating effects of her grief and whilst still in mourning she was getting out and about and came down, to see Arthur, soon after he came home.

During a gentle stroll through Phillips Park, they stopped to sit on a bench and watch the old men, bowling corner to corner across the beautifully kept crown greens. She told him that she was going to spend some time staying at her auntie's house, at Cleveleys near Blackpool, on the Lancashire coast and she wondered when she had settled in, whether he might like to come and spend the weekend with them. This fitted in well with Dan's plans for getting away and as he knew that her widowed aunt had plenty of room, so that he wouldn't be under their feet and as it would save him paying for a boarding house room, he immediately said that he would.

A long spell of bad weather gave way to crisp bright days and early on a Saturday morning, he took the train to the coast. The Promenade at Blackpool was almost empty of holidaymakers at that time of the year and because of the war. Many of the private hotels had been converted to convalescent homes for the wounded or were billeting officers waiting to join their regiments and embark for France. His bag was light and as it wasn't raining, he decided it would do him good to walk the mile or two to the north shore, from the Tower to Liza's auntie's home on the sea front. The tide was in and the heavy swell and strong wind blowing in across the Irish Sea drove great waves into the sea wall, which broke with a thunderous clap, dumping showers of salt sea spray on unwary promenaders and the passing cream and green coloured trams.

He arrived a little damp and flushed with the chafing of the wind on pallid cheeks, more accustomed to the artificial light of the underground world. Liza welcomed him at the door. It was good to see that her complexion had benefited from her stay and a sign of the old twinkle sparked momentarily in her eyes.

"You walked all that way?" she remonstrated.

"Oh that's nowt to what I do most days" he laughingly replied "I walk it on my haunches and carrying a pick and shovel too."

Inside, the house was a model of Edwardian style, much more comfortable, lighter and more airy than the Victorian parlours he had endured as a boy, when making Sunday best visits to his parents friends. The woodwork was light in tone and highly polished and a grandfather clock toned sonorously as he stepped through the vestibule into the hall and felt his feet sink into the plush of the Axminster carpet. It was clear that Liza's aunt had married money and that her late husband had left her well provided for.

The old lady was small and plump but surprisingly spry and cheery considering her age and the arthritis that he knew was slowly corroding her joints. Her companion and helper, Miss Asterbury, greeted him with the reserve of one who whilst sharing his working class origins, had risen to her higher station by dint of her nursing career, which had taken her to the dizzy heights of her profession as matron at Booth Hall Children's hospital, a place which Dan had reason to bless for curing him of scarlet fever as a small boy.

After a frugal but tasty lunch of mulligatawny soup followed by cheese and watercress sandwiches, Liza suggested they went for a blow and at the top of the famous tower he knew what she meant. This great steel mass, modeled on the Eiffel tower in Paris, was the wonder of the north and the views far out to sea and inland across the Fylde to the Lancashire plain, were a sight to behold, on such a clear day. But the wind was awful and the gentle swaying of the tower as it flexed with the blast was too much for Liza's stomach and so, they descended to seek refuge in the warmth of the tower ballroom and the indulgence of afternoon tea.

The afternoon tea dance was a long established tradition and whilst Dan was none too accomplished in this social grace, with Liza's prompting, he made a passable show of a foxtrot and then took welcome refuge in the more manageable tempo of a slow, waltz. Liza sparkled and glided along as if she were in a skiff on a park lake. This was a legacy of her marriage to Ted, of course, and with that reminder of his dead friend a shadow flitted across the brightness of his holiday mood. But this didn't last and soon they were enjoying tea and Chelsea buns and talking of the good times together when Ted was always the life and soul of the gathering and the willing butt of so many friendly jokes.

As they strolled home, arm in arm, along the darkening prom they were confronted by an elegant lady, who had alighted from a very expensive motorcar to walk over to them.

She bade them good day in a pleasant if somewhat haughty upper class tone and without further ado, handed Dan an envelope. He opened it curious as to what this could mean and was horrified when a large white feather fell into the palm of his hand. He was rooted to the spot but not Liza, who swung her handbag catching the unwary woman smack in the face and then pursued her back to the refuge of her car, cursing her in vivid language that he had no idea she knew.

When they returned to her aunt's he was still shaken and was very quiet and uncommunicative throughout dinner and for the rest of the evening. The old lady retired early and this gave Dan the opportunity to plead the effects of an early start and seek the solitude and solace of his bed. For a while he tossed and turned trying to shake the incident out of his mind. But a charge of cowardice and in front of Liza whose husband had so recently been similarly accused, tied to a stake and shot, was not so easily dismissed. But eventually emotional exhaustion combined with physical tiredness lulled him into the shallows of sleep.

He awoke suddenly, conscious of a sound in the room. It was a dark moonless night but he saw what appeared to be a figure dressed in white standing by his bed. He tried to sit up to accost it when the apparition spoke.

"Shove over Dan, sorry to wake you, but I'm cold and heart-sick about what happened and I need to talk with you and get warmed up."

The simplicity and directness of her request was pure Liza, who was clearly unconcerned about the risk of being compromised by coming into his room clad only in her nightdress, in the middle of the night. She knew well how badly he was feeling and took him into her arms and whispered denials of the wretched charge that had been leveled at his manhood by that stuck up bitch. At first he was too deep in self-pity and anger to respond but her persistent soothing words, soft arms and tender endearments brought calm to his mind and relaxed his painfully taught body.

They communicated like this for some time until he became aware of the warmth and closeness of her body through the thin cotton layer of the shift that separated them. He had never considered what a comely lass she was, when done out in her street clothes and with her hair tied up in a very tight and proper bun. He turned to shift on to his back to conceal the growing hardness between his legs when, to his amazement and excitement, he felt her firm but tender grip on his rampant cock. It was all he could do not to come straight away as she simultaneously kissed his cheek and drew him towards her and between her wide-open, welcoming legs. It was a quick and abortive business. His climax, as he feared, came before she had even begun and they parted like teenage first timers, shivering with the exciting novelty and in his case, embarrassed at what, and how badly, he had done.

For a while they lay apart, back-to-back, saying not a word. He wondered and worried about what she would think of him in the morning for taking such advantage with her husband, his friend, not long gone. He turned intending to express his regret when she sat up pulled her nightdress over her head and neatly sat astride him holding his head between her hands and slipping her exploring tongue deep into his mouth. The effect was electrifying, as they abandoned all sense of decorum with him deep inside her warm wet flower and she riding him furiously for all she was worth. Her strength and raw passion were a revelation and he needed all the endurance acquired at his backbreaking job just to keep up with her and hang on. Then, when he thought he could go no more, with a hoarse cry she collapsed on his chest limp and all done. But he was only physically challenged and his lust was not yet fully spent.

Rolling her gently onto her back he parted her pliant legs and thrust deeply and roughly into her fathomless cleft. The frenzy of his need knew no limits, as he grasped her shoulder length hair and deeper and harder he went, until aroused again by his ardor, she cupped his taught buttocks in her strong hands and began pulling him in and urging him on until, with a massive shudder and an almost inaudible groan, he subsided onto her and stayed there a while in response to her plea, *"Please stay in a bit, love. Don't come out yet, I want to feel you in there."*

In the morning they contributed to the polite breakfast chatter as only two old friends would at the home of a widowed aunt. They confirmed, without trace of a blush, that they had both rested well and enjoyed deep uninterrupted sleep. Dan intended catching the noon train, so that he could be home and early to bed, in readiness for Monday's early start and Liza insisted on accompanying him to the station. On the way there, they spoke of everything but what had passed between them the night before. Dan had never felt so relaxed and full of well being since war had been declared and the night with her had been a wonder, but he did not love her and he knew that she felt the same.

He couldn't explain it and he didn't intend to try. He had done his fair share of groping and grappling with rough mill girls in the dark, along the canal banks. But this had been powerfully different. He understood the reason for her hunger but he wondered at Liza's complicity and how she had acquired her undoubted skill. They had both fulfilled a powerful need to vent all their anger, sorrow and fear in one shameless orgy of lust. It had changed their relationship forever, but they knew it for what it was and demanded no more of each other than a deep abiding friendship that would endure, no matter wherever they were. They walked in silent companionship and at the station he took his leave of her, leaning from the carriage window.

As the guard's whistle blew, he told her what she feared most, but expected, *"Liza. I am going to join up next week and I will soon be off to the war!"*

5

Near Mansfield, Victoria, Australia
1914

Charlie's father's letter had done the trick and Pompey had soon assayed his potential as a horse soldier and leader of men. He had joined a squadron of the newly formed Light Horse before Christmas and was working up a string of horses and men in the high country back of Mansfield from where the mountain cattlemen came. It was hard work in the heat and the constant climbing, requiring the men to sometimes dismount and ascend with their mounts at a jog, was building the endurance of horses and men alike and hardening them for unknown trials that were yet to come.

They were mounted infantry, not cavalry, a modern equivalent of the French and British dragoons that Napoleon and Wellesley flung against each other across the battlefields of Spain and at Waterloo. They rode into battle or out on patrol carrying a rifle, bayonet and ammunition, along with sufficient food and water for themselves and their mounts. Whilst the mountain streams of the high plains reduced the need to carry so much water, the load to be borne was a trial for man and beast in the summer heat.

It had been harder to leave Alice than to vacate his place at the bar, but he had pondered on his father's words and he believed that his conscience and duty were clear. Australia had enjoyed the inheritance, bounty and protection of the motherland and the time had come to pay the bill. At a more personal and selfish level he was thrilled to be out in the bush on his horse, being paid for it and feeling that he was fulfilling a noble duty at the same time.

His men, volunteers from all over Victoria, were not so philosophical and made no bones of their delight at escaping the drudgery of factory, office, mine or the family farm, for the excitement of foreign adventure on the other side of the world. Charlie didn't know where they were going but they were to embark in two weeks and the rumours suggested

Near Mansfield | Victoria | Australia | 1914

the Middle East. They were bound to sail through the Suez Canal and he understood that disembarkation orders would not be issued until then. In the meanwhile he was dedicated to bringing his force to a pitch of condition and readiness that even the long voyage could not completely dull.

They camped under a blaze of stars with the Southern Cross clearly marking the southward way. Around the gum-log fires, men yarned and sang, to the accompaniment of mouth organs and even a fiddle, the bush ballads and songs of old Ireland, with a tribute to good old Banjo Paterson thrown in now and then. In the cool of the dawn they stood to, as tradition demanded, to fend off what? Charlie wondered, perhaps a surprise attack by maggies and roos. The call to saddle-up echoed back off Mount Stirling and soon they were winding down towards Mansfield on the way to their Broadmeadows camp near Melbourne and a last fling with the women and booze. Charlie's Sergeant reported that all was in good order and the men in good cheer. Alf Grommet's promotion had been a good one. He was by far the best man in the saddle and a dead shot, whether mounted or on foot. That he was a half-caste Koori from a tribe up Barmah forest way, was at first a problem with some, but his skills, the quiet way he had with him and a light but firm touch when needed with his soldiers, won over all but the most bigoted amongst the men.

"Keep them up to the mark, Alf," urged Charlie, "There'll be longer rides ahead of us and we'll all pay the price for slackers and any who can't keep up."

On his last night in Melbourne Alice and Charlie dined alone. She would miss him terribly but at least she had her work with the young ladies at Methodist Ladies College to keep her busy through the days and to occupy her stray thoughts through the lonely nights. She approved of his going and understood why, but she hated this parting so early in their marriage and couldn't bear to consider the possibility that he might never come back. Of course she would take up volunteer work, especially in support of the men going away and there would be visits to Charlie's parents to share in the news and maintain their spirits.

They spoke of their plans for their lives ahead when he had returned with his duty done and she looked forward to the hope of family and a bush retreat of their own.

They made love through the night with a passionate depth and duration they had never attained before and without regard for the gossip of servants and neighbours, they greeted the dawn on their balcony, wrapped in their robes and toasting each other and their future life with the finest Australian champagne.

Light rain veiled Princes pier and gradually obscured its view, as the tugs pulled the troop ship away starting the long run down the bay to the heads at Queenscliff. The navy band continued to beat out Waltzing Matilda as they turned their faces southward, setting their minds on the long haul across the Bight to the Indian Ocean and leaving behind only their hearts and their love for those they had left back home.

He had been correctly informed about when they would hear their disembarkation orders, but it was to be at Port Said rather than England or France.

Turkey, as a result of a secret alliance with Germany, who had gained great influence over a powerful group known as 'The Young Turks' and the Turkish army, had come into the war in 1914 by attacking Russian forces in Armenia, threatening the Baku oilfields in Azerbaijan, and exposing British India to attack from the north. In late 1914 Britain had occupied the Turkish port of Basra at the head of the Persian Gulf and there was growing concern that the Turks might threaten the Suez Canal from Palestine across the Sinai. It was natural then, that Charlie expected to be deployed in defence of the canal but, after a briefing of Australian Senior Officers, Chauvel told his men that they were to attack Turkey directly under the leadership of the Victorian, John Monash, by landing in force at Gallipoli and then pushing up the peninsula as part of a force that would take Turkey out of the war and threaten the Austro-German Southern front, at the same time, relieving the pressure on the stalemate in the West.

Mindful of military censorship but feeling the necessity to communicate with Alice, in case of the worst, he dashed off a quick letter to tell her of his experiences so far and to reassure her that he was in good hands with Monash and Chauvel in command.

Somewhere in the Middle East

My Darling Alice

I am fit and well and we are safely ashore. I am fully acclimatised and our continued training and the odd bit of footy practice are keeping me trim and up to the mark.

The journey out was pretty uneventful, apart from the disappearance of a corporal, with a rather unsavoury reputation with the men, who must have fallen overboard whilst we were

Near Mansfield | Victoria | Australia | 1914

crossing the Bight, where most of the men including yours truly were violently sick. The horses coped better and landed in fine style, despite being a little sluggish at first after all the inactivity and confinement.

I have seen the Pyramids and ridden on a camel and our blokes gained quite a reputation with the Egyptians for not taking any old slack when their drinks were watered and attempts were made to short-change them. The burning of a merchant's warehouse was put down to them, an action that, as an officer, I cannot condone of course, but the case was not proven and the local traders were much more amenable from then on.

We are somewhere in the Middle East, we are not allowed to say precisely where, but it is clear we will be moving off soon and may see our first bit of action. I love you my darling and want you to know that you will always be in my thoughts, especially in times of danger and of course in my last thoughts should the worst happen, which of course it won't. We are well-trained and well lead by Australian commanders and I know you will pray for me and that I will act honourably and bravely when we go into the fight.

There is no time to write more than one letter if I am to catch the departing mail ship, which will be at sea before we go. So please tell mother and father that I love them and think of them often and hope that they will soon have good reason to be proud of me and our fine men when news of our success comes through.

Goodnight sweet princess, I will hold you in my dreams and for ever.

Your loving husband

Charles.

After a brief period of acclimatisation in Egypt, an Australian brigade, including Lieutenant Charlie Elliott and his command, was dispatched to the Greek island of Lemnos from where they were shipped to the Gallipoli peninsula and landed under heavy Turkish fire at dawn on the morning of April the twenty fifth, nineteen fifteen.

6

Manchester, England
1915

With his mining experience and partially completed engineering qualifications, Dan Bevan was a natural recruit for the Sappers and he was dispatched to Woolwich Arsenal in London, for a crash course in military excavation techniques and the making, detonating and defusing of bombs. His aptitude, education and obvious application, guaranteed early promotion and he had attained the rank of sergeant upon returning on attachment to the Manchester Regiment, which was standing by, awaiting orders to go.

He had not seen Liza since their parting in Blackpool but they had corresponded while he was in London and each week he wrote a long account of his training and when he was granted leave on every second weekend, he recounted all that he had seen and experienced during his visits to the capital's famous sites. He was interested in the history of Parliament in particular and its long struggle to gain recognition by the crown. The great statue of Cromwell, who had ruled the only serious English republic, stood proud and defiant next to the Houses of Parliament and reminded Dan that Manchester had been for parliament in the civil war and that his troops had fought a pitched battle against the king's forces advancing from Salford, across Blackfriars Bridge.

He couldn't get enough of the science museum in South Kensington but the historical venues drew more attention from his pen.

London 1915

Liza.

You wouldn't believe the splendour of the British Museum and all the statues from Egypt, China and Ancient Greece. I even went into the great reading room where Karl Marx sat and did his research for Das Kapital. Mind you, he might have done better to watch the Arsenal round the corner at Highbury on those Saturday afternoons.

Across the river, I saw where Shakespeare's Globe theatre used to be and had a pint and pork pie in the George where Charles Dickens wrote the Old Curiosity Shop. Even further down the road, was the Tabard Inn at which Chaucer had his pilgrims gather before heading off on their pilgrimage to Canterbury in his famous Tales.

I could go on and on and I wish you could be with me to see it all. One day perhaps I will be able to take you to London and show you all this.

Love

Dan

But didn't that remark give him pause. Was it true? Was he being honest? He was not sure. She would always be a welcome companion but after that night, he didn't know how to begin again and get them together, much as they were. He had no regret for what happened between them and the very thought of it aroused him and filled him with delight. But to seek it again might be to take unfair advantage of her situation and yet to meet and just ignore it, also, just didn't seem right.

But, she came on his last night in England to take supper with Beattie, Arthur and Dan. It might have been a sombre affair but for Arthur, who knew what everyone was thinking and feeling, having gone off just like Dan to his own earlier war.

"Now don't be misery guts, you lasses, before you know it, the job will be done and he'll be marching back in that door." Boomed Arthur, as he uncorked some old French Brandy he'd kept for this sort of day. Raising their glasses they toasted Dan's success and safe return and looking into Liza's face he knew that she devoutly wished it and willed him back to her, alive, healthy and whole. This was the last time he was to see her before he went away forever or for goodness knows how long.

His training had focused mainly on trench-warfare and techniques for destroying, pillboxes, undermining heavy gun emplacements and blowing breaches in fortified trench lines. He was amazed then to hear that rather than heading for the western front, where such skills were in great demand and had plenty of scope for application, he was to ship out with an expeditionary force sent to protect the Suez Canal from the Turks.

They set sail on a rainy, early spring morning, mixed in with other northern regiments including the remaining first battalion of the Lancashire Fusiliers, which had recently returned from India. Their main force had left in September with such a large contingent from Bury that it had seemed the town's men folk must have volunteered as one. He couldn't help but wonder, with a whimsical smile, who was left to make the famous black puddings or was this yet another area into which women workers had advanced?

Rolling down the Atlantic coast of France there was no shortage of the Bay of Biscay's legendary mal de mer. It seemed so strange to be passing the country where their allies were struggling against the enemy along a 600 mile line and crying out for support. He could see the importance of maintaining control of the seaways but didn't the Allies destiny lie in France, where victory must surely be won.

The troops poured down the gangplanks, their pallid legs and putty-white faces exposed to a searching examination by Egypt's unrelenting noonday sun. He had never experienced heat like it and wondered how they would even march let alone fight. To get burnt and be put out of action was a punishable offence and he would have to be careful, with his skin, to expose himself gradually and learn to go slow.

In the barracks some troops were resting. Many were tall Sikhs and Rajputs from India, who had seen fighting in the taking of Basra and were waiting to move on.

Dan got talking with one of their British officers, who assured him that the Turks were no push over, especially when fighting to defend their homes or under the command of German officers, who would turn their guns on them rather than let them cut and run.

For the next few weeks all they seemed to do was force march their men all over the surrounding desert, battling sand storms, heatstroke and flies, such that even bayonet practice in full battle order, at midday, was a preferable alternative for which they willingly volunteered. Gradually, the routine became less punishing and those with the right pigment began to be at home in the blazing sun. As a sapper Dan was spared the pains of the footsloggers and drilled his men in destroying mock bridges and rail lines and blowing chunks out of old forts, like those which once Crusaders had fought to defend and fleetingly won. He would shelter under a tarpaulin out of the worst of the day's glare and watch lines of Australian horsemen ride out on patrols to ensure the canal's desert approaches were clear. This had become a regular event since a Turkish army of ten thousand men had moved on the canal in January, but retreated back across the Sinai into Palestine when they saw the size of the forces ranged against them. He didn't envy them their mission but at least they had horses and he had heard that even their Sergeant's mess had cold beer.

Then one day the mood changed. The rumour started with the Aussies, as they liked to call themselves, which they passed on as their water tanks came round. We're going to invade Turkey they said and for sure we'll soon be gone. Unlike so many such predictions this was true, at least for the Australian New Zealand Army Corps, which was landed on the Gallipoli Peninsula on the 25th of April at a place that would ever after be called Anzac Cove. On that same day British forces went ashore on five beaches at the southern tip of Cape Helles with disastrous consequences for the Lancastrians and Irish troops amongst them.

A few days later, Dan got orders to pack his ordinance ready to land at Helles in support of the forces which had become bogged down trying to take Krithia and the strategic hill top fortress of Achi Baba.

7

Anzac Cove, Turkey
1915

Charlie's training had not prepared him for the rain of fire that made hell of that beach. They'd expected to make a surprise landing and to wade in unopposed but the Turks were ready and someone had got it all badly wrong.

He stumbled out of the boat into surf that knocked him off his feet. As he surfaced, keeping low to evade the enfilading machine gun fire from the heights above the beach that plucked men from the boats, scything down those wading ashore and casting them away like discarded rag dolls. He turned to see how his men were faring, but such was the stuff-up with the order of landing and the chaos caused by the unexpected Turkish welcome, there was a mad disordered scramble to the beach, with companies and regiments hopelessly mixed.

Shells were falling at increasingly regular intervals from guns that had been carefully ranged on the landing point to achieve maximum carnage and disruption of the discharge of equipment, horses and mules. They fell amongst both those still in the water and others thinking themselves safely ashore on the beach. Suddenly, Charlie felt a violent tug on his arm as he was hauled to his feet in Sergeant Grommet's powerful grip. Pointing to a sheltered gully to their left, about a furlong away from the shore, Alf motioned for his officer to follow him in. It was not Charlie's nature to fuss over rank and this was no time to care about who was leading whom. Nodding his assent, he stumbled after his Sergeant and both men shouldered their rifles, hitched up their packs and ran, as fast as the shallows and the cloying wet sand would allow. A shell burst away to their right, peppering them with pebbles and rasping their faces with a blast of airborne sand. But they made it unscathed but for minor scratches and cuts as the machine guns began to focus their fire more intently on those poor bastards still coming in.

Anzac Cove | Turkey | 1915

Gasping for air and shaking with exhilaration and fear, they flung themselves down into the welcome shelter of a rocky cleft. Soon, they were joined by a procession of followers, who were either walking wounded or shaken, but all in one piece. It was a mad house. What should they do? Where should they go?

Some of their companions began firing wildly in the direction of the muzzle flashes above, while most sat or lay down shaking, cursing and crying such that it would take more than a Sergeant-Major's parade ground bellow to get their attention amongst that din. The horseback attacks and mountain training had not prepared them for anything like this but they had perfected the art of signaling by waving when coordinating distant riders and attempting a silent advance. It was a natural skill of the bushmen hunters when stalking a fox or a 'roo and when Charlie and Alf began signaling their intention to move on up the defile, the men behind were quick on the uptake and passing the word, began to follow their lead.

In the absence of clear orders to advance and having no idea of what lay ahead, Charlie and his men spent the remainder of the day in getting survivors and wounded off the beach and regrouping units in the shelter of the rocky gullies.

As dawn broke and the sun came up, they were bivouacked in a protected gorge, safe from all but the vertical descent of a mortar shell. The beach behind and below them was empty of the living but the broken bodies of corpses and dead mules littered the sand and bobbed up and down in lifeless resignation as they floated out on the receding tide. He could tell from the concentration of nearby outgoing rifle and machine gun fire that the Anzacs were hitting back and just as his disheveled band was starting to move on inland, in search of food and water and to join in the action ahead, a regimental runner burst in and spotting Charlie's rank, shouted

"All officers to HQ! Follow me sir and make it bloody quick!" and galloped out again as fast as he came in, with Charlie scrambling in tow.

He was amazed to see that the command had already settled into a dugout, flanked on two sides by solid rock walls. Engineers had raised the others out of empty ammo boxes and drift logs and were shoveling a deep layer of sand and earth onto the otherwise unprotected log frame roof. Messengers were coming and going and lines of purposeful men and heavily laden mules were filing by and moving on up to support and supply those who were trying to gain the heights and silence the Turkish guns. He was relieved to see that clearly someone was in charge and parting the blanket that served as a door he entered the makeshift HQ.

"*Ah, G'day to you Captain Elliott, glad to see you made it in one piece,*" boomed a tall, cheerful Brigadier that Charlie could just make out in the gloom at the back. It was Monash himself and that he had been so readily recognised, by the brigade commander was a complete mystery to him. Recovering his poise he replied,

"*G'day sir, it's Lieutenant Elliott actually.*"

"*No it's not!*" Monash asserted, clapping him on the shoulder in response to Charlie's belated salute.

"*You're alive, you're here and I understand you're capable. I've lost too many good officers already today so Captain it is.*"

Charlie was pleased that promotion was his so quickly but embarrassed that it came so easily and all because he had lived whilst watching so many others die.

The squadron had regrouped along with a crew from Western Australia and to his delight most of his men had come through. Orders were being issued left right and centre and he was soon leading his team up the trail to relieve a forward position that had been held by men of the first wave to get in. His best shots were set up to distract Turkish snipers and the hand over was quickly and smoothly achieved without loss or harm to both those outgoing and those coming in.

Over the next few weeks Charlie seemed to live several lifetimes of danger, excitement, boredom, bravery, fear and tragic loss. They had advanced, taken and lost positions close to the unassailable ridge. News came through that the Kiwis had gained the heights for a while, in their sector of the front, but that they couldn't hold on and consolidate. He lost many of his mates to snipers, in futile massed attacks against impregnable positions and sadly, even some to self-inflicted wounds and disease. He was both harder in body and spirit and had faced the most horrendous personal challenge, of bayoneting men to death in desperate hand to hand fighting along trenches and in dugouts, where deciding who was friend and foe was a split second choice, if one was to cheat sudden death and avoid killing a friend. He would never forget the pleading look turn to resignation in one man's olive eyes as Charlie stabbed him with all his considerable power then, kicking him aside like the sack on the training ground, moved on to his next victim. How had it come to this, that he killed without qualm or compassion, but then later, especially in the sleepless reflective hours of the night, felt sorry for the Turks who had so little to defend but fought so bravely for their homeland. After all, he thought, we were invading them. But, then came the dawn and the never ending bluff and counter bluff, bomb throwing, raids to grab prisoners and always the deadly snipers awaiting the unwary head above the parapet.

They started a newspaper and even baked their own biscuits. At home the Anzacs were heroes, whereas all the disasters were down to the Poms. But he had to admit that Australian officers assented to and ordered the suicidal mass charges and though it was rumoured that the Brits sat down after landing on one of the beach fronts at Helles, allowing the Turks to shift forces to the Anzacs front, there had been even more horrendous losses of British, French and Indian troops, than the Anzacs had sustained. It was the high proportion of men lost, however, from such small nations as Australia and New Zealand that was the tragedy, which had not yet hit home for those back in Australia waiting for news.

Caring for and living so closely with his men, his mates as they had become, kept him busy and was all that saved him from going mad. Tough, coarse and brutal as many were, they were equally forthright and respectful of a brave enemy's religion when they tried to retrieve their wounded and sought parley to bury their dead. They grizzled and whinged, as only Aussies can, but when it was needed, they worked and fought like Trojans and their ingenuity and initiative knew no bounds.

It was just over a year since they had landed when, as suddenly as their orders to come, they heard that they were calling it quits and that they were to leave quietly in the dead of night, with putties and socks wrapped around boots to muffle their tread and all that might rattle or clank securely tied down. Monash did a great job and although they had left so many unfulfilled hopes and dead comrades behind, none were lost on that masterful retreat across land, beach and water that were still within range of Turkish guns. Australia had suffered its first major military defeat and its troops had created a legend.

Cape Helles, Turkey 1915

Dan went in at Sedd-el-Bahr a few days after the main assault wave had secured the landing and missed the butchery that befell the Irish regiments and the best that Lancashire and especially little Bury could send. The old collier the River Clyde, from which the Royal Dublin, Royal Munster Fusiliers and Hampshires had charged into a hail of unexpected gun fire and incendiary shells, was grounded in the bay. An airman had reported that the sea was 'absolutely red with blood' for fifty yards from the shore.

The Lancashire landing on W beach had suffered similar carnage and of the thousand men and officers of the Fusiliers First Battalion, with which Dan had left England, only four hundred had survived. The carthorses pulling Dan's gear snorted and stepped shyly as they skirted the piles of dead. The stench was appalling and so much human meat was still strewn around that swarms of 'corpse flies' blanketed the unburied remains, laying their eggs in decaying flesh.

The advance had bogged down a short way inland and he and his men were called up to blast a way through Turkish strong points. The sapping or undermining of fortifications, to collapse them, was a form of military engineering developed in the middle ages but Dan's tool of trade was high explosives. Soon they were digging and tunneling to approach and undermine the Turkish position, without being seen or heard. The blast, when it came, shook the ground for hundreds of yards before and behind the lines and a twenty-yard stretch of the Turkish bastion and all the men in it had ceased to exist.

But the ensuing infantry assault was too slow getting going and so poorly coordinated that before sufficient men could reach and break through the gap, a creeping barrage of shells fell amongst them and a swath of machine gun fire cut down those who were left. His first sap had worked to perfection but he was shocked and shaken by the pointless loss of life on both sides and such wanton expenditure of men. When the whistles blew and the brave and headstrong young officers urged their reluctant but obedient men to follow them over the top, Dan thought of poor old Ted who had refused to go and wondered whether he would be any braver if ordered to do the same.

Four Battalions of Lancashire Territorials, newly formed, untried volunteers, made up the bulk of the fourteen thousand-man force engaged in the first battle for Krithia and by nightfall on 28th April they had sustained three thousand casualties.

As so often in this war, initial movement and dash subsided soon into stalemate and the prolonged slog of trench warfare and the continuing attrition of material and men. This was no place for Dan and his skills. The rocky terrain and natural defences did not favour his unseen approach and soon he and his squad were withdrawn to return to Egypt and await redirection to where they could be of more use. But before they left, they were assigned to help the pioneers prepare the ground for the countless graves and respectfully dispose of the dead. It was a sorry task for a miner, who once went underground digging up its riches to enhance people's living, now fertilising the earth with men's bones.

8

Melbourne, Australia
1915/1916

Alice Elliott paused in the act of pruning her roses and once again, when her mind wandered from the many tasks she undertook to keep it busy, she wondered after Charles whereabouts and well being and missed him so badly that it hurt. Soft tears pricked her eyes and trickled down her cheeks, seeking to ease and relieve the pain in her heart. She missed him terribly and had found it hard to sleep and not worry about him, since the dreadful news of Gallipoli reached Melbourne.

She had resigned from her commitments as school matron and thrown herself into a crowded programme of work in support of the war effort and in helping women whose men had gone and were not coming back. On many a dark evening she had ventured into the none too savoury back streets of Collingwood, Abbotsford and Richmond to provide comfort and what material support she and her friends charity efforts could raise, for penniless, husbandless, mothers with too many young mouths to feed. So many lived in such unsanitary conditions that diseases were rife and she found herself once more drawn back to the medical fold.

As a young girl she had trained as a nurse at the Bendigo Base Hospital and had graduated to working as a theatre sister at Melbourne's Alfred Hospital in Commercial Road. It was whilst working there that she had met Charles when he was admitted for minor surgery to fix one of his many footballing injuries, after a particularly spiteful Melbourne versus Collingwood clash. The hospitals were starting to bear the brunt of the repatriated wounded, as returning troop ships offloaded their damaged and broken human cargo, with little ceremony, at a far from festive Princes pier.

She had taken a refresher course and was soon in increasing demand to make up for shortages and to relieve the overstretched staff remaining behind, as so many nurses were leaving for England and the war fronts.

She was particularly welcome on the unpopular shifts and for emergency surgery at night. Soon, she was working longer and more often than she had intended, as the demand for major surgery began to even outstrip the capacity of the new repatriation hospitals. She found herself working to repair the dreadful damage that the returning young men had suffered at Gallipoli and increasingly in France.

Alice had become hardened to the suffering and wounds inflicted by road and industrial accidents and somehow it was less tragic to tend the physical ravages of old age. But to see the irretrievably smashed bodies and ruined minds of these otherwise fit and handsome young men, was often more than she could bear.

Coming on and off duty, she would visit them in the care wards, hungry for any news of the whereabouts of the Victorian Light Horse and to ask if anyone had come across Charles and might know how he was. Only one from his squadron had come across him and all he could confirm was his promotion but not whether he was still alive, wounded or dead. Then came the good news of their safe withdrawal and as his name was not in the daily casualty lists she clung on to hope for the best.

The newspapers could give no details of regimental dispositions but the dispatches of dedicated Australian war correspondents ensured that what news there was focused on Australian reverses and triumphs. It was clear that Gallipoli had been a failure as was evidenced by the returning hospital ships, full of wounded and the near dead. But there was uplifting news of the heroism and endurance of both Aussie and Kiwi boys and of how they had totally dispelled any remaining British prejudice about the second rate, nature and reliability of colonial troops. The Indians had left behind even more dead than the Aussies, as if to underline the point.

Returning from work one evening, she found a letter on the salver on the hall table. With trembling hands she tore it open and knew in an instant, from the address, that he was alive and out of that Turkish hell.

Somewhere in the Middle East
January 1916

My Dear, Dearest Alice,

I am alive, well and safely returned from Gallipoli, thank God. Many of our fellow countrymen, Kiwis and even more from the ranks of our allies were not so lucky, but I expect you know all of this by now, as the first of the wounded will have made it home and families who have lost loved ones will be bearing the terrible cost of this ill-judged venture.

Churchill's idea was good and had it come off we would have taken the Turks out of the war and relieved some of the pressure on those poor devils on the Eastern front and our men in France. But as the old proverb says so go the plans of mice and men, which don't count for much in the whole of eternity. There was no singular big blunder just a series of incremental failures of timing, intelligence, quirks of sea and tides, lack of experience with that type of landing and gross underestimation of the readiness and fighting qualities of Johnnie Turk when defending his home and land.

But you would have been so proud of our blokes. Never once did they flinch at a duty or even the most suicidal order to charge. No matter where they came from, they were such characters and company that along with them, any man would have been proud to serve and if necessary die. One, in particular, you will be hearing about soon as a great Aussie hero, was Private John Simpson. He took daily risks in leading a donkey carrying wounded down from the front line, despite shellfire and snipers and, tragically, was killed doing this in May. Funnily enough he was what the English call a 'Geordie' from their industrial North-East coast.

All that, you will read about in the newspapers, for you will hear little of the trials we endured, from those who make it home. The dysentery, heat, thirst and flies of the relentless summer, matched the worst of our Mallee at Christmas and the gibber plains back of Bourke. This was followed by winter's icy blast brought down by winds from the Caucasus, freezing the water in our washing bowls in the morning and accompanied by occasional flurries of snow. How right Dad was about his Colt, it really served me well in all weathers.

I don't want to dwell on the fighting, it was as horrible as you may imagine but I must confess to you that I have the blood of many brave men on my hands and sometimes in the night, I jerk awake from nightmares in which the fine balance of the struggle is tipping against me and I am the victim.

Anyway, enough of that, we are resting, reunited with our horses and when next we are called, I am sure it will be for action that matches our training and suits our style. No more will those chinless wonders from Eton and the Guards patronise we 'colonials' and doubt our mettle. Mind you, at the current rate of attrition of British and French frontline officers, there won't be many of those poor bastards left. At least they are brave or mad enough to lead the suicidal charges.

Sorry about the curse my sweet, but I will not strike it out in deference to those I have fought with, for whom it is the mildest of oaths that might come to mind, after what we have seen and done. You will recall Alf Grommet. He is here and also whole and well. He was a rock throughout and a particularly steadying influence on me during the landing, when the shock of going ashore under fire looked likely to overwhelm me. His family works on a station near to Echuca and as I suspect they have very little, perhaps you could send a parcel of clothes, toys and goodies, with his love. There are three children, a boy and two girls all under seven. The address is enclosed.

I must finish now, there is a limit to the amount of paper we have here and I will need most of my allotment to write those letters, I dread, to the families of those we left behind. I know you will rejoice with me that we have come through this first challenge and that we are not afraid to take on more.

Forgive me. This has been all about me. I hope you are well and that mother and father are coping with my absence. I have written to them by this same mail but perhaps you will send them a wire in case it is delayed. I don't want them to worry unnecessarily.

It was wonderful to get all your letters and the parcels when we came back to base and I am so proud of your taking up that surgical work again. I don't know how you can stomach it, I'm sure I couldn't. I hear the call for lights out so I must close. Goodnight my darling. God bless and thank him for preserving me.

Your, devoted

CHARLES

P.S. I had an amusing encounter with a Sergeant from Manchester, the other day, who strayed into our footy practice and copped one of my full on tackles-yes, dear the sort that caused us to meet, only this time the other poor bloke ended up in casualty. But he was only bruised and shaken and we had quite a chat about the differences and similarities between our two great Victorian era cities. They have trams like us, an elaborate town hall, a fine university, they're mad on football and cricket too and their Guardian sounds like our Age.

He was a mining engineer before he enlisted and a nice straight talking fellow. Not at all like some of those stuffed-shirts that we have to entertain in our mess.

We talked a lot about the monarchy and what Australians thought about the crown. Whilst he was never disrespectful, his views were very liberal and I think he was moving towards becoming a believer in an American style of republican government. He was interesting, well read and we had quite a debate around parliament and King that, unfortunately, we had no time to finish. Don't know why, but we exchanged addresses. I can't see that we will ever meet again.

Manchester 1916

Liza was walking home along Broadway at the end of her shift and as usual she was suffering one of her blinding headaches that she was told were caused by too much exposure to the Ammonium Nitrate they packed into the shells. Soon after Dan left she quit the mill and transferred to one of the new armaments factories that Lloyd George was setting up all over the country. She hated the work, but the girls were great fun and her supervisory position challenged her sufficiently that she was never bored. It was good to be backing up those poor souls in France and she hoped that, one day, one of her mines might come into Dan's hands and help him blow Jerry to kingdom come.

She still carried the letter he had sent from Egypt, before going into action. She kept it in her bodice close to her heart and whenever she felt sad and low and pined for Ted, she would take it out and read those words that had gone some way to heal the deep anguish that still woke her, crying in the middle of too many nights.

Somewhere in the Middle East
April, 1915

Dear Liza Love,

Forgive me for such a short letter, but we are not allowed to say much and I will have no more chance to write for a while as we are about to move off and I wanted you to get this news, at least, in case of you know what.

Manchester | England | 1916

We have spent a few days in a large base area where we were training and getting used to the climate. There are men from so many countries and regiments and last night in the Sergeant's mess I got talking to a bloke from Ted's outfit, who told me what really happened. It seems he had been in several bloody attacks, on the night before it happened and had even volunteered to go out into no man's land to snatch a German prisoner for interrogation. Poor lad, he must have been buggered by then and living off his nerves, no doubt.

The next day they copped a dreadful barrage, the like of which this fellow hadn't experienced, before. Many of his mates were buried alive and after the failed attack, he was found by military police, wandering back from our lines, saying he must get home in time for tea with his Liza.

The bastards arrested him and although his officer and chaplain spoke up for him, those heartless brass hats convicted him of desertion in the face of the enemy and condemned him to death.

So, Liza though my tears stain this letter as no doubt yours will too, take heart my Love, in knowing for the rest of your life that your man and my friend, was brave and true to the end and certainly nobody's coward. I must go, we are being called to muster for the off. Go well. Take good care. Here's my love and if I too don't make it, remember me along with your darling Ted.

Lots of Love!

Dan

She remembered how her tears had fallen to splotch the paper and mingle with the stains of his. Dear Dan, he had given her this comforting gift before going away to test his fate. She would be eternally grateful for this and dearly hoped to thank him on his safe return.

That had been many months ago and though she knew he had not gone to France she had no idea where he was. But now, the terrible events of Suvla Bay and Gallipoli were well known and she guessed he had been there and that he was probably alive, as his name was not amongst the fallen in *The Evening News*. Homes all over East Lancashire mourned their loss and the widows and grieving mothers of Bury were too numerous by far. She could understand the comfort and companionship of going to war with neighbours, relatives and workmates, but she questioned the tradition of local Pals regiments that led sometimes to the loss of two and even three men from one family at one go.

Everywhere, women wore black and able-bodied young men were becoming a rare sight on the streets of northern cities and towns. There were lots of men in her factory who did the heavy and specialist skilled work, but most of these were too old or unfit to go.

She knew how the poor lasses felt and she did what she could but there was nothing for it but to get on with life and do your bit, as the alternative was either to top yourself or go stark staring mad. Liza was made of tougher stuff than to contemplate any such way out. In a way, she had developed a freer life that in some ways was preferable to the one she led before the war. Not that she would have wished Ted out of it of course, but she could do as she liked and the extra incentive money from war work had enabled her to help her mother with the upkeep of her younger siblings. She did not want for women friends and now and then, but not indiscriminately, ever so discreetly and certainly not close to home, she had indulged in an occasional man. They had met a need but none had served her anywhere near as well as Dan had done on that amazing night at her aunt's.

When she thought of it now, she could see his hard, alabaster-white body beneath her, all muscled from the mine and looking like those Roman gladiator busts on the post cards he had sent from the British Museum. The skin of his body was milky and soft in comparison with the calloused palms of the hands that gripped her so tightly as he penetrated and pleasured her, on and on, as though he might never stop and she might come all night. She flushed at this self-indulgent recollection, pulled her coat collar up to keep out the icy moorland wind and scurried along faster, heading for home.

She stirred up and refueled the fire that had not gone out and the smell of the slow simmering hot pot on the hob reminded her she had not eaten since noon. As she hung up her coat behind the door, the firelight revealed a letter lying on the floor. She snatched it up. Ripped it open and let out a deep sigh of relief and then a shout of delight, as she saw that he was alive and safe, after surviving that terrible place. She took out a bottle to settle her frayed nerves and toasted his health with several noggins of Gordon's gin. She would never love him as she had Ted, but he had been a steadfast part of her life at telling moments and his devotion and caring when she had needed it most, would ensure she always maintained a privileged place for him in her affections and frequently in her thoughts. She would go and see Beattie and Arthur tomorrow to make sure they received the good news and to revel in the warmth and good humour that Arthur was bound to dispense in celebration of the survival of his surrogate son.

Arriving in France 1917

It was over a year later that both Liza and Alice, at their opposite ends of the earth, heard news of their men's further parts in the seemingly endless war. Dan found plenty of opportunities to play his part in Maude's successful campaign to take revenge on the Turks for earlier losses and capture Baghdad, whilst Charlie was to the fore in the dashing contribution of the Light Horse to Allenby's advance on Jerusalem, with their celebrated cavalry charge to overrun the Turkish garrison at Beersheba.

The world was in even wider turmoil. Ireland was suspect since last year's abortive Easter rising and the ill-advised execution, soon after, of many of its leaders. The Russian war effort had collapsed and the March revolution that had deposed the Tsar had given way to the Bolshevik takeover of government, to the delight of the starving, mutinous soldiers returning from the collapsed Eastern front. This freed up German reinforcements and made the plight of the Allies even more desperate in contesting the future of Europe in the West. Their situation had been rendered even more uncertain by mutiny in the French army earlier in the year and so, the entry of the Americans into the war came not a moment too soon.

Dan had been withdrawn from Mesopotamia and, at last, had gone to France to try his skills on the intractable German front line. Charlie was a little later in coming and when Alice heard he was bound for the western front, she could no longer bear to wait at a distance. Although she couldn't be with him, she decided to get a lot closer by enlisting as a nursing volunteer and going to work in one of the hard pressed casualty clearing stations close behind the front line in France.

9

Western Front, Belgium/France
1917/18

Messines near Armentières

Dan called a halt to the digging with a downward cut of his arm and at once all the excavators who had been following his lead, stopped digging and put down their picks and shovels, careful not to make a noise. He put a stethoscope-like instrument to his ears and applying it to the forward wall of the chamber he began to listen for any sound that might indicate that the enemy was digging a counter sap under the allied positions. He was part of an enterprise that was the most ambitious planned so far in the war. Its aim was to bust open the German's otherwise impregnable Hindenburg Line of defences, to enable a decisive thrust to their rear.

They dug stealthily to avoid alerting the enemy above. It was their task to dig out one of sixteen chambers at the end of long tunnels, one hundred feet underground. Then it was planned to deposit nineteen mines in these holes with a combined weight of high explosives of around a million pounds. Guy Fawkes would have salivated at the thought. This was what Dan had trained for and he was both professionally committed and excited at the prospect of being partially responsible for an action that could turn around the allies' fortunes, with minimal loss and damage to the men on his side.

Having heard no sound of activity in front of them, Dan signaled for digging to recommence. He had made it a cast-iron rule to check hourly, after an almost fatal experience, on an earlier sap, when his team was ambushed by a squad of German shock troops who broke through a sidewall of their tunnel. It was only the quick thinking of one of the former Durham miners in their ranks, that had saved all their lives, by chopping away a roof prop and entombing the intruders beneath tons of earth and clay. His men came mostly from mining and civil engineering backgrounds and he had drilled them to chop and shovel out earth, almost soundlessly.

The whole exercise required meticulous planning. The earth had to be extracted and disposed of stealthily and dispersed via camouflaged trench-tramways, well away from their position to keep their ploy hidden from observers in the enemy lines and in the air above

At the same time the delivery and handling of such a vast quantity of explosives was a very delicate operation, especially with random barrages likely to fall on their positions at any time. Any mistake could cause a deadly home goal for his side. Also they had raced against the weather ensuring they were done before the forecast rains of August made the ground too wet for the attacking troops to get across.

Everything was ready in early June for Plumer's second army to move up and take advantage of the breach. When the detonation was ordered, Dan and his men had moved back to a position in the rear where they could observe the result of their work without obstructing the assault wave. Nothing in his life could have prepared him or any man present on that day, for the devastating consequences of the simultaneous discharge of a million pounds of explosives. A great chunk of the fortifications and the ridge, on which they were built, completely disappeared as though vapourised. With it went some ten thousand German defenders. Retreating infantrymen told him later, that there were almost no human remains, just rags of clothing and shards of steel helmets to mark the passing of a complete football crowd's worth of men in one colossal bang.

The explosion was a total surprise, but the attack had been expected, it was impossible to hide the build up of troops in such flat terrain, but the usual stuff-ups between the planning and execution on the ground, led to the subsequent assault barely clearing the line of the ridge. So much effort and skill wasted and fearful loss of life, to achieve so little in the end. From here on Dan's cynicism went beyond the usual level of disdain for Generals and staff officers, which was the norm amongst soldiers on the Western Front. It began to harden deep inside him and made him question, what he was fighting for and what sort of society he might return to, if it were led by people such as those who professed to lead them here.

Somewhere in France 1917/18

Liza drove the heavy vehicle as carefully as she could down the rutted lane and into the clearing amongst the shattered pines. A row of large white tents stood in the misty gloom of a winter's afternoon, which almost obscured the Red Cross markings on their weather-stained roofs and walls. The men in her ambulance were in too bad a way to cry out at the bumping and jolting as she drew to a halt alongside lines of stretcher-bearers and orderlies, ready to race the wounded soldiers through the open flaps of the casualty reception area and in to resuscitation or on to surgical care.

She had tired of the constant headaches and monotony of the munitions plant and after a Manchester night out with a group of nurses and orderlies on leave, she was persuaded to sign up, learn to drive an ambulance and soon found herself across the Channel and into the thick of the action.

She was cold and exhausted from the endless trips in the dwindling light, along the treacherous shell-holed roads and took the proffered cigarette and steaming cup of Bovril from the kindly Salvo, with gratitude and unconcealed relief. Sitting next to her at the otherwise empty trestle table, which usually served as a lying in wait stage for those who had some hope of cheating death, was a beautiful but gaunt nursing sister whose ash-blonde hair and honey coloured skin were marred by her sunken eyes, rimmed with dark shadows of fatigue and the lines of stress and strain that traced their way from her eyes, to her cheeks.

"*Want a cig love?*" said Liza, pulling out a crumpled pack of Woodies.

"*No thanks, not one of my vices.*" The other woman replied, as she gave Liza a long appraising look.

"*You look as buggered as me.*" She added, stuffing a stray strand of her golden tresses under her prim nurse's hat.

"*Yeah, well I've not stopped driving backward and forward since last night's gas attack in which those poor devils were caught.*"

"*Yes, I know.*" She said. "*That's why I've got time for a break. There's not much we can do for them in surgery and for most of them it's the end already or a life of blindness and hacking and coughing their lungs up, that will see them off before too long. God! I thought the Anzac boys coming back home from Gallipoli had it bad.*"

"*Oh, you're an Aussie,*" acknowledged Liza, looking at her companion with renewed interest. "*Where are you from?*"

"*Melbourne.*" Came the reply "*and you?*"

"*Me? I'm from Manchester and I only got here a few months ago.*"

For another hour they exchanged histories and experiences but mostly they spoke about women's issues, such as the move into new

Western Front | Belgium | France | 1917/18

occupations, votes for women, what it was like for Australian women to have the vote for so long. They reflected on how the war had taken them in directions they could not have dreamed of a short time ago.

"I wonder where it will all end," mused Liza. "I'm certainly not going back to the drudgery of a mill job!"

"Yes!" said Alice. "The genteel life of the lady of the house in an East Melbourne mansion will not do for me either."

They both admired the Pankhurst women and what they had done for their British sisters. Alice had been inspired by meeting and working with a nurse, called Sarah Britain, who certainly blew a breath of fresh air through the starchy hierarchy of nursing. Liza was curious about life down under, which seemed so far away. Was it so different from England and how did women cope with the heat and the terrible fires she had heard about.

"It's not unlike the Mediterranean", Alice said, "Warm dry summers, lovely autumns and springs and a cold but not even frosty winter. We even have autumn leaves." She enthused, "and with St Kilda beach's promenade and pier on the bay, a mere tram ride from the centre of town, it's easier to get to the seaside there than you can get to Brighton or Blackpool at home".

The mention of Blackpool gave Liza pause, for a brief moment as her mind turned to thoughts of Dan. She hadn't heard from him since he left the Middle East and she wondered whether he was still alright.

"But what about living and working, especially for women?" Liza asked.

Alice thought for a moment before responding, "It's like a smaller version of England, We're more stuffy about some things and more relaxed and easy-going about others but nowadays women are getting a better go."

At last, Liza spoke about her life, about Ted and how his death had changed it and soon they made the inevitable connection between Dan and Charles and marveled at the coincidence of it.

"More casualties, Sister! The surgeons are scrubbed and ready to start," a nurse called from the entrance to the surgical tent.

"Got to go", said Alice, reluctantly and wearily. "Duty calls. Good to meet you Liza."

"And you too love. Take care," replied her newfound friend.

"Perhaps we'll meet for a drink in London or even better, in Melbourne, one day when all this is over," suggested Alice.

"I'll drink to that and God bless 'till then," agreed Liza, as they parted to pick up their parts in the war. But although their meeting had been so brief, they had tied a knot of common understanding that was more binding than that of the two men.

Cambrai, France 1917

Just when he had become accustomed to criticising the aged Generals for lacking any new ideas and fighting this war with the tactics of the past, Dan was fortunate enough to witness one of the most innovative and daring attempts at a final breakthrough to end the deadlocked conflict with one decisive blow.

He was safely housed in a concrete observation post which commanded a panoramic view of the ground between the German and allied positions and from which he was surveying a distant fortification on a slight rise, to assess what it would take to blow it away. This would open a gap and threaten the flank of a suspect Bavarian regiment that was thought not to have the same stomach for a fight as the Prussians.

The smoke was clearing after one of the heaviest barrages he had experienced since coming to France and he feared he was about to witness another futile infantry assault over open ground, in broad daylight with the consequent slaughter of the innocent and obedient participants. No wonder they were referred to as the 'poor bloody infantry.'

It was the unexpected growl of heavy engines, like those of overloaded lorries grinding desperately up steep moorland roads, which made everyone in the lookout-post put up their binoculars and gasp at the sight that could have come straight from the pages of HG Wells' *'War of the Worlds.'* Lumbering across the terrain from the British lines, with squads of infantry following in the shelter of their bulk, were hundreds of huge steel monsters moving on tracked wheels like those he had seen on steam-driven tractors at a farming show.

"*What are they?*" another Sergeant asked and their officer who had been a mechanical engineer in civvy-street said, "*Those my boys are our new secret weapon. They call them tanks.*"

Judging by the ease with which they were crossing deep, flooded shell holes and crushing their way through the tangles of defensive German wire, seemingly indifferent to the stream of machine gun and rifle fire directed at them, this was a weapon with a future. It would certainly win the approval of the steadily advancing men tucked safely into the wake of their protective iron skirts.

The effect on the enemy was devastating. Positions which had withstood weeks of attacks crumbled in minutes. Total panic was evident in the ranks of the enemy's élite troops and the sudden about face and dash to the rear by those defending the salient, confirmed the suspicions about the temperament of the southern German troops. Cheers erupted from the allied trenches and helmets flew in the air as the first sign of positive, infantry-friendly tactics began to unfold before their tired and incredulous eyes. The more than three hundred tanks soon blasted a major breach in the defensive positions and rolled on through to create mayhem in the enemy's rear. Their artillery was ranged to rain down fire on to static positions and not these moving monsters which fired back. They were incapable of comprehending let alone coping with this threat.

Dan was thrilled and wondered where and by whom they had been designed and built. He bet that Rolls Royce, back in Manchester, had had a hand in it somewhere.

Then when the initial excitement had abated and the tanks moved on out of sight, driving a confused and demoralised enemy before them, he wondered whether the stream of cavalry and foot soldiers that filed by would be enough this time to keep up the forward momentum and hold what had been so hard won.

"Silly, old buggers!" He exclaimed, "Most likely they'll stuff it up again."

He recalled a few lines from an officer poet called Sassoon, about a General, which was doing the rounds:

'He's a cheery old card', grunted Harry to Jack,
as they slogged up to Arras with rifle and pack.
But he did for them both with his plan of attack.

Over the next few weeks, tragically, he was proved right. Despite advancing six miles and taking thousands of prisoners, the predicted bad weather hampered the cavalry and insufficient infantry were made available to follow through and hold what had been so cheaply won. Within fifteen days the British had been driven back to almost where they had started.

What was the point of using twentieth century weapons when the tactics predated even the last century? Dan would now transfer to another sector and the deadly slog of probing fire began again as he packed up his kit and moved on.

10

Western Front, France
1917

Casualty Clearing Station
Somewhere in France, 1917

My Dear Charles,

I wonder how long it will take you to recover from the shock of receiving this letter and knowing that I am here in France. Like you, I can't say where I am but as you can see, I have come as a trained operating theatre sister and am based with an Anglo-Australian Red Cross hospital team, in a casualty clearing-station, not far behind our lines.

Being so far from you became too much for me and I thought I could do more to help the injured men closer to the action, where speed of evacuation and medical care make all the difference between survival and death. It's surprising what little things one learns that make the greatest difference. For instance, by leaving the severest of wounds open to the air rather than covering them, and keeping them free of the bacteria in the soil where men have lain, gas gangrene is best avoided. But, alas, as you will know we are so overwhelmed by the numbers of wounded that at times we are forced to sedate many whom we cannot treat. I am hardened by now to the most horrendous wounds but the pitiable condition of the gassed is still hard to bear, particularly as we can do so little for them.

Then there are those troubled in their minds, as I would be if I had suffered the horrors and risks that they and you, my darling, experience as part of your daily round. It is a crime against humanity that the French and British execute many such poor men who otherwise have done their duty beyond the limits of human endurance. I hear that far more Australian troops than

British go missing without leave but thank God our Generals and politicians will not allow our men to face a firing squad. On the positive side there is hope for the future as more and more doctors are becoming alienists and studying the possible causes and new kinds of treatment. For some the simple 'talking cure' developed by Freud and Jung seems to have a beneficial effect and they say there is a hospital for officers in Scotland that is specialising in battle stress cases. But other poor souls will have to be confined at home for the rest of their lives.

Goodness, what am I doing going on with all this morbid stuff when you are in so much more danger than me. You will be amazed to hear that I chanced on a woman friend of that Manchester soldier you 'bumped into' in Egypt. She drives an ambulance that delivers casualties to our post. Poor woman, her late husband was one of those poor sods (sorry Charles, see how this life is coarsening me already) who cracked and was court-martialed and shot. She doesn't know where Dan is, but he survived Cape Helles, Krithia and Mesopotamia and is over here now and probably involved in every attempt to blow a way through the lines.

I liked Liza, she's down to earth, tough, intelligent and resourceful, one of the new post-war women in the making, whose ability and ambition are defying the confines of her class. How the British cling to this comfort blanket of social hierarchy. They seem to know instantly all about their fellow country people's social and economic situation and where they come from by the way they dress and speak. Still, I suppose we are not entirely innocent with our 'squattocracy' and the way we measure people by the school they attended and which church they belong to. But we are so far ahead socially in the way we treat each other and I weep for those French and British soldiers when I think about the meager rewards they will return to after the war. Even skilled engineering soldiers like Dan get only one shilling and eight pence a day whereas our boys get five bob.

You men will face an even bigger challenge of change when you return home because women are on the march. So watch out my boy, you need to be aware that many of them, like Liza and even me, will not go back to pre-war life and traditional women's roles.

Enough of this social lecturing! How are you, my love? Well and safe, I hope. God forbid that you ever appear at our tent door or on *the table. I'm glad that Alf is there to stand by you. I did what you asked and received the sweetest note from his wife thanking me for sending on dad's gifts and it was signed by all the children.*

I am tired and drawn, not as lovely as you remember me and now I can imagine the stress and fatigue you face at every waking hour. Charles, you must talk about what happens and your feelings, no matter how terrible your duty and who better to confide in but your ever-loving and devoted wife, especially now that I appreciate more the horrors you face.

Goodnight sweet man. I don't know what happens about leave from the front with things as desperate as they are. But I'm sure you have the resources to find me, even if Alf has to track me and how wonderful it would be to get together, no matter how briefly, in Paris or London or just some little shell-hole somewhere in France.

With all my love,

Your wife,

Alice

Somewhere in France, December 1917

So much for dash and movement, thought Charlie, as through the tangles of wire, he surveyed a sea of mud, with shell holes filled to the brim with fetid pools of water and he all but gagged at the dreadful smell of thousands of unwashed, lousy men in close proximity and the decomposing remains of many thousands more who were beyond caring. It was an instant death sentence to rise above the parapet and even his periscope attracted the occasional chance shot from bored snipers.

"Jesus, Alf, what a hell-hole. I'm not sure what smells worse, us or those poor dead sods out there."

"Yeah! Thank God for what we learned at Gallipoli. Yesterday some poor green subaltern raised his arm to test the wind and lost half his hand, in the blink of an eye."

But even that hardship had not prepared the Aussies for the dreadful resignation of this place. It was as if men on both sides had abandoned all hope and were merely passing their time in a queue shuffling along to their inevitable deaths.

Western Front | France | 1917

"At least the armchair warriors have given up ordering those suicide charges. The French mutiny must have given them a fright."

"Might be that the top brass are starting to listen to Pompey Elliott and word is that Monash is getting involved in planning and rehearsing attacks."

But still the Generals had ambitions for one last great push that would end it all with a single triumphant blow. The Germans were far from done, however, and had given the allies some close run fights. But the sheer weight of the new American manpower and their military manufacturing capacity ensured that it could only have one end. But the question on every combatant's lips was *"When? Please dear God, when?"*

In the meanwhile death came in daily doses, delivered by shellfire, snipers and gas. Real man-to-man fighting was rare, but the occasional night raid to test enemy alertness brought the threat of a lucky bomb throw and brief barbaric melees which involved slithering, blindly, around in mud and darkness, hoping to get in the first deadly blow with whatever was at hand. Picks, shovels, knives, spiked knuckle-dusters and even modified car springs and bike chains were employed in these primitive encounters. It was positively medieval, more like the field of Agincourt than a twentieth century battle.

Suddenly, a mist began to roll in enveloping Charlie's position and at once he screamed *"Gas!"* as men whirled bullroarers, sending defenders scrambling to don gas masks. But it was smoke not gas and that could mean only one thing, an attack was coming in. It was too late to call down artillery support and he noted with approval that Alf was moving steadily amongst the newer arrivals, ensuring they knew what to do and that panic didn't take hold.

"Steady!" yelled Charlie. *"Hold your fire 'til I give the command."*

He could see the first wave of gray-clad ghosts, snipping and wriggling through the coils of perimeter wire and when they were far enough into the killing ground, but still short of bomb throwing range, he unleashed a hail of fire down on them from pre-ranged heavy machine guns and fusillades of rifle fire from hundreds of Lee-Enfields in the hands of Australian infantrymen for whom this had become as easy and natural as riding a bike or swimming in surf.

Alerting his reserves at the rear of the trench with the order *"Fix bayonets!"* he couldn't help feel a shiver of primal fear race up his spine at the rattle and clack of dozens of deadly blades being locked into place, ready to dispatch any brave souls who survived the lead storm and made it into the Aussie frontline trench. In one hand he brandished his father's deadly Colt and in the other he held a Mills bomb primed for the throw. Very few came through and those who did fell quickly to a volley of shots and a brief and deadly bayonet charge by the reserves.

Sensing a withdrawal, and then hearing the trill of German officers whistles recalling those of their men who were left, Charlie hurled his bomb in their direction to speed them on their way.

"*Sergeants secure parapet!*" Charlie ordered. He had been caught out before, by standing down prematurely. Then he turned to check the butcher's bill as the medical orderlies scurried to provide aid to the wounded. It was not as bad as usual, their position was well prepared and as veterans his men were very well rehearsed. Driving rain swept away the last wisps of smoke and as the soggy gray twilight clamped down on friend and foe alike, Charlie slipped into his dugout to smoke his pipe and read again the amazing news from his wife.

"*Happy Christmas, boss!*" Alf greeted him, as he came through the dugout curtain.

"*To you too, Alf, and many more of them in happier places than this.*"

Christmas! he had forgotten that it had come last night and wondered at what devil's work he had been engaged on the eve of Christ's birth

He had been stunned by Alice's letter and was both troubled and impressed that she had come to the front. What a woman he had married and what a different future they would make together, if only he could get out of here alive.

11

A Home Fit For Heroes

Manchester, 11 November 1919

It was the eleventh hour of the eleventh day of the eleventh month, exactly one year since the war to end all wars had concluded. It had cost the lives of eight and a half million combatants and over thirteen million civilians had died from war-related causes, famine and epidemics. Dan and Liza stood to attention as the final strains of the last post echoed off the ancient walls of Manchester cathedral. Both had a host of memories of lost comrades and Dan could recall the unearthly silence that fell over his position on that day, a year ago, when the ceasefire was declared. There had been no bird-song in that wasteland for the past few years and the cessation of human activity left a threatening soundless void, which the men seemed unwilling to fill, even with their own voices. It was still hard to believe that it was over and that now they had a new future to face, without the daily grind of duty and the ever-present fear of sudden violent death.

The majority of women in the congregation, at the memorial service, pointed to one of the challenges to come. Three in ten of the boys and young men aged between thirteen and twenty-four in 1914 had been killed and the bravest and best of a generation had gone, leaving the country to be led by many of those rear-échelon warriors, whose tragic tactics had made this disaster. Manchester suffered more than its fair share of this deadly reaping. The war poet, Wilfred Owen had died fighting with the Manchesters within a week of the armistice and Henry Moseley, a leading scientist at the University, fell at Suvla Bay.

The service and ceremony were hard on the still raw emotional wounds and afterwards Dan and Liza strolled arm-in-arm under the flags in the Manchester Regiment's memorial chapel. Some were so old, that they dated back to battlefields from India to Waterloo and finally, the Somme. They hung fragile as gossamer, unruffled by the still air of the darkening Cathedral interior. The memorial book, recording those who had died was on display and a page would be turned every day for eternity or until Christianity quit this ancient site.

"*At least the demand for monumental masons, undertakers and doctors will provide plenty of jobs for some for the foreseeable future,*" mused Dan bitterly, as he thought of the honeyed promises of politicians to build a home fit for heroes.

"*But at least there will be more choices for women to develop careers and use their talents,*" Liza countered.

For most it was a disaster and a betrayal of all that they had sacrificed especially their youth and their idealism. Where women had not taken over, the most venal and disreputable of men, who had earned up to five pounds a week at war work compared with the Tommies five bob a week fighting pay, seemed to have a strangle-hold on the best jobs.

"*Aye! After all that underground killing there's no way I'm going back to the mine now and what sort of government will we get with the loss of the brightest and the best?*"

The monarchy was desperately trying to hold things together as their Russian, German and Austrian relatives were either murdered or banished and to give him credit, George had appeared in the front line and signed personal letters to all the officers and men who returned from captivity. But societies in Europe were shaky and in some cases under threat of revolution.

"*Where, will it all end? Perhaps that Marxist orator on that wet night in Ancoats was right after all.*"

"*I don't want to go back to my old work either. Pankhurst and the Suffragettes are on the right track and I might see what I can do to help women get ahead.*"

Though they walked hand in hand, their thoughts and feelings were not in tandem.

He couldn't settle with Arthur and Beattie, despite their love and understanding. It was all too soft, confining and unreal compared with the comradeship of those men bound in a forthright brotherhood by a trade of imminent death and daily destruction. He couldn't accept the King and country for which he had fought but nor did revolution hold any appeal or answer his questions about an uncertain future in a world without the unifying purpose of war. Manchester also had lost its inspiration for him and there was no future for him with Liza, because she was bound up in causes he did not share and was leaning left and all but red.

For Liza, the ending was a new beginning. She had endured as much as any man and more importantly, as a person, she had grown. She had a new confidence and courage that had not been necessary in the days when she had floated along under the wing of Ted's protection and influence. But now she could think and fend for herself. At last, Mancunians had had enough of sacrificing their working lives to the enrichment of the city and its merchant aristocracy. The new and growing Labour Party was the future for them and Liza threw herself into the cause.

It had been surprisingly easy to move from supervisor to union organiser as she knew all the tricks on both sides of the fence and it wasn't long before she achieved office in the ranks of the cotton operatives union, just as cheap Asian textiles were starting to challenge the comparatively high-paying Lancashire industry's future. For the next few years she learned how to campaign, door-knock and make herself heard at factory gate meetings, even when heckled and abused by the men.

She demonstrated in defiance of the police for a further extension of the women's vote, which had been limited to those over thirty since 1918. She lost touch with Dan, it was as though his light had gone out as hers had flared up and he had vanished without trace and nobody, including Arthur and Beattie, knew what he was doing nor where he had gone.

12

Taking to the Dream Road

Derbyshire, December 1919

Dan was still battle fit, hard and young and even a winter's night outdoors held no fears for him, having slept so often under shellfire in Flanders' freezing winter fields. So he had filled his army pack with a few belongings and donning his military-issue boots, puttees and gas cape, slipped out into a freezing cold Manchester dawn and followed the same route he had taken in that innocent summer of 1914, on the way to the Derbyshire dales. It felt far from a home fit for heroes to Dan as he warmed himself by the fire in the Nag's Head, supping a consoling pint before braving the elements on the Pennine route that would take him north, along the high spine of northern England, in search of his own land.

Money had been made out of war industries and it was being spent freely. But little of it trickled down to those who had either served or whose lives had been blighted by losing breadwinners for freedom's cause. At the top of the social pile the aristocrats had lost a generation who might otherwise have inherited and modernised their land and property holdings. They were now being forced to sell off assets to meet crippling death duties. At the other end of the scale, the wages of industrial workers and farm labourers were being depressed by imports and international competition, as cheap Asian textiles threatened the Lancashire cotton trade and American manufacturing, which had been boosted by the war effort, began to steal Britain's traditional heavy engineering export markets. Rail and coal strikes had aroused fears of Communism and a Labour government encouraged de-mobbed officers to strike-break and even called out the navy to stand by in Liverpool, just in case.

Although Dan had been promoted to Lieutenant in the field he felt neither at one with that class, once out of the war zone. Nor could he sympathise with the miners and workers, with whom he had grown up. After what he had been through he couldn't return to the mine nor to his studies, but his disdain for authority in the shape of politicians and armchair Generals was not so great as to make him a revolutionary in the Russian mould. He was aware that some of his former comrades had stayed on in the army and had gone to Russia to fight against the reds. But this held no appeal for him.

His desire to give up and run away, to which he had almost succumbed on many desperate occasions at the front, finally found its fulfillment in a novel solution to his lack of purpose and interest in peacetime life. He realised that apart from his time training in London and trips to Blackpool, he had seen none of his own country, although he had learned much about it from the array of people from different parts, he had served with. So, he had decided to set out heading north in winter to see where he might end up.

The lack of a fixed plan and destination suited his mood of uncertainty and added a pleasurable sense of expectation to his departure. All he knew was that he wanted to escape the depressing confines of the dark and dirty industrial slums and get away from the crowds of people who seemed stuck in a powerless acceptance of their lot or looked to politicians to get them out of it. He hoped to find another brighter more hopeful England populated and led by the likes of those classless, competent men and women with whom he had gladly served and fought. Derbyshire was known to him and seemed as good a place as any to start.

After an hour's hard upward slogging to gain the main ridge track, Dan had overcome the initial resistance of both his body and mind. He had crossed the pain barrier that he recalled from his school cross-country running days and was moving fluidly with an easy ground-devouring stride. The cold and madness of attempting to walk such country in mid winter had given him pause, but as the effort warmed his body, his spirits soared above their bodily confines and he felt a first glimmer of hope and delight in a venture that had no clear purpose but which, at least, had propelled him out of his dulling lethargy.

Although exposed to the bitter wind, the rain held off and the air had a rare winter clarity that enabled him to see for miles and to contrast the harsh loneliness of the soggy upland water table with the black smoke stacks and endless rows of terraced houses, spilling over their city bounds to gobble up more and more of England's countryside. So far, he had made good going but as he approached the peat-bogged terrain of Bleaklow, his lightened mood gave way to a growing unease at the prospect of crossing this treeless, trackless expanse of black, oozing peat.

This was the early stage of vegetable decomposition that covered a vast area deep in compost-like silt and which, given thousands more years of compression, would become coal, the cause of his spending so much of his youth underground.

His map showed no track and whilst it was unsafe to attempt a direct crossing of the peat, there was the option of threading his way along the beds of many streams which drained the bogs, making a meandering pathway to his destination on the other side.

He had not gone far when a rocky outcrop offered him the chance to take his lunch, in a dry spot, sheltered from the biting wind. The cheese and onion butties reminded him of his working days and he smiled as he recalled Beattie in her kitchen, cutting the thick slices of bread and telling him approvingly that

"There's a right pair of dossers' wedges to keep yer goin."

It was then that he realised what was troubling him about this place. For the past hour he had tramped only the firm gravel-bedded streams with water lapping up to and sometimes over the lace holes of his boots, winding through deep gullies whose black, loamy peat banks rose on either side to a height of ten feet, shutting out any view of the surrounding terrain. All he could see was the brown gravel stream bed, the pewter gray sky and the black, oozing flanks of the gully.

"That's it!" he cried out. *"It's a bloody trench line".* If it weren't for the total silence and absence of human company, he could have been back in the hellish rabbit warren back over there.

Suddenly a voice cut into his reverie, causing him to jump up and drop his sandwich into the mud.

"Are you thinking what I'm thinking?"

Spinning round, Dan saw a short, stocky figure dressed, like him, partly in civvies, tweeds and tell tale items of military issue that had seen hard service along with their owner who, despite his cheerful freckled face, bright blue eyes and flaming red hair, had that watchful, awareness about him and the gaunt look of the hunter too long in search of his elusive prey.

"Yes" replied Dan, *"Add a fire step, a dug-out, some duck-boards and wire and we'd be back there."*

"Why aye bonny lad." The stranger continued. *"Just when you think*

you've escaped and even in such a quiet and lonely place, as far as you could get from the crowds in this tiny island, the memories flood back to haunt you."

Having recovered his composure, Dan introduced himself.

"I'm Dan Smith, late Lieutenant in the sappers and survivor of the Dardanelles, Mesopotamia and France".

"That's a more impressive record of survival than mine" responded Captain Angus Armstrong of the Durham Light Infantry.

"I was taken prisoner early in the piece and sat out most of the war in a Jerry prison camp. Still that was no picnic as I had wounds that got limited attention and the food got worse and less and less as Germany ran out of resources."

They shook hands, squatted down together and were soon sharing their rations and chatting away like the lifelong friends that time in the trenches made of complete strangers.

Angus was walking back from the war to his home in Durham where he hoped to resume his studies at the university. Despite his Scottish name, the Geordie lilt in his voice was ill-disguised beneath his otherwise polished English and was explained by the fact that his father, a pit-man from Lanark, had come down from Scotland to work in the Durham coal fields and encouraged his son to take a scholarship at a grammar school and go on to start reading philosophy and economics at Durham, before the war intervened.

Dan had met lots of Geordies in the sappers and he knew that there was always one to be found where there was a shovel, a soccer ball, a beer or a fight. But this one was different, he had those cheery but steely contradictions alright, but overlaying this was the abstract thinker who subjected all ideas and especially 'givens' up to the light of scrutiny and surprisingly often found them to be suspect or wanting in ways that Dan had never considered before.

The Crowdon valley had been taken over for rifle training during the war and the youth hostel, which had barely reopened after its finish, should have been closed for the winter but the warden was an old sweat from the South African war and was all too willing to accommodate these winter wanderers. After a plain but filling meal of thick pea soup and crusty bread, they gathered by the fire to exchange experiences, helped along by tots of malt whisky from a flask that Angus produced from his pack.

"Strictly forbidden under YHA rules, except, of course on medicinal grounds" said the warden, with a wink, as he took a swig of the pure water of life.

What started, that evening, as a relaxed, friendly conversation, developed during the next day's northbound trek into a brisk debate that would have done justice to the best tradition of Oxbridge tutorials.

"Dan, You must admit our heritage of defending the rights of free men and distributing wealth. It began with Magna Carta, then followed Parliament's resistance to a tyrannical king and even under Cromwell, the Diggers and Levellers amongst his troops wanted to distribute land to the people. Workers rebelled against enslavement by the new machines and those brave Tolpuddle Martyrs were exiled to Australia for their Unionism. Even in your home town the massacred Chartists were only asking for the vote for all and freedoms we now take for granted."

Just when Dan thought he had tagged Angus as a Bolshevik supporter of socialism, he revealed his complete dedication to anarchism. For him there was no state of society that could ever satisfy his ideals of individual freedom.

"That's all well and good, Angus and I can readily meet you part way in your beliefs. In your review of our history you conveniently neglected to recognise that it was the new constitutional monarchy, laws enacted by parliament and the formation of trades union that have won and preserved our rights and liberties. Rebels have certainly highlighted injustices but seldom righted them.

The complete disregard for and rejection of any kind of system of law and order, make me more than just uncomfortable. I can't ignore the rioting, looting and worse that broke out in newly liberated French villages before order was restored and some of my mates who went with the unsuccessful British expeditionary force to Russia described sickening scenes of cruelty and depravity perpetrated by both the Red and White armies in pursuit of your sort of lofty rights and entitlements."

"So you're a monarchist then Dan and you the working class son of mining stock! You ought to be ashamed of your self!" Angus taunted.

"Well yes, I suppose I am in favour of keeping the King" Responded Dan, rather tentatively. "If that will maintain social stability and only if he is ultimately accountable to a democratically elected parliament." He concluded, with much greater conviction.

"The fact that communism has made much less progress here than in Russia and Germany is down to our governments' legislation which is curbing the worst extremes of the bosses and recognises the rights of workers."

Angus derided this as rubbish but, despite the continuing polarity of their positions, they were amicable in their agreement to disagree.

Their exchanges continued to be bold, spirited and to an observer, unfamiliar with hard-headed debating tactics, might have appeared over-direct, certainly impolite, possibly rude and seeming at times to suggest the onset of violence. But how they loved it, as the miles reeled off and they argued their way through rain and sleet-squalls, across bleak moor and fell, contributing their own torrent of words to the spindrift carried away on the biting wind.

Along the way they diverted to visit interesting locations, such as Richmond, the home of the Yorkshire regiment, the Green Howards, which had distinguished itself in France and some of whose members had been imprisoned with Angus in Germany. In the market square below the castle they renewed their acquaintance with ripe local cheeses and Tetley's ale.

Continuing on their northern way, as they forded swollen streams and waded across boggy saturated plateaus, they marveled that this was the birthplace of the major rivers on which the industrial and harbour cities of the north had built their prosperity. On bright sunny winter days, Dan could not conceal the delight he felt when intermittent patches of sunlight and shadow rippled across the landscape switching on and off the purple hues of heather and spot-lighting the dirty-white fleeces of grazing sheep. Charlie had spoken fondly of his memories of the strong Australian sunlight and dry astringent scent of the trackless bush and Dan wondered how he was settling down and what he would have made of Angus and his philosophy.

13

Back Down-Under

Melbourne, Australia 1919

Dear Liza,

Thank you for your recent letter and Christmas greetings. I was concerned to hear that Dan had disappeared but in some ways it is not surprising, as many men here have found it so hard to readjust to civilian life. In the coastal cities there is a flourishing lifesaving club movement, which gives them a chance to maintain their comradeship and army-style disciplines, but many have taken to drink and abusing their wives and families

Charles is doing well. His work at the bar, commitment to the rehabilitation of less fortunate comrades and occasional escapes to the family property, have prevented him suffering the malaise that is preventing so many from moving on in their lives. I regret to tell you that Charles' mother and father have died of the flu that has swept across the country. As though it weren't enough to suffer sixty thousand war dead, ten thousand more have been taken by the Spanish influenza epidemic.

Charles says little about what happened at the front, not that I need telling after my work with the wounded at the casualty stations. But it might help him to relieve the pressures that I see when he awakes suddenly, watchful and alert, in the middle of the night, muttering about 'standing to' as though readying for some enemy action. His wounds have healed but he has a disconcerting habit of suddenly rubbing his hands together violently, as though desperate to keep warm, and at the same time he shuffles backwards at great speed until he stands several feet away. Strangers are shocked and disturbed by this, whereas children find it great fun and typically he laughs with them to hide his embarrassment. Fortunately it hasn't happened in court yet but if it did, I am sure his shell-

shock would endear him to any jury in this current climate of hero worship of those who have served. I find it best to keep my own counsel but Charles, although having fought willingly for his king and country, seems to see some points in favour of all sides.

But enough of this woeful stuff-Melbourne is marvelous again and a world away from the dark days and gloomy weather of wartime London and Northern France. Women are being pressured out of factories and professions by the returning men but the shortage of manpower still offers them new opportunities and with the growth of veterans' health services and the repatriation hospitals, there is considerable demand for my services.

How are you going Liza? What are you doing with yourself? Going back to management in the mill or have you been lured into women's politics? I wish you and Dan had got together and made a go of it, then perhaps you could have come out here and joined us. Australia needs get ahead people like you two.

Let us know as soon as you find where and how he is.

With love from me and Charles,

Alice

PS. I am enclosing some clippings from our main newspapers, the Age and the Argus. I hope they will answer some of your questions about Melbourne and give you a picture of life in Australia since the war.

Australia Bounces Back

Now that the horrors of the war are behind us and most of our men are back home, the city is shaking off its gloom and once more, can it be said to be "marvelous Melbourne."

The war has brought social changes and our economy is expanding at a great pace. There is much more manufacturing to compete with farming for workers and this has created an acute shortage of skilled labour.

Though, sadly, many of our women, are bereaved and must devote themselves to the care of wounded fathers, husbands and sons, new employment opportunities have opened up for them. Everywhere, they've abandoned service, the kitchen, the nursery and the drawing room to work at all the jobs and professions that once were the sole preserve of men.

Whilst women are continuing to serve as they did in war time it is vital that we replenish our working population from sound stock so that one day we will be able to stand on our own feet, free of ties to Britain and any other 'old world' powers.

The Age
Melbourne

Enemies Within

There is growing tension between the returned soldiers and those in the powerful union movements, especially the wharf workers, whom many consider betrayed the men at the front by some of their actions. Some see a threat from those International Workers of the World, One Big Union radicals and Irish Republican sympathisers, who opposed conscription and accused those brave men who fought, of being 'mindless lackeys of Empire'.

This is sad when we know how many loyal Irishmen of all denominations and trade unionists enlisted and fought for their principles. On the other hand, there are some sinister shadowy figures that are rumored to be conducting secret military maneuvers on remote properties, in case of a Bolshevik uprising.

Such is the concern of our returned servicemen at the breakdown of law and order that, in July, two hundred diggers burst into the Premiers offices complaining about the attitude of the Victorian police.

This has led some to question the selflessness of some of our politicians including the 'Little Digger', Billy Hughes, but our servicemen laud the benefits he has won for them.

Melbourne's Catholic Archbishop, Cardinal Mannix, appears to be too close to the Irish Republican cause for an Australian cleric, but the persecution of father Jerger, the German born Catholic priest and push to deport him, seems to us a shameful act of prejudice.

Perils Without

We have seen what Japan did to the Russian navy and now that revolution and civil war have crippled her further, there is no great power at hand which can protect us, if the Royal Navy could not come to our aid. In Australia we can no longer hide from the world. Should the European Empires in the Pacific and Asia ever crumble, we are so vulnerable, so far away and alone.

We need more European people to secure our isolated outpost in an otherwise Asian sea and what better source exists than those men and women of British stock that we fought alongside in Europe and the Middle East.

The Argus
Melbourne

14

Law Without Order

Durham, England 1920

The smashed glass on the pavements, the result of flying brown ale bottles thrown by truculent, drunken miners, should have alerted Dan to impending trouble, but it wasn't until he heard the jingle of harnesses and the scrape of horse shoes, seeking traction on slippery cobblestones, that he realised he was in peril of becoming an innocent victim of a mounted police charge. He had no previous experience of such tactics but recalling the legendry massacre of Chartist demonstrators by undisciplined Yeoman cavalry in Manchester's St Peters Fields, he began to run through the mob as they desperately dug up cobblestones to hurl at the oncoming mounted men.

What was he doing in such a predicament? He had so recently turned his back on the war to end all wars and set off North to find a new direction and purpose, far away from violence and the getting of coal, only to find his self shoulder to shoulder with Geordie miners, in the front line of industrial strife.

At Angus' invitation, Dan had terminated his pilgrimage and taken up residence in Durham and to his surprise, found himself living once more in the shadow of pithead winding gear and sharing evening pints in company with coal miners and their wives.

The day had broken fine and he had welcomed Angus's invitation to go and enjoy the fun of the annual Durham miners' Gala and such fun it was. After the impressive parade of pitmen beneath their gloriously colourful union banners, marching in military precision behind the most famous of the great brass bands, carefree crowds of colliers, their wives, children and sweethearts gathered to hear and heckle the leading Labour politicians of the day, who promised an even more utopian home fit for returning heroes. After this they were to disperse and enjoy all the fun of the fair.

But then, as he had seen at that pre-war gathering in Ancoats, something had happened to change the cheerful mood of the crowd and turn it into a restless mob looking for a target for its growing hostility. At first, Dan had taken little notice of the bus loads of seemingly merry, inebriated men who had joined the throng, assuming them to be miners who had stayed on longer at the pubs after their march and who now wished to join in the fun of the political rally. But at various strategic locations in the crowd, agitators began to call out strident objections to state-sponsored welfare and voiced ever louder demands for freedom from control of bosses, politicians, police and even the king. The Russian experience was highly praised and recommended and it was not long before opposing factions formed and turned on each other, with fists and sickening kicks from iron-shod clogs.

As Dan moved to distance himself from the disarray, he noticed what seemed to be organisers back by the buses giving instructions to runners who carried their orders into the throng. Foremost among these was the familiar figure of his good friend Angus. So much for his much vaunted bill of rights. Suddenly what had been but the harmless banter and debate of the moorland trail had become the rallying cry for true anarchists who respected neither the lives, limbs nor liberties of these innocent citizens, who were out for a day of recreation and fun.

Dan had run hard away from the mob up Saddler Street and was beginning to slow up along North Bailey towards the imposing Cathedral when he was tripped and pinned to the ground by an enormous policeman, who enclosed Dan's head in his cape before manhandling him into a nearby Black Maria. It was well after dark before the cell door opened and he was amazed at the cheery greeting of his captor.

"Well now Lieutenant Bevan what were you doing in such disreputable company. I've a good mind to put you on a charge!"

"Hells bells," replied Dan, "It's Sapper Purvis, isn't it? You were on my team at Messines."

"That's me, sir," he agreed holding out a steaming mug of tea and a thick bacon sandwich. "I was one of yer champion diggers on that fine occasion. Aye, It were me that brought down the roof on them Jerry shock troops. So what brings yer to these parts and what d' yer mean by joining with them there anarchist scum?"

"It's a long story." Said Dan, "and not nearly as bad as it seems. But how did you get on to me? Were you looking out for me or was our meeting an accident?"

"It were pure chance yer running past me then," replied Purvis. "But yer was on a list of folks we was looking for. The powers that be are reet worried about the increase in strike action and now troops and tanks 'ave been sent into Glasgow to control what they call 'Red Clydeside', anyone associated with troublemakers is under suspicion. So, although we know y'er not as involved as yon Captin Armstrong, it'd be best if yer made yerself scarce and got out of 'ere as soon as possible."

"So I'm not under arrest?" Dan queried.

"Why no me canny lad" Purvis retorted, reassuringly. "Ah kept yer name outer the charge book and the men thinks as yer just a drunken Toff sleeping off an 'eavy night out."

Having thanked Purvis profusely for his comradely loyalty, Dan made haste to get out of Durham. Making his way across to Carlisle in the West, he stopped along the way at the sites of the Roman garrison forts, which were important staging posts along Hadrian's Wall. From a high point on this northern rampart of the Roman Empire, he peered out over bleak country under a black rain-sodden sky, recalling that Charlie's ancestors might have raided this far south, preying on isolated farmhouses and communities somewhere out there.

Carlisle was full of troops returning from the troubles in Glasgow and others on the way to keep an on-going watch, although things had settled down since the worst of last year. The unrest must have been serious thought Dan, when he learned from a group of Tommies gathered round a station pie stall, that about twelve thousand soldiers had been involved at the height of it.

Purvis had given Dan the address of a cheap, rundown bed and breakfast place in the grimy back streets of Carlisle, whose landlady and transient guests were disinclined to ask or answer questions about their business, where they were heading next and why? This suited him fine.

In the back bar of a nearby pub he had a cold and gristly pork pie for his tea and was invited by a group of ex-servicemen who had seen service with the Durham Light Infantry in France, to join in their game of darts. There was unspoken acceptance of a former comrade in arms and he had no qualms about sharing with them his disillusion with 'civvie-street' and lack of any future plans.

He enjoyed their easy acceptance and readily agreed to go with them to a nearby ex-servicemen's club where they were to farewell some mates who were about to serve overseas.

The club was uncomfortably warm and smoky with a friendly crowd of members, who accepted him as a brother, despite his accent making it obvious that he didn't come from round there. A circumstance that would have guaranteed much more reserve in pre-war days. To his surprise, the overseas posting was not with the regular army, but to do police work in Southern Ireland, where former war service officers and men were being employed as a paramilitary force to relieve the Royal Irish Constabulary in combating IRA terrorism. He had heard about this newly formed force, which the Irish called the 'Black and Tans' because their uniforms, made up of a mix of police dark-green and ex-army Khaki issue with black belts, reminded people of a pack of Limerick foxhounds bearing this name. But so far they had seen little action and their atrocities had not yet hit the headlines.

By the end of the evening, he had drunk more than he had intended and in the morning, despite his mental 'fug' and aching head, he recalled his agreement to go with the new recruits to see about enlisting himself. Despite some reservations about this work, he needed the money and to get away to a place where the British authorities might lose track of him. Where could be better than in their employment when their eagerness to win recruits had overcome their caution about the backgrounds of those they were engaging. Also, it meant leaving England and across the water he would be less likely to bump into anyone who knew him and about his Durham escapades.

But before he boarded the train that was to take the new recruits to Liverpool for embarkation to Dublin, Dan picked up the evening paper. The news was all about strikes and disturbances and he was about to turn to the sports pages when he spotted an item about a demonstration by suffragettes in Manchester. A group of them had chained themselves to the railings around the central gardens in Piccadilly square and some had been arrested and even imprisoned for this and violent resistance to arrest. Three constables had sustained severely bruised shins and black eyes.

"My God!" exclaimed Dan, as he read that one of the women who had been put away for twelve months was a union organiser called Eliza Miller.

He would have to write to Arthur and Beattie as soon as he got to Dublin to find out where and how she was and he realised it was about time he let them know that he was safe and well and serving in Ireland.

Manchester 1920

Dear Dan,

It was a relief to get your recent letter, Beattie and me were right worried about you and it's good to know you are safe and sound, although from what we hear about the Irish troubles and what some of those Black and Tans are getting up to we fear you might be back in harms way. Anyway, we pray that it will soon be settled and that you will come, safe home.

Afraid the news of Liza is not good. On top of her twelve month sentence she has made things worse by going on a hunger strike and when we last saw her she was a shadow of her usual sparkling self. We were mortified to hear that she had caught pneumonia and is in the prison hospital, where we cannot visit her.

We are sure that news of you will encourage her to buck up and although her mail privileges have been withdrawn, somehow her women friends get messages through and so we have passed the word to them that you are fine and send her your love and support. We thought it best not to mention Ireland.

Times are bad here, but what's new about that in Manchester. The returned men feel let down by the politicians and even those in work are restless and resentful of the employers who lined their pockets during the war and don't want to share some of their good fortune with their people. I fear it's going to lead to even bigger strikes than we have had already on the railways and even worse, there may be a total breakdown of law and order.

Winston Churchill, you know, who got blamed for the muck up at Gallipoli, has been up here speaking in his electorate about the need for restraint and warning about the evils of Bolshevism. He's not that popular, especially with the suffragettes and miners, but at least he served in the front line in France when he lost his job at the Admiralty. Which is more than you can say about Lloyd George – they say he spent most of his time serving the women. I don't know what to make of Winny. He's reactionary about some things and radical about others-he even supports Irish self-rule, but not the Republican version.

Well best be off to bed-early start in the morning. I'm still doing a bit up at the pit and have to be up at 'sparrer's fart'. Now you take care, do you hear? Beattie sends her special love and so do I and I have no doubt Liza would too if she could.

Arthur

15

Irish Troubles

Dublin, Ireland 1921

Dan's rank and war service had been recognised by the recruiters and his experience in making and defusing bombs had made him a natural candidate for the squad responsible for detecting and dismantling the booby-traps and land mines, that the IRA delighted in placing along roads and under bridges in anticipation of passing dignitaries and military patrols.

This work had taken him beyond the confines of Dublin and gave him both an appreciation for the beauty of the Irish countryside and familiarity with the grinding rural as well as urban poverty suffered by the people. He couldn't help sympathising with their wish for independence from Britain, especially as he observed the callous behaviour of some of the Anglo-Irish landowners and British officialdom. But as the violence mounted and began to take the lives of so many innocent civilians, he could not endorse the rebels methods and wondered whether it was worth all this strife to escape the rule of a comparatively benign sovereignty.

Terrible atrocities were being committed by both sides and especially the rogue group of former British army officers, known as the AUXIS, who had mutilated victims and burnt people's properties at will. But Dan was really shocked when the IRA raided the lodgings of British Intelligence officers on a quiet Sunday morning and gunned down fourteen of them in their beds or whilst they were dressing. This was then followed by equally vicious retaliation by the Black and Tans who slaughtered innocent football supporters.

As a result it became increasingly perilous for British soldiers, especially in their off-duty moments, to walk the streets unaccompanied in many parts of Dublin.

On one particular night, Dan was walking home from attending a performance of one of Sing's comedies at the Abbey theatre, when he was confronted by three youths who had emerged suddenly from a darkened side street. Dan tried to joke his way out of the situation but, as they backed him against a wall, calling him all manner of filthy names, he knew they intended him harm and that he would have to fight before he could run.

Whilst Dan had confined his work to bomb disposal and kept out of the raids and reprisal activities of some of his comrades, he was no angel when it came to 'rough house brawls' and especially when defending himself. Survival at the front had often depended on the quicker reflexes of those engaged in hand to hand combat in narrow trenches, half full of water and mud, together with proficiency in the use of extraordinarily primitive weapons that suited the close quarters struggles in confined spaces, where rifles and bayonets were useless.

As a precaution, therefore, Dan had continued to keep a short, razor sharp stabbing knife secreted in his puttees, close to his calf where he could draw it when crouching, as though hurt or if he were knocked down. In the pocket of his trench coat was a length of bicycle chain that when swung in a vicious arc around the head was a very effective deterrent to attackers with knives or clubs.

But on this occasion he relied on a ruse he had learned from Scottish troops in France. Like some of the Highland regiments, he often wore a forage cap in Ireland and as the men charged him, he grasped the tails hanging from the back of his headgear and swung it sharply across the faces of the first two assailants.

The effect was stunning. Both men collapsed, without landing a blow, covering their faces with their hands as blood trickled out between their twitching fingers.

"'E 'as blinded me!" Shrieked one of them and, seeing their plight, the third assailant took to his heels and abandoned his mates.

What they had not known was that sewn under the front edge of Dan's cap was a collection of lead shot and sharp razor blades. Ignoring their whimpers, he parted the hands of the two on the ground, checked that their injuries were more cosmetic than life-threatening and ran before curious onlookers could join in or summon the police. It had got so bad that one had to be careful even of pretty, seemingly accommodating colleens who often lured soldiers into fatal ambushes or kidnap. Even children were used to serve as decoys and lures. You could trust nobody and the strain was beginning to tell.

At times like this, he longed for the comfort and solace of Elspeth, who would feed his inner man and blunt all other appetites. So he set off for her house in Merion Square.

He had met Lady Elspeth Leonard at a dinner dance for officers and their ladies at a leading Dublin hotel, earlier in the year. She was the widow of an infantry officer killed on the Somme and had come to the dance as the guest of Dan's commanding officer. Though born into a lower middle class family of farmers she had married well and had inherited her late husband's title, wealth, property and superior manner. She seemed just the type that Dan despised and would steer clear of.

She was short of stature but her striking, junoesque build and crystal clear tones of speech commanded attention and her cool green eyes missed nothing, whilst assuring you that she was giving you her total attention. For some reason Dan was attracted rather than repelled by her cool patrician manner and when she responded to a male companion's somewhat risqué tale with a hearty earthy laugh, he suspected that her riding expertise was not confined to horses.

She accepted his invitation to dance and after some polite conversation and two circuits of the ballroom floor he thought he detected the sudden exploratory pressure of her knee against the inside of his thigh. But when he reciprocated by allowing his hand to slide down her back and gently caress her ample posterior, she withdrew instantly to arms length and as though concluding a conversation on country house etiquette, loudly declared,

"I can't accommodate men who insist on pursuing game out of season and come uninvited. But at the right time and in the right place I am all in favour of men shooting away to their hearts' content!"

Then, she looked him straight in the eye and without batting an eyelid, thanked him graciously for the dance turned elegantly and swept across the floor back to her friends. Dan was not sure he had heard correctly, nor what conclusion he should draw from this exchange.

All the next week he was unable to get her out of his mind and he wondered how he could contact her and whether this would be wise, when through the mail, he received a formal invitation card, from Lady Elspeth Leonard, requesting the pleasure of his company at a Dublin address, where she would be 'at home' on Saturday afternoon.

At the appointed time and wearing a hired lounge suit-he thought it unwise to be seen in his uniform without knowing who her other guests might be-he pulled the bell of the grand Georgian house. A smartly uniformed parlour maid let him in and escorted him to a beautifully appointed sitting room that appeared to double as a well-stocked library. It was an overcast day and lamps had been lit whose light was reflected from the mahogany shelves and leather spines of well-worn volumes. On a side table, he caught sight of a silver tea service and plates of sandwiches and cakes, which reminded him he was hungry. But where, he wondered, were the other guests? And, when his hostess swept into the room, he fully expected to be taken to join the assembled party.

But, instead, after a perfunctory greeting she offered him tea and waved him towards a much-used chesterfield facing a grand marble fireplace. In the mirror over the mantle shelf, he watched her pour his tea herself and wondered what had happened to the maid.

For the next hour or more, which flew by, she questioned him so skillfully about his life, experiences and opinions that she learned all about him, whereas he gleaned little about her. She confessed that she had been intrigued by their brief conversation at the dance and that, unashamedly, she had invited only him so that she could find out all about him. She was particularly impressed with his progress in the mines from coalface to management and his war experience and promotion in the field. She passed no comment on what had brought him to Dublin with the Black and Tans and was entranced with the story of his winter walk along the Pennines.

By six o'clock, drizzle and mist had set in and this indication of a premature dusk caused her to draw the drapes and turn up some of the lamps. Noting his quizzical look, she explained that it was her practice to give her maid Saturday evenings off. Then having invited him to relax and smoke if he wished, she excused herself and withdrew from the room, leaving him to his own devices.

The books looked inviting and with due care, he began to take down and riffle through volumes on biography, history and philosophy whose titles he had heard of but never before been in a position to read. Half an hour had passed and he was so engrossed in a book that he hadn't heard her return and it took her discreet cough to catch his attention.

Turning slowly towards the direction from which the sound had come, he started at the sight of Lady Elspeth Leonard reclining on a blanket, on the chesterfield, wearing nothing but a string of cultured pearls.

Rich brown aureoles crowned her pert red nipples and the profusion of her rich black bush proudly contrasted with the alabaster white of her inner thighs.

"God, but you're lovely!" He gasped.

"Dan", she replied, "come here and brighten-up this dull afternoon!"

What followed was beyond even his most vivid imaginings. She certainly could ride and having reluctantly quit her bed late on Sunday morning, he slipped out of the grand house by the rear lane, exulting in spirit but bearing the bruises and deep scratches in his back and buttocks that could only have been inflicted by a woman hell-bent on extracting satisfaction.

South Western Ireland 1921

The Irish troubles provoked increasingly vicious acts of violence and there were even signs of a split in the nationalist ranks between one group prepared to settle for a free state, subject to some English jurisdiction and the diehards for whom nothing but a Republic, totally free of British Imperial rule, would suffice. Such was the feeling of enmity between them that it might soon lead to Irishmen fighting amongst themselves.

The ruthless Auxis were so deeply despised for their wanton depravity that there was little grieving on either side when an IRA force annihilated a column of these irregulars on a lonely back road in County Cork. Ambushing regular Black and Tan units, however, was another matter and an informer had given warning of such a plan that was to take place near to a village just outside of Cork. A land mine was to be secreted in a culvert under the main road into the village, along which a Black and Tan contingent would surely come to deal with a false report that an IRA unit was drinking in a village bar.

It was determined that the terrorists must be taught a severe lesson and the expertise of Dan and his unit had been called upon to prepare a nasty welcome for the IRA flying column that would follow up the ambush to kill survivors of their trap. The Republican bomb makers knew their trade, but as much of their skill and techniques had been developed under German tuition, nothing in their repertoire of deadly tricks was new to Dan and his team, who had put their lives on the line so many times playing the deadly game of setting traps and counter traps to undermine enemy tunnels and fortifications during the recent war.

The informant's story was sound and Dan had no difficulty in disarming the culvert bomb, even on a dark, moonless night. How much easier it had been without the distraction of heavy artillery barrages and the constant fear of running into enemy sappers tunneling towards him with the same deadly intent.

The dismantled munitions were loaded onto a donkey, led by two of his men disguised as locals and taken a mile further up the road, away from the village, where Dan placed them under a hump-backed bridge that the vengeful Irishmen would have to cross. The original culvert bomb had been replaced by a smaller charge which at the appointed hour, close to dawn, would be detonated under a derelict army truck of the sort favoured by the Black and Tans.

The men who should have set off the trap and their watchers had been rounded up shortly before Dan's arrival. The target Black and Tan unit would set off as expected after receiving the false report and then an Irish loyalist soldier from Dan's team would phone the IRA commander to advise that the ambush was underway.

Shortly after 5am, the Black and Tan truck arrived at the culvert, crossed over and put down its occupants in a side lane from which they dispersed taking up positions behind trees and surrounding hedges to await the outcome of the counterstroke. Dan had rigged his bomb to create more noise than destruction and supplemented this with an incendiary device that would ignite a drum full of oil-soaked rags and send up a billowing cloud of thick black smoke.

The roar of the farm truck's engine could be heard a mile away as it raced along the lonely country road. The commander had taken the bait and the IRA flying column was right on-time. Dan's explosion would have destroyed the latest model of armoured tanks and the effect on the canvas-topped vehicle was devastating. The truck and its unsuspecting complement of twenty men was tossed high into the air and shredded by the force of the blast and the hail of ball bearings he had included for good measure. The following 'staff car' fared little better as shards of steel and glass cut a swathe through its interior, killing the driver before he could brake or steer the vehicle away from the gaping hole opened up by the total destruction of the bridge. The blast brought down a rain of metal and masonry fragments, followed by several minutes of eerie silence, before the ignition of the car's petrol tank produced a flash of flame, turning dawn into brightest day and incinerating any who might have survived the bomb.

"*Serve the murdering buggers right!*" spat a Glaswegian sergeant.

Dan had done worse to other men whom he had considered braver and more honourable enemies than these, but the irony and insensitivity of this remark was not lost on him. He kept his thoughts to himself and having delegated responsibility for clearing up the scene, he packed up his gear and set off back to Cork for a hot bath, breakfast and a few hours in bed.

Dublin 1921

After the successful ambush in the west, Dan returned to Dublin. It was clear that the British Government had had enough of the Irish problem. A truce was declared after Michael Collins lost more than a hundred men whilst holding the customs House on Dublin Quays and negotiations were underway for the granting of Free State status. Under these circumstances Dan and his colleagues saw little need for continued hostilities and so apart from joining necessary self-protective actions, he did all he could to avoid involvement in aggressive patrolling or any other confrontation with Irish factions. He was content to respond to bomb threats and, in his leisure hours, he enjoyed all the solace and comforts that Elspeth so willingly and artfully provided.

As a result of his work in the west and the losses they had incurred fighting with their brother insurgents, the IRA had become much more cautious and protective of their assets and Dan had thought no more of it until early one evening, at Elspeth's house, when her maid slipped him a note saying that she had important information for him and urging him to join her in a city bar, later that night.

Whilst he trusted Elsie because of her association with Elspeth, Dan was too experienced an Irish hand to discount the possibility of an assassination attempt and so he was careful to arm himself with a service revolver and to reach the bar well ahead of the appointed time to watch the comings and goings of the patrons and to assess the risk of entering alone. A few shillings bought the compliance of a young peddler who was wandering from bar to bar selling cigarettes and matches and when he confirmed that a woman answering Elsie's description was sitting alone in a back bar, Dan entered by a side street entrance and slipped into the settle beside her.

She wasted no time in getting to the point.

"*I'm sorry to bring you 'ere sir but through some relatives of mine down Cork way I 'eard that the IRA 'ave put a price on your 'ead and* want you dead or alive. Yer know that explosion what killed the flying column near Cork, well it turns out that one of 'em was the brother of one of the IRA's top men and so they're out fer revenge."

"Why do you think they are picking on me, Elsie?" Dan responded with a quizzical look.

"Well, sir, a lot of yer mates 'ave been boastin' about it and sayin' as you was the master mind be'ind the bomb. Naturally, IRA men got to 'ear this and the rumour is that a murder squad is getting' ready to do yer in and I'm right afraid fer lady Elspeth as well as you. They're mad enough to kill yer both."

Dan questioned her further about the sources of this information and was soon convinced that she could be right and that he must take immediate steps to put himself and Elspeth out of harm's way. He thanked Elsie warmly for risking her own neck to warn him and tried to slip a fist full of pound notes into her handbag as a reward, but she would have none of it.

"No! You've always treated me proper and I'm that devoted to 'er ladyship that I couldn't bear to see 'er caught up in this." With that, she jumped up and slipped out of the door into the night.

Dan allowed her time to get clear and then seeing the chance to join a group of departing revelers, he left through the front door and lurched along, as though one of their merry party until they reached the better-lit and more populated main road, where he was able to slip safely away weaving and dodging through the crowds of people on their ways home from window shopping expeditions to the city centre. He was out of immediate danger but it was clearly time to consider getting out of Ireland.

16

Manchester Once More

Melbourne 1921

Charlie had adjusted better to civilian life in Melbourne than most of his returned comrades. His legal work had prospered; his war record had enhanced his reputation and made him a popular patron of good social causes. He was not short of invitations to seek political office but in the newly federated Australia, the political scene was still too fragmented for his liking and he saw signs of potential trouble in the policies and activities of all sides. Like many of the returned soldiers, he held politicians accountable for the failure of the conscription referendums and he had not forgiven them for not providing the additional manpower needed to support the thinning Australian ranks at the time when they were fighting for their survival.

Many men of property and business conspired with organised labour to exploit high protective customs barriers that procured their rorts, maintained higher prices and secured the white Australia policy, keeping out competition from cheaper Asian labour. In Brisbane a Federal Labor Party Conference adopted as a policy objective *'The socialisation of industry, production, distribution and exchange'* and although they could not agree about its application, events in Soviet Russia made this move a cause for concern.

But despite these worries, life for him was good and he was never more happy than when catching up with his army mates and when he could get away from his legal work for a while to ride on the Gippsland property and try to stem the inevitable neglect and supervise the manager's work, now that his father was not there to give it his loving care.

He would dearly have loved to maintain contact with Dan and hear what he felt about returning to his old life in England, but Alice had told him of his disappearance and he wondered what would become of him. Britain, he knew, was in turmoil with, serious strikes and such political upheaval that they had committed troops to trouble in Glasgow, to the Russian civil war and to deal with rising rebellion and violence in Ireland. Charlie wondered which side Dan would take in all this and what a debate they might have had over a few whiskies late at night in his Gippsland den.

He was jolted from this reverie by the sudden halting of the cable tram as the grip man applied his brake and alighting rapidly, Charlie made his way into the Supreme court for his first appearance of the day.

After a frustrating day of delays, postponements and difficulties with witnesses and the jury, Charlie was glad to call into his club, on the way home, to unwind over a few drinks with his colleagues at the bar. He was amused to hear one recount the outrageous antics of John Wren and his rogues and how, yet again, they had thwarted detective Ryan's attempt to shut down the Collingwood tote and city gambling club. Less amusing was the news that Mannix had been denied access to Ireland and that his British instigated 'dumping' ashore in Cornwall had worsened the unrest on the Melbourne waterfront. Also, the police were unhappy and had clashed with diggers.

Manchester 1921

In returning to Manchester, Dan had come full circle since he had left two years ago on his walk to the North. He was no clearer about his future direction but there was more than enough for him to reflect on in his recent past. He had set out with peaceful intentions but once more found himself involved in the trade of death. He still espoused liberal politics and ruefully recalled how he had almost been seduced into fascist causes. His love life had been satisfied at a physical level but his mind was still troubled and now he had to face up to a return to those he loved most and had left so abruptly, without explanation and then there was Liza languishing in jail

On a typically rainy Manchester afternoon, under a slate-gray sky, Dan knocked on the door of the house that before his travels had been his home. Arthur heard him and shouted with delight for Beattie to

"*Cum quick our Dan's back!*"

As usual, Beattie eyed him speculatively and like a teacher preparing to admonish a truant and without any hint of warmth or welcome, said, "*So you're back and 'ow long for this time?*"

But Dan knew as he folded her into his filial embrace that hidden beneath that dour façade and indifferent greeting was a powerful sign of her hidden love and painful awareness of how insecure and rudderless he was.

Pushing him away she told him not to be *"Such a daft 'a''porth" and that 'e was lucky she just 'appened to 'ave a steak and kidney pie in t'oven that should serve for three,"* as though she had not known the prodigal son would return that day.

After a meal that would have fed a squad of soldiers, they settled round the kitchen fire. Arthur lit his pipe and Beattie sat in her rocking chair and continued to finish a rag rug for the fireplace. Over lunch Dan had told them all he felt able about his recent experiences and now it was their turn to tell him about themselves and Liza.

Not much had changed in their lives except that problems with Arthur's partially amputated leg had forced him to reduce his work at the pit and he had used the available time to further his interest in philosophy and history and he was a mine of information and opinions on the triumph of Socialism in Russia and its prospects for gaining an equal political footing in mainland western Europe and particularly in Britain.

Liza was on the mend but hating her lack of freedom and was as much a thorn in the side of the prison authorities as she had been a scourge of oppressive bosses and politicians who vetoed the right of women to vote.

Hardened as he was by the memory of his months of living in a front line dug-out, under regular artillery fire, he was still shocked by the conditions under which Liza was detained at his majesty's pleasure. She was too weak to see him in the public meeting area and so he was escorted to her cell where she was sitting up on her hard bed. The dark green painted wall and bare flagstone floor conducted the soggy, damp chill of the rain-drenched streets into the room and a film of moisture glistened on the ceiling. A bucket served as her privy and her blankets were of coarse shoddy wool that barely protected her from the cold. It was far worse than any billet he had experienced.

"Hello Liza luv! How now?" he said with a feigned cheerfulness that did not match his worried look nor hide the sudden watering of his eyes.

"*'Ee Dan it's right good to see you!*' she responded, *"But didn't they feed you in Ireland?"*

The Mancunian ritual of seemingly uncaring and disparaging small talk continued for some time before they settled into their old sense of intimacy and comfort with each other and despite the presence of the warden at the door, Dan sat on the edge of her bed and held her cold and newly calloused hand as she told her story.

After her war service, Liza had continued to represent the cotton operatives as a union official but more and more she was drawn to the larger political injustice of denying women a more equal social standing with men.

"After all," she declared with vehemence, "*didn't we suffer and serve like men and some women even lost their lives behind the lines or were maimed for life working in those munitions and arms factories, filling in for the absent men?*"

She railed against the way they had been rewarded with dismissal and denial of future access to the challenging jobs and expanded career and income opportunities that the needs of the war economy had opened up to women, as soon as the men returned. So, she had become an active and one of the most militant, members of the suffragette movement.

Dan saw the justice in her case but at the same time he was all too well aware of the emotional and physical sacrifices that his returned comrades had made and he had to assert that

"*It wouldn't be right for them to be denied some preference in getting the chance to at least take up where they had left off in their trades and careers, to do their duty. Even though, I must admit, all too many of them are severely limited in what they can do by the damage to their bodies and minds.*"

He could have said more but, bearing in mind her passionate beliefs and frail state of health, he kept these thoughts to himself.

That was not all he kept hidden from her and she from him as the warmth of his hand radiated up her arm bringing promise of comfort, caring and protection. Neither of them referred to what had occurred between them in Blackpool, but the unspoken memory of their coupling and bonding hung between them. Dan could sense the depth of her feeling for him by the way she clung onto his hand and the intense looks she gave him from her dark-rimmed eyes whose size and depth grew and grew as time went on and the barriers of estrangement dissolved.

As he stood up to leave, in response to the warder's indication that his time was up, having sensed her leaning towards martyrdom, he assured her that she could do more good for her cause on the outside than in there and he promised to see what he could do to gain her release. Ironically, despite Dan's military record and connections, it was the influence of Lady Elspeth Leonard that turned the key and freed Liza on strict conditions of parole.

Elspeth knew what Liza really meant to Dan and although she had delighted in their Dublin affair, she was under no illusion that it had been more than that and demonstrated her lack of any jealousy and abundance of worldly wisdom by pulling all the considerable aristocratic and personal strings at her disposal to set Liza free. After all, she reasoned, she too was a woman who expected to get her own way and couldn't see why the rest of womankind shouldn't have a better deal in a world so dominated by the wants and whims of mere men.

Arthur and Beattie dedicated themselves to Liza's convalescence and when she felt strong enough, she accepted her aunt's invitation to take the bracing sea air at her Blackpool home. Dan was a regular visitor, reading to her from the latest Fabian literature and Suffragette tracts as well as from the novels of Dickens and Austen. Their walks along the prom became longer and more vigorous as her rude health returned but neither showed any inclination to resume their physical intimacy. Despite the ease of their conversation and the delight they took in each other's company, Dan sensed there was something important that Liza was holding back from him that somehow related to their relationship and there were other things that puzzled him and about which she couldn't be drawn.

Most intriguing of these was her insistence that he must never call on her at weekends, when she said she devoted herself to her political cause and needed the time for quiet reflection, to read and write without the distraction of visitors and even close friends. He wondered about this and entertained the possibility that she might have a new man in her life, perhaps even a married one that she could only see occasionally and in secret. He had raised this suspicion with Arthur, but met as strong a wall of obfuscation and silence as Liza had built around this secret and clearly special part of her life.

In quiet, reflective moments Dan tested his commitment to Liza by considering how he felt about the possibility of her loving another more than she loved him. He was surprised at the jealousy aroused by the thought that she might be enjoying another, perhaps as deeply though more permanently than they had achieved. But at the same time, he could not see himself committing to love and live with her forever, as the ultimate bond of matrimony required. Also, as well as not knowing what he wanted to do with the rest of his life, he was conscious of the constant threat of retribution by the IRA whose brotherhood was deeply rooted in the migrant Irish populations of the major cities of Glasgow, Liverpool and Manchester and he would be hard pressed enough preserving his own life without exposing other innocents, especially Arthur, Beattie and Liza, to the threat of their ruthless killers, who offered no mercy to man woman or child.

It was the arrival of a rare but welcome letter from Charlie, sent via Liza, more in hope than expectation of its getting to him, that provided the prospect of a possible solution to his problem and the more he considered Charlie's proposition, the greater grew a glimmer of hope that there might be a brighter future than the grim uncertainty and violence of his recent past.

Melbourne 1922

Melbourne 1922

Dear Dan

No doubt this letter will surprise you, both because I have stirred myself to write to you after so long a silence and because of what it contains.

Although we met for such a short time in Alexandria there was something about you and our conversation that made me wish that we might have become better acquainted and now that I am home, knowing that we both went through similar experiences in Mesopotamia and France, I suspect like me you have feelings and questions that you find it hard to share with anyone but those who served with you and some even deeper, possibly darker doubts and fears that you could only reveal to what we Australians call a special 'Mate.'

This intense nature of 'mateship' between Australian men, grew out of our pioneer settler life and this war has given it a new meaning, that only we returned soldiers can understand and express. Whilst I have many such comrades that I respect deeply and indeed a wife I revere and love to distraction, one is often only prepared to share ones greatest vulnerabilities, hope and fears with a stranger who at least will listen with the understanding that comes of having survived the same test of violence, the constant chance of disability and risk of death.

So, Dan, forgive me if I burden you with more than you are willing to bear, but in short, I believe you could be such a 'Mate' to me.

All I know of you since you returned has come to me via those other veterans of the Western Front, my Alice and your Liza, who have corresponded continually, like chattering Magpies and from their letters I learned of your pilgrimage and experience of further service and action in that hellish Irish situation. Like the good lawyer that I am, I have deduced from this evidence that in searching for an understanding of our times and a clearer path into a better future, we are both embarked on a quest like that of Pilgrim but, so far at least, with none of his certainty and progress.

So let me get to the point of this letter. I have heard that things are not so good in the old Dart – as we call the source of our convict forebears-and even that you may be in some personal danger because of your Irish service. As you are an experienced mining engineer with particular knowledge of explosives and with no dependants, I wondered would you consider coming out here where we badly need men of your skill and character and knowing that I would stand guarantor to the government for your capability and probity? Alice and I would be delighted to accommodate you until you get established.

Close to our country property is a coastal coal mining community called Wonthaggi where I am sure I could find you a suitable position and just think of the time we would have introducing you to horse riding in the bush and solid man to man discussions in the evening with the help of my late father's stock of single malt whiskies.

Think about it and do say you will come.

In friendship and soon to be mateship,

Charles Elliott,

Or, to you, just plain Charlie.

17

Melbourne Unrest

Bourke Street 1923

The jingle of the bridle, clopping hooves and arrogant snort of his horse as it shook its head to dislodge some bothersome flies, reminded Charlie of his days in Palestine. But instead of peering through his goggles at a sand-blasted vista of desert terrain, he was riding down the centre of the tram tracks in Bourke Street.

Most of Victoria's police had gone on strike and on Melbourne Cup eve, there was mob rule in many Melbourne streets, where the feverish contagion of misrule had tempted usually sober citizens to get involved in rioting and looting of property. Along with many of his ex-service colleagues, Charlie had volunteered to maintain the peace and was on his way to investigate reported trouble in Niagara Lane, where a mob was said to be intent on torching a warehouse. As the contingent of horsemen prepared to turn from Elizabeth Street into Little Bourke, bystanders called out a warning that the crowd's blood was up and that they were beyond reasoning with.

At sight of the horsemen, the rioters paused but then began to jeer and hurl cobble stones, which they had prised-up from the lane's roadway. Faced with this hostility, Charlie called on his men to draw their batons and proceed at a canter into the laneway, pushing through the resisting crowd and striking those who sought to injure horses or riders, with sharp, stinging blows to their heads and shoulders. It was all over in a moment. The mob had retreated and dispersed as smoothly as a receding tide, disappearing into the many laneways that offered alternate escape routes northward out of the city.

Charlie acknowledged the grateful thanks of the warehouse's owners and as he and his squadron rode away, he was conscious of the appreciative shouts and applause of passing citizens, paying respect to these upholders of the law whose uniforms confirmed their service with the legendary Light Horse. Whilst he was reassured by this endorsement his satisfaction was tempered by the fact that it had become necessary to risk their hard earned reputation by turning out against some of the citizenry whose freedom they had fought to defend.

Later, when he had joined a group of his regimental mates for a drink at the Mitre Tavern, Charlie fell in with the debate about the state of the nation after the war and what needed to be done to improve it. One well-oiled warrior complained,

"I think it's all down to the damned labour unions and those who want a Bolshevik republic along Russian lines." Charlie saw some truth in this and said that,

"The labor politicians haven't helped by adopting the clause that commits them to a policy of socialisation of industry, production, distribution and exchange."

A big bluff Sergeant from Essendon cursed Mannix and the Sinn Feiners, "Look at those rebels who attacked a harmless troop of veterans, unarmed lancers and their horses and then took armed possession of the Dublin Post Office, whilst many of their betters were fighting and dying alongside us in France."

Charlie had no sympathy for Mannix who had cheered on the anti-conscription vote, whilst ever decreasing British and Australian forces tried to hold the line against desperate and nearly successful German counter offensives. But he warned the company about attacking the Irish and Catholics as a whole,

"I must remind you that there were eleven VCs and many other soldiers of Irish origin who marched peacefully on Saint-Patrick's day. What we need is stronger national leadership that can maintain law and order. Like the leadership the Duke of Wellington displayed after Waterloo when, as Prime Minister and despite being a noted conservative, he recognised the justice of electoral reform and Catholic emancipation. But I fear, however, that the current British monarchy and those who ran the war leave much to be desired and it might soon be time for Australian leaders such as Monash or Chauvel to exert some influence on the corrupt politicians, war profiteers and socialist troublemakers, amongst our workforce."

This was greeted with a murmur of approval amongst the gathering and on the strength of these views Charlie was invited to join a group of like-minded brother officers at the Australia Club, later in the week, to discuss this further.

The Australia Club, Melbourne 1923

The meeting at the Australia Club was held in an upstairs suite. Entry was by invitation only and judging by the size and hardened look of the two men controlling the door, Charlie guessed they had seen service overseas. He was greeted with a familiar but respectful,

"*G'day Sir!*" by one of them and the other took his coat and hat.

"Thank you Sergeant," responded Charlie and the curt but amicable nod this evoked confirmed his assumptions about these guardians.

The room was warm, brightly lit and the combined efforts of a sizable gathering of cigar, pipe and cigarette smokers had filled it with a dense haze of blue smoke. He was greeted warmly by a tall lean fellow who Charlie recalled had been on Monash's staff at Gallipoli and later in France.

"*Good evening Charlie, Glad you decided to come. We need clear headed fellows like you.*" They exchanged pleasantries and after updating each other on what they had been doing since returning to civilian life, Charlie's host took him by the arm and steered him through the raucous throng to join a small and more intimate group of older men, who were seated by the fire. At his arrival the group stood as one and, with a notable absence of formality introductions were made on a first name basis only.

Charlie shook each of them by the hand and their friendly, knowing looks suggested they knew more about him than he knew of them, but as they all had held ranks of major and above in the army, he really needed no further introduction and could easily have reeled off their ranks, units and battle experiences.

But, before he could begin to ask the questions that had been on his mind since receiving the invitation to this meeting, the assembly was called to order and all eyes turned to the end of the room where a tall, elegant, silver haired man stood behind a table covered appropriately, given the company, with a gray army blanket. He wore full-dress uniform whose gleaming buttons and insignia sparkled as they picked up and reflected the firelight.

Charlie was stunned. What was a man of his eminence doing here, he wondered. He had expected a much more low-key affair but the presence of such a senior and distinguished commander put a much more serious stamp on the evening.

The speech that followed was a masterpiece of oratory, better than any Charlie had heard at the bar. He opened with a reminder of what they had achieved together under the flag, then neatly and dispassionately summarised the post war economic, social and political situation in Australia. He then nominated the threats to civic harmony and stability that recent strikes and political and religious demonstrations had represented, and he closed with a passionate appeal for his former comrades to join with him in coming to the defence of Australia and their King.

This short speech was heard in complete silence but as soon as he sat down, the gathering erupted into rapturous applause and spontaneous cries of;

"Well said sir!"

"I'm with you all the way!" and

"Where do we sign on?"

Charlie was stirred by the challenge thrown out by such a famous leader and the passionate response of those battle-hardened, cynical and usually taciturn men. But before he could escape to a quiet corner, where he could gain control of his thoughts and reflect on what his reaction should be, the staff officer was at his elbow once more to deliver a polite invitation for him to join the speaker in an adjoining room.

As he entered, his guide withdrew and Charlie found himself alone with the great man in what looked like a cross between the library of a law firm and a well-appointed study. He accepted the invitation to join his host by the fire and the offer of a large glass of whisky, then sat down and prepared to listen to what this man had to say to him.

"Captain Elliott," he began, "I'll get straight to the point. You heard my speech, you know what we are about and I want you to take a leadership role in our organisation. But before you reply, I must stress that although your military record is of paramount importance, it is your standing as a respected barrister and dedicated worker for returned servicemen's rights that are of most interest and value to our cause."

Charlie had anticipated that the evening would end with an invitation to join an organisation but he had not imagined such an offer from such a man. Calling on all the courtroom skills he had developed appearing before the most exacting judges, Charlie asked questions, summarised responses and generally played for time whilst another part of his brain decided how best to respond.

"Firstly sir," he asserted," I must stress my sympathy with your views about the need to secure the stability of our new nation. I agree that the loss of the cream of potential European leaders in the war and the weakening of the unifying power of monarchy by deposing of the Czar, the Kaiser and Austrian Emperor, exposes their countries to anarchists and revolutionaries. I have heard that some of Germany's officer corps have similar concerns and have started to form societies of ex-servicemen and have begun training to maintain their military readiness in the event of social breakdown.

But, secondly, I must remind you that I am a senior member of the legal profession, sworn to uphold the laws of the land and I would have to be assured of the legality and probity of your plans before I could give you a firm answer."

The commander said that he could not have received a more worthy response and invited Charlie to think it over and get back to him with a decision by the end of the month. Whilst endorsing the importance of the law, he reminded Charlie of the role that Cromwell had been forced to play to limit the dictatorial behaviour of a dissolute monarch and a rogue parliament. He assured him, however, that whatever might be done, it would have to have the full backing of the Australian Parliament. But he warned that politicians of the like of Hughes and the up and coming Lang and the influences of Cardinal Mannix and his creature, John Wren, would need to be checked by loyal, upstanding men of Charlie's ilk.

Alice had stayed up to hear Charlie's news upon his return and after he had settled by the fire with a warm glass of milk that she had prepared for him, he recounted all that had happened.

"What I have to decide, Alice," he concluded, *"is whether it is right for me to join such a secret army."*

18

Dan Down-Under

Gippsland 1923

The sky was blue from horizon to horizon and the light and heat were of an intensity that Dan had not experienced since his time in Mesopotamia. The rolling hills, unlike the treeless Pennine moorland, were densely covered by eucalypts whose variety and individuality were concealed at a distance by appearing to share a dusty dark green conformity, not unlike some of the camouflage thrown across guns and dugouts in France. But it was their smell that stopped him in his tracks as its aromatic scent tingled in his nostrils, reminding him of the ointments that Beattie had insisted on rubbing on his chest when he was down with a bad cold. He found it hard to absorb the conflicting messages of extreme heat, blinding light and the memory of dismal sunless Manchester days of snuffling and coughing, brought simultaneously to him by this unique scent of the bush.

As Dan's equestrian experience had progressed no further than the riding of donkeys on the sands during seaside holidays, he had declined Charlie's offer of a mount and he had elected instead to tramp around the property, as Charlie called his farm. Although it was only mid-morning the heat was oppressive and Dan was glad to reach the shade of the trees and take a draft of cool water from the hessian bag that Charlie had insisted he carry.

He had been instructed to take frequent drink stops, to keep his shirt sleeves rolled down, his collar turned up and always to wear his hat whenever he was out in the sun. He was beginning to appreciate the wisdom of this advice but he thought Charlie had been unnecessarily alarmist when he had suggested that in some circumstances that following these cautions could make the difference between life and death.

Dan's work down the pit and his military service had made early rising an ingrained habit and in the warmth of a summer dawn, it had been easy to quit his bed. Following the sound of men talking and laughing loudly, he had found himself at the door of the cookhouse where the contract shearers were gathered for their breakfast break, having already relieved a first batch of merinos of their thick heavy fleeces.

Many of these men would have served overseas and although they were aware that Dan had been an officer and was a friend of the boss, their greetings showed no sign of deference or respect for his former rank. At the same time, although they chided him for being a *'new chum'* and *'another useless pommy bastard'*, there was an unspoken acceptance of a comrade who had shared the same unspeakable horrors and survived. He could sense this in their chorus of invitations to

"Pull up a pew and 'ave a bit of tucker!" and in the way they shuffled along the benches to make a space for him to sit at the large refectory table.

He had seen newly arrived Australian troops going noisily up the line for the first time in France, especially the veterans of Gallipoli who arrived with all the swagger of battle-hardened men, greeting their weary British comrades with provocative questions such as,

"'As youse been in a fight-or just in France?" Then, after their first experience of German artillery barrages and their losses at Fromelles, there were no more vainglorious comments. They had returned silently, after action, with that far-away look in their deep-set eyes that spoke of days and nights under relentless siege.

So, he knew their banter for what it was, often a screen for deeper, hidden attitudes and feelings that they would only own to with their closest mates and even then only after sinking a few beers. But how they had fought and always given good account of themselves, even when assigned the untenable positions or suicidal attacks. With all this in mind, Dan approached them with both caution and well founded respect.

The strong, scalding tea they offered him was welcome, but he could not face the mountain of meat that seemed to be their staple diet. A couple of eggs had sufficed and although this confirmed their perception that all pommies were lilly-white and somewhat lilly-livered, Dan was soon drawn into their circle and gave as good as he got in their banter about their countries respective cricketing prowess, lousy English weather and the inability of new settlers to cope with real men's work under the unforgiving Aussie sun.

The shearers' cook had packed him a huge wedge of cheddar cheese and what seemed like half a loaf and, towards noon, Dan was glad of this as he rested on a log and contemplated his first experience of entering what Australians' called the bush. The grass was sparser and tougher than in England and gave way to what to him seemed like occasional tufts of straw, beneath the canopy of evergreen Eucalypts. When he considered the lush pastures of Cheshire and the Lancashire plain, he wondered how sheep could thrive and grow so fat on such poor feed. But then everything here seemed bigger than its counterpart at home and this applied especially to the men he had seen, stripped to their singlets, digging holes for fence posts, felling huge trees with axes and sawing them into logs, seemingly immune to the blazing sun.

On closer inspection the trees revealed subtle differences in the colour and shape of their leaves and bark that often hung half way down a tree's trunk like a partly peeled banana. It was dusty underfoot and the ground was strewn with fallen twigs, gum nuts and desiccated leaves. It was no wonder that a lightening strike could soon turn this natural fuel dump into a roaring inferno that might burn for weeks and devour miles of trees, undergrowth, sick animals, houses and even the occasional person.

What appeared, at a distance, to be unrelenting olive green drabness revealed bursts of brightly coloured tree blossoms and delicate flowers which defied the dryness and flourished in the heat. The most exotic birds flashed across the glade in pursuit of insects or in search of nectar and nuts from what he had thought to be lifeless trees. Having slipped into a light doze, Dan awoke at the thud of approaching hooves and was pleased to see Charlie walking his horse out of the depths of the bush.

"G'day, Dan! How are you going?" Charlie called, as he tied up his mount and settled down on his haunches, as comfortable in that exacting position as Dan was sitting astride a log. He asked Dan for his first impressions of the bush and laughed when Dan wondered at the ability of sheep to prosper on what to his eyes was very poor pasture.

"If you think this is bad mate, you will really wonder at the big sheep runs inland, which to you will look like a dust bowl with only occasional tussocks of grass."

Then Charlie went on to talk about the business of rearing sheep and the good and bad points of the country and the climate and the wonderful endurance of the Merino breed.

Later that evening, after a substantial farmhouse dinner, Charlie and Dan settled in the study to reflect on the day and drink a nightcap or two. Charlie had been talking with some of his local contacts from his football days and told Dan that there were opportunities for experienced men in Wonthaggi's state coalmine. Charlie acknowledged that Dan had turned his back on the underground trade but he put it to Dan that it might be better to get a start where his skills were in demand and the money was good and assured. Also, Charlie added,

"It's not a bad place, near the coast, with plenty of opportunity for fishing and boating in your time off and not far from here when you want a change of scene." Dan was less than enthusiastic but he took Charlie's points and as a newcomer, he was anxious not to become a burden on anyone and especially to seem to 'bludge', as they called sponging here and to outstay Charlie's welcome and hospitality.

19

Liza, Elspeth and Bill

Manchester 1923

Liza had been surprised to be released at the intervention of a titled lady but it was through this connection with Elspeth that she came into contact and under the influence of people who might once have seemed to her to be her natural enemies. Some Manchester manufacturers had done well out of the war and were using their wealth to establish fine homes in the Cheshire countryside south of the city.

Elspeth had quit Dublin soon after Dan and she was a frequent house guest at weekend romps where skill at dancing the Charleston was more appreciated than who you were or where you had come from.

Liza was both intrigued and flattered to receive Elspeth's invitation to join her at a party at the home of a particularly influential Mancunian magnate. At first, Arthur and Beattie had been doubtful about the propriety of this but they conceded that,

"Lass needs a bit of fun" and their concerns diminished upon hearing that lady Elspeth Leonard was to act as chaperone.

The fine Georgian house was set in beautiful parkland just out of Congleton and Liza was tickled by the thought that the eighteenth century grandees who had built it with the proceeds of investments in slave-based sugar and tobacco plantations, were being succeeded by a different class of men but who also shared a talent for making money out of the sweated-labour of others.

The Saturday night party was in full swing and their host had spared no expense to ensure its success, even to the extent of hiring a well-known dance band from Manchester. Elspeth ensured that Liza didn't want for partners but whilst she danced fit to drop, she found none of them worth talking to. At ten o'clock a supper break was announced and Liza excused herself from the unwanted attentions of a frightfully boring former Guards officer and took the opportunity to escape the dining room throng by setting off to explore this handsome house.

Couples occupied the conservatory and other discreet outdoor locations and the lounge and gunroom had been commandeered by noisy parties of gamblers who were playing poker and roulette. She was about to give up the search for some peace and quiet when she came upon a short passageway leading off the main hallway and as she turned into it, she noticed a faint light shining through the partially opened door of a room at the end of the corridor. Curiosity got the better of etiquette and having pushed the door further ajar, she passed into a dimly lit room and found herself in a very well stocked library.

She moved towards the nearest shelf and was about to take down a work of county history when a voice from the far end of the room suggested, *"You'll find more interesting works over here."*

She turned to locate the speaker and saw a young man, sitting in a corner of the room with an open book on his lap that he was reading by the light of a standard lamp, which shone down over his shoulder, leaving his face in shadow.

"What have you found that could possibly be more interesting than the story of the Lancashire witches?" Liza replied.

"Ah you have a point there," he conceded, *"but I am more disposed towards this history of civil aviation."* Then, as though just having recalled his manners, he sprang up and holding out his hand said,

"Hello! My name's William Brennan, but you can call me Bill."

Not to be outdone by his directness Liza said she was pleased to meet him and with the firmest handshake she could muster and in an equally forthright manner advised him that she was Elizabeth Miller but better known as Liza.

He was of medium height and slight of build and now that he was fully exposed to the lamplight, she took in his thick mop of brown hair, a tanned face with a strong tracery of lines radiating from his deeply set blue eyes. It was the face of a man who had spent a great deal of time outdoors and yet the skin of his palm was soft and un-calloused by manual labour.

Liza was suddenly conscious that she was alone with a stranger in a partially lit room in a quiet part of the house but then, as though he had read her thoughts, Bill sat down, invited her to take the seat opposite him and taking out a silver case from his breast pocket, asked her if she minded him smoking and offered her a cigarette. She encouraged him to go ahead but declined herself.

"Filthy habit." He said and confided that of the many he had picked up in the war, this was the one he had failed to give up.

Oh, here we go thought Liza, the bloody war again. When would the stories ever stop? But to her surprise, he began to ask questions about her and such was the steady and disarming way he did it and so intently did he listen to her answers, half an hour had passed before she realised that he knew most of her life story, whereas she knew nothing about him.

"But what about you?" she managed to ask him as he paused to light another cigarette.

"Oh there's nothing much to tell." He replied evasively, suggesting that he was more protective of his history than she had been of hers or that he was genuinely more interested in the stories of others than in his own. Liza was not so easily deterred and soon discovered that he was an Australian from the west and that he had grown up on his family's large cattle property in the tropical north of that state.

"I suppose you came over for the war" she suggested, *"But what keeps you here now that it is over?"* Liza had heard all about the Australian soldiers from Dan and she had carried some rough specimens in her ambulance, back from the front. But this one was different-his reserve and quiet unaccented speech gave no indication of his colonial origin. His answer to her question was not at all what she had expected

"I'm a pilot with KLM airways working mostly on the London-Amsterdam route. I came over with the first contingent of the Australian Flying Corps at the start of the war and fortunately for me, I am one of the few who made it through the lot without any severe damage."

So, that explained the weather beaten face and the lines around his eyes, she concluded, but he was so different from the devil may care fly boys she had seen whooping it up at the Midland hotel, drinking and roistering as though each evening might be their last and sadly for too many of them this had turned out to be all too true. Clearly his main interest was flying and he spoke earnestly but economically about his civilian work but he neither gave nor sought any opportunity to talk about his military experiences.

It was only when he responded to questions about his home that his eyes lit up and an increasing warmth and animation, bordering on passionate feeling, illuminated his stories of growing up in a vast, sparsely inhabited land where, *"The climate alternates between almost crippling droughts and the life-saving Monsoonal downpours that we call the 'wet'. In the 'dry' season, animals and people are almost at the end of their tether, praying for the relieving storms, rainy deluges and floods that turn dry creek beds into serious rivers. In the 'wet', dusty plains become carpeted with lush grasses and delicate flowers, which lure back thousands of migratory birds to breed and nest by the transitory lakes and overflowing billabongs."*

Liza was entranced and felt as though she could see this place and it took the sonorous boom of the gong, calling guests back to the party, to break into her reverie and draw her back out of what seemed like a deep, dream-filled sleep.

"How about a dance?" Bill asked and Liza assented, returning dreamily to the dance floor, wondering whether this man could step it out as well as he could talk.

She found that he could and the rest of the night passed in a blur of conversation and energetic dancing until Elspeth suggested that as it was after midnight, it was her duty to convey 'Cinderella' safely back to Arthur and Beattie, who would certainly be mounting an anxious night watch in expectation of Liza's return.

Before departing, Bill had told her of his plans to go home soon. Two new Australian airlines had started up, one with the strange sounding name of QANTAS and the other which had been the first to get into operation was based in Western Australia and it was with Western Australian Airlines that he hoped to get a job working with another well known pilot called Kingsford Smith. He had expressed the wish, however, that he and Liza might meet again before he set off and she had told him,

"That would be nice!"

20

Down, Up and Out of the Mine

Wonthaggi 1923

Despite all he had been told about Wonthaggi by Charlie and his mates, Dan found it hard to accept that a coalmine could exist in such a delightful rural setting, close to such beautiful coastal scenery. The mine itself was much the same as Bradford pit or any other coal mine of that period, but there were no mean streets of cheaply built terraced houses surrounding it and instead of the dark, sulphurous, coal-fired and chemical induced smogs, the skies were clear and blue and the sun shone more often than not, even on the coldest of winter days.

The Wonthaggi mine had only been open since 1909 and by making Victoria's railways no longer reliant on NSW for fuel supplies it had become a vital contributor to the state's economy. As Charlie had predicted, both Dan's industry background and military service had made him a welcome recruit to a position with responsibility for production and safety at one of the major coal seams. The management had welcomed him enthusiastically and both his experience of managing militant Manchester miners and leading battle-hardened front line troops, prepared him for what he would have to contend with when confronted by his Australian work force.

Unlike many British newcomers he knew the importance of underplaying his knowledge and skill and as he had done with Charlie's shearers, he approached his team with respectful deference to their local knowledge, but also determined not to take a backward step when sure that his professional judgment was correct. This aspect of his work turned out to be easier than expected because of the way he seized a fortunate opportunity that occurred in his first week underground.

He was particularly early at work on the day in question because he had been woken prematurely by the day breaking much brighter and warmer than he was used to. Having gone down to the face, well ahead of his shift and even before the safetymen who were required to declare the galleries safe for men to start work.

Ever since the death of his father and Arthur's accident, Dan had made his self, familiar with the most common hazards. He was particularly fresh and alert on that morning and something about the changing atmosphere he encountered as he approached the face caused him to turn back halfway down the tunnel and quickly return to the foot of the lift shaft, taking particular care not to risk striking a spark.

He met the safetymen and miners as they were about to alight from the lift cage and as expected there were many ribald comments about the possible reasons for his having quit his bed so early and starting ahead of time. He wasted no time on greetings and explanations but ordered the miners to return to the surface immediately. He was quick to share his concerns with the safetymen, who set-off at once to test the atmosphere along the road leading to the face. Dan was aware that he ran the risk of needlessly delaying the shift and affecting output and the men's bonus pay and after an anxious wait he was relieved to hear from the returning safetymen that there were dangerous pockets of gas in the atmosphere and that it was far too unsafe for work to commence.

As a result of the subsequent enquiry into the stoppage, Dan was commended for his initiative but also cautioned that in future he should not take it upon himself to suspend operations without first consulting his superior.

Management's endorsement was one thing but the reaction of the miners was an entirely different matter. They knew that he had risked his reputation and job security by backing his hunch and putting their safety ahead of production. As a result the barriers of reserve between them evaporated as quickly as morning mist on a summer's day and he was initiated into the mysteries of mate-ship in a small but vibrant country town. A few days later, after dinner at his digs, his landlady, herself a former miner's widow, confided in him that the union had disciplined the safetymen for allowing a boss to call a safety halt before the union could declare the area black and put the management in the wrong.

Charlie had been right about Wonthaggi being set in delightful country. Dan's new found popularity opened up a range of invitations to fish, hike, join in beach picnics, and dine at the better class homes of those who considered themselves to be what passed for society in that town. He decided to make the most of it and even began to get the hang of Australian football. But whilst he indulged himself to the full in months of good living the work was very much the same.

He had left Bradford pit as a deputy, survived the war, served with the Black and Tans in Ireland and here he was seemingly back where he started as part of the management of a small rural coal mine at the other end of the world. Dan had not followed a conventional plan and so far his life and career owed much to seizing the positive opportunities that came along and bearing the less welcome blows of fortune. But despite this haphazard approach to work and life, each stage had brought new challenges which he had overcome and learned from. But now he felt stuck and needed fresh inspiration to move on. When he received Charlie's message inviting him for the weekend to the Strezlecki property, it seemed as though his mate had read his mind and he was right.

After the pleasure of Alice's table, the two friends set themselves up by the fireside in what had been Charlie's father's study which was essentially as he had inherited it but with subtle added comforts that reflected the tastes of a successful city barrister. Charlie's sword and his father's colt, which had served him so well, as his father had predicted, in Turkey, Mesopotamia and France, were mounted above the fire place. The firelight reflected back from the bright steel of the sword and sparkled in the crystal tumblers that contained generous drafts of single malt whisky with a touch of branch water.

Before Dan could broach the subject of his discontent, Charlie told him that General John Monash had heard of his safety exploit at the mine and had requested that Dan come to see him at the Melbourne headquarters of the newly formed State Electricity Commission. Despite much enquiry and several tumblers of malt, Charlie would reveal no more than the date, time and address at which he was to meet Australia's most celebrated soldier and innovative engineer.

Melbourne 1923

Monash's office was well appointed but true to the man's recent field experience, its features were utilitarian and included a full scale model of the proposed power industry in the Latrobe valley and Dan was all too familiar with the folded campaign bed in a corner, which suggested that late night working was not uncommon.

He wasted no time in getting to the point. The general had been charged with the task of setting up an organisation that would exploit the State's brown coal deposits and build power stations to boost the supply of electricity to meet the growing industrial needs of Melbourne. The war had taken so many good and skilled men and in particular he needed leaders who could win the confidence of a largely independent-minded, ex-service labour force and who could overcome the delays and obstacles thrown up by the State's abundant and all powerful bureaucracy.

"I am familiar with your action at the Wonthaggi mine and of course I have checked your military record. It seems to me that you could blast your way through the kind of obstacles that slow my enterprise, as you did to German strong points and IRA ambushes. How would you like to come and join me? The pay will be no worse than what you get now and I can assure you of more challenges and excitement than you have seen since you were discharged from the service."

Dan could not believe his luck. His only question was about accommodation and Monash indicated that the widow of one of his Sergeants ran a respectable guest house in Hawthorn that would suit Dan down to the ground. He thanked the General, shook his hand, and made his way out into the Bourke street crush of shoppers and homebound office workers. It certainly was a city on the move and would need all the power it could get to feed its growth.

Charlie was delighted to hear his news and they repaired to his club to celebrate over a few drinks. Alice welcomed the return of the revelers and treated them to a hearty dinner and began to plan introductions that would quickly ease him into Melbourne's social whirl. Federation gentility had died with the war and the new Jazz age of flappers and the Charleston were all the go.

After Dan had departed, Monash stood at his office window, taking in the view of the bustling, restless city and smiled with smug self-satisfaction at what he had just achieved. In the aftermath of the Melbourne police strike and subsequent riots, Monash had been called on to assemble a paramilitary force which, independent of the police force, could act as strike-breakers and guarantors of social order in the last resort. The General had assembled five battalions, officered by many of his former comrades from the actions in Gallipoli and France. What Sir John had not told Dan was that he had just recruited him to that élite, brethren.

21

Elspeth Plays Her Hand

Manchester 1924

Lady Elspeth Leonard luxuriated in her scented bath and contemplated with pleasure and a hint of excitement the dilemmas that faced her and the opportunities to intervene in and shape other people's lives, especially those of the men she had in her sights. Her late husband had left all her material needs provided for and so she was free to fully indulge her hobby of pursuing her wants, especially those of the carnal variety. She was not constrained by the strictures of conventional morality but according to her own lights, she was a good and honourable woman.

The developing liaison between Liza and the oh so charming Bill had amused her, at first, but now that Alice had begun to press Liza to come out to Melbourne she saw this as an opportunity to enact her primary plot and to consign Bill to a very different future.

She and Liza met for tea at the Midland hotel and over a refreshing pot of Lapsang Souchong and delectable friands, Elspeth began to explore Liza's intentions. Long ago she had detected the change in Liza's demeanor and in particular the softening of her sharp edge. A combination of feminine intuition and the astute employment of a private detective had revealed the secret of Liza's weekend absences to visit her love child and she had a shrewd suspicion as to who his father was.

Liza was amused by Elspeth but was too astute not to have seen through the courtesan image that she so carefully cultivated and that fooled so many, especially the men who thought they could exploit this merry widow. Beneath this façade was a serious streak of compassion and care of which she had been a beneficiary whilst locked away in Strangeways prison and in helping to rebuilding her social life after her release and convalescence.

It was clear to Elspeth that Liza was set on going to Australia but that she was conflicted by the choice of a certain and secure entry, under the protective care of Charles and Alice in established Melbourne and the exciting and risky chance of flying into the frontier west, with Bill. They were both aware that Dan was in Australia and about to base himself in Melbourne and though he was in both their thoughts, neither woman mentioned his name.

Elspeth was too shrewd a tactician to try to persuade Liza to adopt one or other of these courses of action but rather sought to influence her by example.

"I invited you to tea dear, so that you would be the first to hear my news. I have decided to take a trip to Melbourne to visit the wife of one of my late husband's fellow officers, who served with George in South Africa. Her family made a fortune from providing food and supplies to the miners on the Victorian goldfields in the 1850s and which they increased by investing wisely in trade."

Elspeth volunteered with a studied nonchalance, as though she were announcing that she was taking a trip down to Brighton for the weekend.

Liza's surprise at this audacious decision was soon overtaken by a touch of pique, that Elspeth had stolen a march on her due to her own indecision and by the realisation that she was being abandoned by those dear to her who, despite their tragedies and disappointments, were getting on with their lives. She felt the first pin-prick of fear that she was going to be left alone.

"But this is so sudden, Elspeth, I had no idea that you had an interest in going to Australia. What has brought this on?" enquired Liza.

"The decision may be recent but having danced and dined with so many gallant Australian officers on leave in London and listened to their endless praise of Melbourne as the Athens of the south, for some time I have thought that it might be interesting to see for myself how marvelous a city it really is. At least a long relaxing sea trip will be good for my health and offers all manner of social opportunities. Then of course Dan is there and so I will have a delightful and oh so good looking man to escort me to parties and balls. But enough of my plans, what about you Liza, haven't you been invited to go and join Dan's friend Charles and his wife Alice, in Melbourne?" Elspeth enquired, archly.

22

The Secret Army

Melbourne 1924

Charlie was greeted at the door of the private suite in the Australia Club by the same former Sergeant who had acted as doorman on his last visit.

"Good to see you back again sir! Let me take your coat and hat. The leader is expecting you, please come this way sir."

On this occasion the Leader, as the Sergeant had designated him, was dressed informally in a fine, impeccably tailored brown suit of houndstooth pattern and as he rose from his desk to greet his visitor, Charlie realised that he was not alone.

The other men in the room were those same former army officers he had mingled with by the fire, before he had met with the man and he was soon to learn that they now comprised the leadership of the newly formed secret force.

The leader welcomed Captain Elliot to the gathering, expressed his pleasure that Charlie had agreed to join them and having invited him to take the only vacant seat at the meeting table, he began to address the assembly.

"I believe that introductions are unnecessary and as you are probably aware gentlemen, as well as having a distinguished war record, Captain Elliott is one of Australia's leading barristers. We are fortunate to have welcomed him to our cause as it must be our essential aim to preserve the constitution of our new Commonwealth by frustrating those who would flout the rule of law, without willfully breaking it ourselves. So, in a sense, captain Elliott will prove to be a valuable umpire as well as being an active player in our team.

I am sure you all share my unbounded admiration and respect for Sir John Monash and would join me in asserting that the somewhat more clandestine nature of our organisation and its proposed operations must *complement and support his official force and in no way cause him any embarrassment. Sadly, there are those both in government ranks and who have the ear of prominent politicians, who do not have the best interests of our country at heart. We must ensure that we do not give any government the excuse to turn our respective powers against each other.*

As many of us enjoy joint memberships of both bodies it is especially important that we seek to avoid putting ourselves in positions of conflicting interests. The dangerous nature of these times and the fledgling state of our new Federation will occasion us to walk a fine line, and at such times we shall need balanced counsel to keep us within the bounds of legality. That is enough about our objectives and values and now gentlemen let us get down to the business of strategy and actions."

Later that evening Charlie and Dan met for a drink at the Mitre. When Dan had described his first few days in his new job, Charlie took him into his confidence about his membership of the new secret army and its broad intentions. Dan felt very beholden and loyal to his friend but he heard what Charlie said with growing unease.

"*Charlie you know my reservations about the politicians and military geniuses who got us into the last lot of strife and I have no love for Anarchists, Bolshevist trade unionists and anti-Imperial, Irish Republicans, but in Ireland I saw what terrible atrocities paramilitary forces, operating outside of the law, with government connivance, can perpetrate on innocent men, women and children. The horror stories told to me by pals of mine who served in Vladivostok trying to stop the red forces gaining control, kept me awake at nights and equally frightening were the reprisals carried out by the retreating white forces, claiming allegiance to the late Tsar. I believe you to be a decent man with honourable intentions but I urge you to be cautious and although I would take your side and back you up at any time you might be in danger, I could not in all conscience sign up with such a movement."*

Charlie acknowledged the honesty of Dan's forthright views and reciprocated the assertion of personal loyalty to him, but maintained that it was his role and intention to ensure that nothing illegal was undertaken by the new force.

They agreed to differ on this point and then in earnest of their mutual loyalty and affection, they left the pub and set off arm-in-arm intent on enjoying good company, music and dancing at the house of one of Alice's well-heeled friends.

The house stood high above the Yarra in one of Hawthorn's most affluent streets and such was the size of its river front grounds that they accommodated both tennis courts and a small vineyard. Buckingham palace sized wrought iron gates guarded the entrance and a tower that might have graced a Roman palisade for keeping watch against raiders from over the Rhine, glowed with lamplight revealing the owners collection of telescopes and betraying his more innocent hobby of star gazing.

The party was in full swing. A small band was beating out the new Afro-American rhythms and a singer aped the latest Hollywood drawl. Drink was flowing freely and it was clear from the original oils on the walls, expensive period furniture and general décor that the owners had not suffered financially and had probably benefited from the recent world war.

Charlie was soon swept away to join a throng of professional associates and Dan was intrigued and mystified when Alice told him that there was someone in the gazebo at the bottom of the garden who was looking forward to being reacquainted with him. He was advised to take two glasses and a bottle of the very best champagne with him and so he set off expectantly towards the river bank, wondering who this mysterious party might be.

The garden was empty of revelers as they were too intent on making the most of the jazz and the booze. As he approached the gazebo, all he could make out in the gloom was the shadowy outline of a person through the frosted- glass window and the glow of a cigarette. He walked around to the riverside entrance and as he put his foot on the first step, his heart leapt when he heard a soft, seductive female voice say,

"Hello Dan. Come here and brighten up this dull evening!"

"Elspeth!" He gasped. "What the hell are you doing here?"

"That's a fine way to greet a lady that has travelled to the far side of the earth to see you, you ungrateful wretch!" She rejoined, with an orgasmic laugh and stubbing out her cigarette, she glided across the gazebo and slipped into his strong embrace.

He was prevented from saying anything more by her searching tongue probing the roof of his mouth. Elspeth was a head shorter than him and more than just comely, but the way she clasped his shoulders and sprang up to clamp her open legs around his waist would have satisfied the lithest of gymnasts. All Dan could do was to brace his legs to take her full weight and rest her back against a pillar for support. At the same moment he realised that she was wearing nothing under her sheath dress but her garter-less stockings and that she was carefully unbuckling his belt to let his trousers fall.

She was in need of no foreplay and he entered her massively with his first thrust. Her sheath was silky smooth and moister than he could remember and as he increased his rhythm she purred contentedly in his ear, clasping his buttocks to draw him deeper in and spurred him on with injunctions of

"Fuck me darling! Fuck me harder and more!" Elspeth came first but urged him to *"Give it to me, deeper!"* and to thrust in her more and more, until Dan felt her body tremble with the rush of her second orgasm, and he finally caught up and let go, with one long shuddering groan.

The champagne tasted the better for their love-making and they talked late into the evening, she leaning against him on the bench, his jacket around her shoulders to ward off the dew and his glass-free hand tenderly stroking her hair. Dan had never tried to understand this relationship. The sex was pure delight and Elspeth had taught him all manner of new things to enhance his and her pleasure. But also, there was good, deep and satisfying conversation that flowed easily between them and often contentious and sparkling debate about matters of great moment to both of them.

As in her approach to loving, Elspeth was pragmatic about life and saw all the big issues through the realistic filter of hard, unrelenting experience. She approved of Dan's decision to join Monash and of his refusal to enlist in Charlie's quixotic venture. After all, her late husband had been all for such cavalier action and that is why he got his head shot off, considerably shortening the duration of their marriage. Finally, they got round to Liza and he was both pleased and strangely perturbed at the news that she had decided to come to stay with Alice and Charlie. Elspeth assured him that she was over the worst of the after-effects of the pneumonia and said that the better climate of Melbourne and new opportunities would restore her to her original vitality. She held her counsel about the son.

The house belonged to a friend of Elspeth's and as she was staying there, Dan did not have to escort her far to her door, where she thanked him for a super time and bade him goodnight but not goodbye. He did not meet her again for several weeks until one day in Collins Street, she approached him on the arm of a handsome man who introduced himself as Bill Brennan and said that he was a pilot with Western Australian Airlines. Elspeth told him that Bill was a friend of Liza's and as they parted she turned and gave Dan a knowing smile.

23

Brothers in Arms

Melbourne 1924

Dan soon settled into his job and as Monash had hinted, the bureaucrats proved to be a far greater challenge to progress than the mostly ex-service tradesmen and engine drivers. The free masonry of the returned soldiers had been at work and news of Dan's exploit at the Wonthaggi mine and his reputation for being a firm but fair boss preceded him and the men and unions were prepared at least to give him the benefit of the doubt.

His initial challenge was to drive through the construction of the infrastructure to ensure the timely delivery of brown coal from the open-cut mines to the power stations that were ready and those which were under construction. Melbourne's manufacturing industry was not nearly self-sufficient in supplying all the needs of such a major project and there were delays in getting major machinery components from overseas. His dealings with the labour force had gone well until a few weeks into the job he began to experience some trouble with a strategically important branch of the builders union.

It wasn't until after a particularly acrimonious meeting with a group of shop stewards, that one of his foremen had snorted, "*What can you expect of the bog Irish?*"

Dan turned to rebuke him with the observation that many good Irishmen had died coming ashore at Cape Helles in support of the Anzacs and then he recalled that one of the most intransigent and hostile of the unionists went by the name of O'Sullivan. This was the name of the Cork IRA commander, whose brother Dan had blown to kingdom come, when he had turned the bridge ambush back on the IRA flying column.

The suspicion that there might be some family connection deepened considerably when a few days later he received a note, in his office mail, cut in the shape of a shamrock leaf, which was signed by *the Avengers of Cork*. Dan lost no time in advising Monash of this threat and within days members of the Victoria Police's Aliens squad had visited a number of homes throughout Collingwood, Abbotsford and Richmond, making plain to the residents of Irish Republican origin and allegiance, what sort of retribution might fall on them and their families if such terror tactics were to be repeated on Australian soil. A few weeks later it transpired that O'Sullivan's criminal record had not been revealed when he first migrated to Australia and he soon found himself deported back to his Irish Republican home. Unsurprisingly, Dan's problems with his work force disappeared as fast as they had begun.

There was an unfortunate aftermath to this development when Dan heard that some overzealous members of the secret army had taken it upon themselves to teach the Irish patriots a lesson and proceeded to beat up and harass the families of law-abiding Irishmen, some of whom it transpired had been decorated fighting with Australian forces in alliance with the British Empire. His warning to Charlie had begun to come true. The Irish community had long memories and a history that made them great haters.

Now, Dan could look forward to Christmas and the arrival of Liza in Melbourne. He wondered how she would be, what she would feel about him and how their first meeting would go. His feelings towards her were very conflicted and not at all clear to him. But events were to keep him wondering even longer, when militant Wharf workers decided to picket the Bryant and May safety match factory on Church Street in Richmond, where their pickets and barricades prevented all raw materials from getting in and finished product getting out.

Many homes and businesses depended on gas lighting and both coal and wood fires for heating and producing steam. Safety matches were considered an important strategic product and the government moved quickly to declare them so and to make the blockade of the factory illegal. Police forces alone were not considered to be strong enough to take on the pickets which were barricaded behind overturned lorries and surrounded by razor wire.

In accordance with his charter, Monash had ordered his force of mounted troopers to back up the police and Dan was attached to the squadron which was to carry out this duty, after midnight, on a dark and rainy night when it was thought the defenders of the blockade would be at their lowest ebb. The troopers had moved off from their Albert park barracks and were proceeding up Swan Street at a steady walking gait, when a motor cycle dispatch rider gave its commander a message warning him to watch out for members of a particularly militant Bolshevik faction which had infiltrated the blockaders and who might be armed.

The same intelligence had come to the attention of the Leader and he had deployed a crack platoon of secret army members to shadow the mounted force and to provide any support that was needed to rout the rabble at the factory gates.

Charlie was the leader of this group and on his first assignment he was anxious that discipline and good order would prevail. But he had cause for anxiety because the secret army's intelligence sources had reported that a quantity of explosives had gone missing from a cargo landed at Port Melbourne and it was suggested that it might be in the hands of the blockading wharfies. He was aware that Dan would be amongst the regulars and he had sought his advice on the power of this amount of explosives and how the defenders of the blockade might use it.

Dan wore the official uniform of the regular militia including an officer's Sam Browne harness with a powerful Colt revolver in his holster. As Charlie's father had foretold such a weapon was less likely to malfunction on such a dirty night and its stopping power was considerable. True to his experience in the trenches and Ireland he had arranged some contingency weapons and he had managed to acquire a Mills bomb from a serving munitions officer whose acquaintance he had made during the mining of the ridge at Messines. This was concealed in a small knapsack which was slung across his shoulders.

Charlie on the other hand, being an irregular, was not in uniform and concealed his revolver under a standard Burberry trench-coat which with his trilby hat gave him some anonymity amongst late returning revelers from illegal drinking clubs and protection from the steady drizzle.

Dan could not recall later what brought to mind the devastating assault the IRA had perpetrated on a passing mounted military band in Dublin, immediately before the uprising began. The injury and carnage sustained by the horses had sickened and alienated the horse loving Irish public such that had not the British made martyrs of the revolutionary leaders by their summary execution, the rising may not even have got off the ground.

As the horsemen drew close to the first of the barricades, Dan noticed that a tram car was stopped with its lights extinguished, forcing the troopers to bunch up to pass it in preparation for a charge. His experience of IRA ambushes and roadside bombs aroused his suspicions and he ran towards the commander of the mounted infantry and sought permission for a delay which would allow him to inspect the tram and ensure it was safe for them to pass. There could be no element of surprise in their approach and so the commander was happy to allow Dan to reconnoiter the tram.

To assist the assault party all street lighting had been extinguished, whereas the barricades were bathed in the harsh beams of search-lights. This enabled Dan to approach the tram in the shadows, unseen by the defenders and it barely took him a moment to spot the charges, taped under the fenders which prevented pedestrians from slipping under the wheels. There was no sophistication about the bomb's assembly and no sign of the variety of booby-trap devices with which he had become familiar during his bomb squad service. All it took was a cutting of the detonator cable with his jack knife and the explosives were rendered harmless.

But he had underestimated the capability of the insurgents and just as he rolled out from beneath the tram the first shot, fired by a sniper posted somewhere in the darkness away from the illuminated barricades, sparked off the bluestone pavement edge, missing his head by no more than an inch. With the survival reflexes of a trench-war veteran, Dan reversed his exit move and rolled back under the protection of the tram, with bullets thudding into its metal side plates.

This caused the mounted troops to dismount and scatter, taking up positions from which they could rain fire on where the muzzle flashes appeared to have come from. But by this time any self-respecting sniper would have changed his position or been long gone. Dan was not equipped to resort to the proven trench techniques of putting up a periscope but he tried throwing out all manner of decoy items to see if he could draw more fire and give his mates time to nail the bastard. But it was no use, the marksman had gone. With great caution he began to slither from under the tram on the side hidden from the factory when to his horror he heard and felt the pounding of boots on the road surface close to where he was coming out. A familiar voice cried,

"*Look out Dan he's behind you!*" followed immediately by a thunderous shot that came from immediately above Dan's prone position, then the heavy thud of a fallen body and the all too familiar desperate cry of a wounded man.

Instinctively, Dan sprang to his feet and fortunately, at that instant, a search light swiveled to illuminate the scene. As he rose, un-holstering his revolver and brandishing the Mills bomb in his other hand he was confronted by more than one black-clad assailant and took in at a glance a body dressed in a military issue trench-coat lying on the ground. He roared out the standard warning that he was about to throw a grenade and this brought the advancing armed thugs to an immediate halt, as if they had been turned into stone. This suggested some familiarity with military training and probably an appreciation of what an exploding Mills bomb could do to them at this close range.

Although it seemed an eternity, this stand-off lasted but a few seconds when the one closest to Dan and presumably the one who had shot the poor wretch on the ground, continued his charge and began to raise a high-caliber game rifle to his shoulder. Having already adopted a firing position, Dan braced himself and shot his assailant through the face at close range. The effect on the man's head was devastating and such that he emitted no sound as his dead body crashed to the ground.

His comrades were either less brave or much more prudent and at the sound of numerous rifles being cocked and no doubt aimed in their direction, they slowly lowered their weapons to the roadway and raised their hands in sullen surrender.

Dan's attention turned to the man in the trench-coat who no doubt had shouted the warning and to his horror he saw that it was Charlie lying there attended by medics who were just starting to check for vital signs. The after-shock of what he had experienced and done in those critical seconds hit Dan suddenly and as he sank to his knees to puke in the gutter, he heard Charlie exclaim

"Take it easy you blokes I'm not dead yet!" and Dan barely had time to thank his maker before he fainted and fell, face-first, into his own vomit on the cobblestones, in the street.

24

Going West

Manchester 1924

Liza's bags were packed and her trunk had been collected by the carters to be forwarded to Liverpool docks. She had moved in with Beattie and Arthur for the past few weeks and though they both appeared calm on the surface, inside they were already grieving for the impending loss of one who was like a daughter to them and it would be particularly hard for Beattie to let go of young Daniel, Liza and Dan's son, whom she had both schooled and scolded whilst his mother was away working and engaged in pursuing her cause.

"*There's a letter for you Liza,*" Arthur said, as he placed the day's post on the kitchen table. When her eye caught the Australian stamp, Liza picked up the envelope and went to her room to read it. How fortunate that it had arrived a day before she was due to leave.

Melbourne
August 1924

Dear Liza,
I hope that this letter reaches you before you set off to join us and in case not, I have written to Arthur and Beattie also.
I am afraid that Dan is in trouble again, through no fault of his own and in order to avoid wrongful arrest and an unfair trial, he has been forced to leave Melbourne immediately. He is unharmed and got away safely last night for a destination it is not safe to reveal in a letter. Be sure he has many supporters here, especially amongst former service men and because of the courageous and selfless thing he did, which I will always bless him for, because he saved the life of my dearest Charles. He will not be without friends and helpers along the road wherever he might go.

Dan was a member of a legally constituted paramilitary organisation whose members were mostly returned servicemen and whose purpose was to support the police in times of serious public unrest, such as the riots we had during the police strike. Both he and Charles (who is a member of a more informal and secretive organisation which does not have government recognition) were involved in an armed confrontation with a Bolshevik-inspired group of trade unionists who were barricading the entrances to Bryant and May's match factory.

A bomb that would have killed many troopers and their horses was spotted and made safe by Dan but then he was in danger of being killed by a group of gunmen who bore down on him. Charles ran from the shadows shouting a warning to Dan and was shot by one of these attackers and would surely have been executed on the ground had not Dan threatened them with a hand-grenade and when their leader refused to surrender and was in the act of raising his rifle to fire, Dan shot him dead.

Charles has a serious but not critical wound in his shoulder from which he is recuperating at home under my care. But even though Dan was on official duty dark forces with connections in government began to spread the rumour that Dan had shot and killed an unarmed and defenceless man. Unfortunately, the dead man was an Irish-American and even though the US government would not sympathise with his cause, they take the death of their nationals in foreign countries very seriously and demanded that either Dan was tried here or extradited to the United States.

Charles felt that, in time, Dan would have been acquitted but there are those in government who are uneasy about Monash's force and downright alarmed at the secret army of which Charles is a member. Questions have been asked in State parliament as to what a distinguished former soldier and leading barrister was doing in Richmond late at night with a pistol under his coat and as Dan is not an Australian citizen and not a veteran of the AIF this makes him an easier target for the Tammany hall Irish element who look for inspiration to Jack Lang in NSW, and who have really got it in for him.

Dear Liza, I am sorry to be the bearer of such news as you plan to depart. You must still come. Melbourne will be a good and safe place for you. Charles and I will guarantee that. Rest assured also

that we and very powerful friends will move heaven and earth to ensure that Dan remains safe and free. We look forward to hearing that you are still coming and to celebrating Christmas with you in our house and your new home.
With all our love,

Alice and Charles

When Liza returned to the kitchen where Arthur and Beattie sat in their habitual places on either side of the fireplace, she could tell from their faces and the crumpled letter in Arthur's hand, that they had received the same news.

"*Now sit thee down here my love*", said Arthur as he drew another chair closer to the fire for her and Beattie poured her a strong cup of tea with more than a drop of the whisky, Arthur reserved for special occasions, stirred into it.

They discussed Dan's misfortune until late into the afternoon. They wondered at his topsy-turvy life.

"*Just when he is settling and things are looking up for him, something always seems to come along to put a spoke in his wheel.*" Beattie observed.

But Arthur, being of a more optimistic bent and very aware that Liza must be doubting the wisdom of taking her son to a country and city where such terrible things could befall an honest and innocent man, assured her

"*Dan can look after himself and you should not consider changing your plans for the sake of Daniel, who will get a great new start in life in such a thriving city and under the protection and sponsorship of kind and influential people like Charles and Alice.*"

It was just the right thing to have said, as she was very much in two minds about going, but the argument in favour of Daniel's best interests carried far more weight with her than any benefit she might gain or lose, by going or staying.

Across the Nullarbor 1924/25

Whilst a strong case proving Dan's innocence could have been mounted the consensus of his friends and sponsors was that the political times were so uncertain that he should leave Victoria at once and get as far away as possible. Western Australia suited this purpose as a destination because of its distance from Victoria and relative detachment from the political and legal affairs of the Eastern states. The problem was how to get him across the 2000 miles of inhospitable country that lay between Melbourne and Perth, without attracting the attention of the Victorian and South Australian police, who would be looking out for him, along with the agents of his many enemies.

It would have been most convenient to go by sea but there was no doubt that the wharf workers and maritime union members would have all the major ports under watch and it appeared that the IRA had put a price on his head. Sir John was sympathetic to Dan's plight and had ensured that a message thanking him for what he had contributed to the SEC and especially for saving the lives of his men, had got through to Dan, along with the pay that was due to him and a very generous cash bonus that probably came from Monash's own pocket. But he could not be seen to become directly involved. The Leader of the secret army, however, was under no such restraint and he too felt obliged to help Dan because he had saved the life of his most valuable officer and legal adviser.

Dan was kitted-out to look like the many diggers who had failed to find work after returning from the war and who wandered the land relying on the good will of country people toward an ex-soldier down on his luck. He wore the insignia of Charlie's regiment, whose story and names of its key officers were familiar to him. So urgent was the need for him to get away, that there was no time to see Charlie who was in hospital and under sedation. But he bade an emotional farewell to Alice who promised to let Arthur, Beattie and Liza know what had happened and that he was safe and well.

Later that night a Sergeant of the secret army drove him to Spencer Street station to catch the night train to Adelaide. Relays of former diggers came and went throughout the train journey. Some engaged Dan in conversation to give credibility to his appearance and ensured that there were no suspect characters on the train that might be a danger to him. His insignia won him respectful treatment by railway officials. Male passengers didn't hesitate to offer him a smoke and women whose dress suggested they were widows of the war, greeted him kindly and a particularly forward one suggested she had a spare room in her Adelaide house that he might like. Under the circumstances he had neither the time nor the inclination to follow up such an obvious come on.

He was tired, confused and angry that yet again his life had been turned upside down just because he had done the right thing. He had no idea of where he was going nor how long and arduous the journey would be. He may as well have been standing at the start of the Pennine track again without having resolved any of his doubts and fears in the intervening years. Why was it that every time he seemed to have put his military trade behind him and found a progressive peace-time occupation, he was called upon to demonstrate his capacity for violent action and his cool indifference when facing death.

He spent minimal time in Adelaide where he transferred to a cattle truck returning empty to Port Pirie, on the edge of the outback, and was helped to move on to Iron Knob, a mining boom town, where he was able to pass as a visiting English mining engineer come out to sell and inspect equipment. The plausibility of his cover, the remoteness of the town and the itinerant nature of its workforce enabled him to stay long enough to rest and get ready for the hard road ahead.

Little did he know that it would take him almost a year to complete his journey, having started in Melbourne in the final months of 1924 and not arriving in Perth until later in 1925. He worked on farms droving sheep and cattle, which greatly improved the rudimentary riding skills he had started to pick up at Charlie's property. He crewed on fishing boats out of the small ports of Ceduna and Fowlers Bay, where the authorities had little presence, and he seized every opportunity to take passage on small local craft heading for ports further to the west. He rode with carters carrying supplies and mail to farms and small communities along the way.

One helpful farmer gave him a rusty but serviceable bicycle and at times of sheer necessity he even shouldered his swag and set out to walk, learning where to find bore water and earning a feed by doing odd jobs at remote stations. Whilst doing this at one sheep property a desperate shearing contractor asked him if he knew how to cook and at four the next morning he found himself grilling mountains of chops and frying dozens of eggs to satisfy the gargantuan breakfast appetites of shearers who had been at work since first light. The cook he replaced had drunk himself to death, even resorting to drinking food flavourings and methylated spirits, when regular alcoholic drinks and his money ran out.

In the free time between meals Dan seized the opportunity to learn as much as he could about the rearing of sheep for their wool and meat. He observed the station hands at work and of course had to kill and butcher his own sheep for the pot. The station owners tolerated his curiosity and marked his intelligence and willingness to pitch-in when they were short-handed. He was able to help them excavate new dams, applying his skill with explosives to break through rock barriers and stubborn tree stumps. He was soon respected as a very versatile and reliable bushman, even though he would always be a poor bloody pom.

As the contractors men came from towns across the western border, at the end of the season he was able to move into Western Australia with introductions to sources of work, food and a bed, in towns all the way from Eucla to Norseman and by this time nobody would mistake him for the former English army officer who had fled Melbourne, where he was wanted for murder.

25

No Peace in Perth

Perth 1925

As Dan looked so different now from when he left Melbourne, he felt safe completing his journey from Kalgoorlie to Perth by train. The city was so quiet after the hustle and bustle of Manchester and Melbourne. It was only when he made a later visit to King's Park and looked out from its heights, that he appreciated its beautiful setting on the banks of a wide sweep of the Swan river.

He had few belongings and being accustomed to long walks, he set off on foot to find the home of Bill and Lady Elspeth where he had been invited to stay upon his arrival in the west. When he reached the ocean beach suburb of Cottesloe, he appreciated how well Elspeth had done for herself in settling down with Bill. The houses were palatial, each with their own grounds and some even with a tennis court at the back. It would need a very convincing cover story to explain the arrival of a disreputable, swaggy, at such a prestigious address.

Despite his uncouth appearance, he was welcomed with open arms, by Elspeth herself and after a luxurious, hot bath and the replacement of his travel stained clothes with fresh, clean ones, it was agreed that he should pose as an eccentric geologist who had been prospecting on behalf of a consortium of wealthy English would be investors. He was glad that Bill was away up north, flying the newly introduced Perth to Geraldton service, as it allowed Elspeth and he to speak freely about what had happened to him and to consider what he might do next. Whilst there was still a strong sexual attraction between them, Dan understood, without a need for words, that she had committed herself to Bill and that despite her previous somewhat courtesan lifestyle, she was a woman of her word.

Bill returned at the weekend and made Dan feel almost as equally welcome as Elspeth had. He confirmed that news of the Melbourne incident had barely registered in the west and that there were neither wanted notices nor any kind of hue and cry. As if to emphasise the truth of this, they organised a party at the weekend, after Dan had been suitably kitted-out by Bill's tailor, and foremost amongst the influential and affluent guests was the local chief of police, who welcomed Dan heartily.

Having been informed of Dan's war service in France and the Middle East and his experience in Ireland, the chief was quick to assert the need for men of Dan's pedigree in Western Australia and more than just hinted that the police force might offer exceptional prospects of rapid career advancement.

This allayed Dan's fears of arrest and for the first time in months he relaxed and stopped feeling like a hunted fox which was but one step ahead of the hounds. The evening was very enjoyable, there were music, singing, cards and later, dancing in the modern jazz style. Having arrived from England fairly recently, Dan was expected to know the latest steps and when he proved that he did, it delighted both the local spinsters and lively matrons and Elspeth ensured he was kept under her protective and somewhat wistful gaze.

The businessmen who were present, represented all of Western Australia's key enterprises and from their conversations, Dan learned that primary industry was the main stay of the economy, which was in a downturn after a post war boom. But he could see that his experience in mining and development of infrastructure, in Melbourne, would make him readily employable here.

There was only one slightly sour note in an otherwise relaxing and encouraging evening, when a leading Roman Catholic Bishop, of Irish origin, made a few disparaging insinuations about the British handling of the troubles in Ireland and sought to interrogate Dan about his time there. But, fortunately, Elspeth was alert to this indiscretion and asked Bill to take his Eminence to join the men for cigars and brandy in the library.

For the next few days, Dan relaxed, took early dips in the surf and over-indulged in the fine food, putting much needed flesh back onto his almost skeletal frame. On his return from a morning exercise session, he noticed that there were two letters addressed to him, sitting on the hall stand. One was from Alice and the other from Charlie. He took them into the dining room and opened the one from Charlie first.

Melbourne 1925

Dear Dan,

We were delighted to hear from Elspeth of your safe arrival in the west. What adventures and privations you must have faced in that arduous overland journey. At least it sounds as though you have really developed your bush skills and now you must be a much more accomplished horseman.

Great news! Liza arrived yesterday and we collected her from the boat at Prince's Pier. Of course, Alice had not seen her since their time together in France, and we were both shocked to see how pale and skinny she was. But don't worry! Plenty of sunshine, solid food and some time on our property in the bush will soon fix that. More news of Liza is contained in a separate letter from Alice and so I will confine myself to news of your situation.

You will be pleased to hear that the Victorian political climate has moderated and now that the old conscription battles and influence of cardinal Mannix are becoming history, bitter sectarianism is on the wane. Your influential military friends are backing an action I am leading in the Victorian courts to quash the charges laid against you, in respect of the Chapel Street 'incident', and there are good prospects of its success.

Both Alice and I are well, my wound has fully healed but I must admit it has slowed me down somewhat and Alice thinks this is no bad thing. We are so sorry that your welcome to our country was so marred by this unjust charge and we are eternally in your debt for saving my life.

I will say no more as I know that the news in Alice's letter will give you more than enough to think about. Suffice it to say you have our love and support and you have only to ask for any help we can give, until your innocence is proven.

Your loyal friend (and mate!)

Charlie

Dan was pleased to hear that Liza had arrived safely and was in good hands and the possibility of legal redress added to his feeling of wellbeing and confidence in his future in Australia. He was intrigued, however, as to why Alice had written separately and wondered what her news might be.

Melbourne 1925

My Dear Dan,

Charles and I were thrilled to hear of your safe arrival and I join with him, once more, in expressing our gratitude for what you did and our love and support in the consequent privations you have suffered.

Now it has fallen to me to give you some long overdue news which I believe to be joyful but which will shock you and I suggest you sit down before continuing to read this letter. There is no easy way to break this news and so I will plunge in. Liza did not arrive alone. She had with her a handsome boy, called Daniel, who is her son and you are his father.

Had Dan not been seated, he would have staggered and might have fallen. A rush of discomforting thoughts, conflicting emotions and disturbing questions surged through his mind. He was the father of Liza's child. It would have happened a long time ago and now the boy must be ten years old! Why had she kept it from him? He had a son but had missed his childhood. He must find a means of supporting them both and make up to Liza the lonely years of struggle she must have faced in raising the boy. Then came a flash of anger-how could she have done this to him and allowed him to go to the other end of the earth with not so much as a word about his son's existence?

He cast the letter aside, swept past a startled Elspeth in the hall, grabbed his coat and stormed out of the house with the curtest of farewells. For several hours, he tramped up and down the Cottesloe beach, his emotions surging and ebbing as in sympathy with the boiling surf. First came disbelief, then anger and finally tenderness and concern for Liza and pride in having a son.

Having reached this calmer state of mind, he turned for home and there he found Bill and Elspeth waiting for him in the parlour. She gave him a tender hug and Bill handed him a very large Scotch. It was clear that they had read the letter that he had dropped on the floor.

Later, in his room, he resumed reading where he had left off.....

Don't be too hard on Liza for not telling you herself. She kept it from you because she felt that you had enough problems, after the war, in trying to sort out your life and she was very determined that you should not feel trapped by your one night of passion.

Arthur and Beattie have been all for her telling you long ago but now that she is here, Liza cannot maintain her secret any longer and in making her decision to come to Australia, where you are already, she recognised that it was time you were told.

So, the duty has fallen to me and I do it with the joy of knowing you have such a fine son by this wonderfully strong and independent woman and, also, with great tenderness and concern for your wellbeing when you have recovered from this shock.

Charles counsels that you must not rush back here yet as the legal situation is not cleared up but, of course, the first thing is for you to communicate with Liza. She is very eager for this and sends her love.

With my love and caring,

Alice

Melbourne 1925

Liza was delighted by Melbourne. It was not unlike Manchester in its Victorian era civic architecture but with such a mild Mediterranean climate and to be so close to the sea was a great joy. It was so good to live in fashionable East Melbourne with the comforts of Alice's beautiful home and the seaside at St Kilda was just a short tram ride away.

She was relieved that Alice had written to Dan on her behalf but also apprehensive about his reaction and whether he would accept and own Daniel as his son once the shock of fatherhood had subsided. Though in some ways she dreaded it, she felt an urgent need to speak to Dan but Perth was so far away. He could not return to Melbourne safely and she could not go to him with such uncertainty between them.

It was Charlie who came up with a possible solution. Whilst there was not yet a direct telephone service between homes in Perth and Melbourne, he believed a private conversation could be arranged from his chambers to those of an affiliated law firm over there. Liza jumped at the idea and Charlie undertook to cable Elspeth and Bill so they could put this proposal to Dan.

Melbourne and Perth 1925

Both Liza and Dan approached this conversation with an equal mixture of anxiety and excitement. Neither had slept well the night before and both had rehearsed their lines incessantly.

When they spoke, all their best laid plans failed them. They started haltingly and even quibbled about the time with him saying,

"Good afternoon!" and she *"Good morning!"* with neither making allowance for the East-West time difference. Then they moved to:

"How are you?" and *"How are things in Perth and in Melbourne?"*

It was not until Liza's innate directness and honesty came to the fore, that the real, necessary exchange began.

"Oh Dan, it's grand to hear your voice and such a relief that you know that Daniel is your son. I am not ashamed of it but I am very sorry to have kept it from you until now. At first I felt guilty on account of Ted but then I realised that if I were to settle for another man, he would have wanted it to be you. But, whilst this banished the guilt, I then feared that if I had told you, you would have felt obliged to do the right thing by me and you had enough worries out there in the war. After that, when you came home, you were so confused and conflicted that I couldn't risk ruining your freedom to find your way back into normal living, whatever that is.

So, I'm sorry Dan, but I'm right proud and happy that you are the father of our darling boy."

Having got that off her chest, her voice faltered and the tears began to flow. Every sob tore at Dan and he responded instinctively.

"Now then, Liza, don't fret so and blame your self for something that we did willingly and which has made us a son. It should be an occasion for joy and we should be toasting with Charlie's best champagne.

Now listen to me. This has been a great shock for me and I must admit that I have thought hard things of you for keeping him and his childhood from me. But you were right. After the war, I was a very disturbed and unsettled man, not fit to be a father and what with the events in Ireland and then the killing in Melbourne, I wonder whether I will ever be able to settle down and take on my full responsibility as a true father should. But, I assure you, I will see you both right and you will no longer have to carry an unequal burden.

I must confess to confusion in my feelings for you. I have always seen

you as a sort of special sister, a soul mate, without the complication of love and sex but after that night in Blackpool, I haven't known what to think."

"Oh Dan, lad", Liza cut in, "apart from Ted, and especially after his death, you have been the most important man in my life. Although you were mostly far away, I knew you were there for me, as you demonstrated when I was in Jail for my suffragette protest, and at bad times I clung to my memory of you as I would to a rock in a stormy sea. It's not the right time to decide about us now, but let's see when we can meet and whatever happens I want you to know that I will carry my feeling for you in my heart for ever."

Neither could bear to speak further after that and the operator indicated that their allotted time was up.

Cottesloe

All the way back to Cottesloe, Dan replayed their conversation in his head. He was both elated to have a son and heart-sick that Liza had brought up Daniel without his help and knowing. At the same time she had managed to represent her union, champion the suffragette cause and even survived jail. How had she coped? His pride in her strength and determination overcame his feeling of angst and the more he thought about how she had done this and kept it secret for so long, in order to protect and care for him, deeper feelings of tenderness overwhelmed him and to his consternation, he began to cry.

Elspeth and Bill could see from his drawn expression and his red-rimmed eyes that Dan had been deeply affected by whatever Liza had had to say. Both knew better than to voice their curiosity about what had transpired but showed their concern by fussing over him, urging him to take a nap in his room and soak in a hot bath before joining them later, over a pre-dinner drink.

As soon as Dan had sat down with his first drink, the flood gates opened and, with minimal prompting, he told them the details of what he and Liza had said to each other and how it had affected him. By the end of dinner he had confirmed his wish to bring Liza and Daniel to Perth so that they could be together at last. But by then he had to find a means of supporting them.

His hosts were eager to offer their support and Bill reminded Dan of the prospective employers he had met at his welcome party and suggested that he could easily make enquiries on Dan's behalf. Dan went to bed with an easier mind now that he was set on a course of action. He was sure he didn't want to take up the offer to join the police but wondered how best he could secure suitable work that would assure him a steady income. But despite Bill's influence and connections it was mother-nature that found Dan a job.

During the night, Dan had been conscious of high winds thrashing the branches of the great gum trees in the garden and the staccato rattle of hail stones on his bedroom window. After breakfast, news came that the storm had caused the Swan River to flood. The North Fremantle railway bridge had collapsed soon after a passenger train had crossed safely and volunteers were being called for to assist the residents of South Perth, which was partly under water.

Bill and Dan were quick to respond and were soon employed in filling and stacking sand bags to protect buildings threatened by the rising water. The scene was chaotic and although Dan had started with a shovel in his hand, by the end of the day, because he had introduced order and discipline, he found himself in command of the operation. He had become well acquainted with sandbagging operations during his service in Flanders and this was sufficiently apparent to the main body of volunteers who saw the sense of his directions and allowed themselves to be formed into more productive squads without complaint, apart from the customary barbs of wry wit.

When darkness forced operations to cease, an unbreached wall of sandbags was preventing the river encroaching further into the suburb and although there was considerable damage in some places, no lives had been lost. Dan and Bill welcomed the invitation to join some of their new 'digger' mates for a drink at a nearby bowls club which ignored the restrictive licensing laws with the compliance of the local police who not only turned a blind eye, under these emergency circumstances, but were more than ready to join the tired and thirsty throng.

Dan finished his first beer and as he turned to compete for another at the crowded bar, he was confronted by a man returning from the crush who thrust a beer into his hand.

"You've earned that", he said. *"I could see that we were in trouble when I arrived this morning and I was impressed with the way you brought order out of chaos and got the men working to your direction without too much complaint. It looked as though you had done this sort of thing before."* Dan thanked him for the beer and his complimentary remarks and went on to admit his frontline service as an officer with the sappers.

"So, what brings you to Perth?" the man responded.

Bill joined the conversation at this point and explained that Dan was visiting from England as a guest of he and his wife and that, after a spot of prospecting up north, he was looking for work in Perth.

Dan recalled seeing the man, during the day, standing on the back of a truck from which he could observe the whole flood protection operation and issue instructions to men who ran off to do his bidding. Clearly, he was in a position of authority and when he introduced himself as Chief Engineer of the newly formed Main Roads Board, it was no great surprise.

Melbourne

Liza had welcomed Dan's invitation to join him in Perth and although he had sent money for the train fares, she was as determined as him to improve their financial security and not become solely dependent on him. Alice offered to find her administrative work in one of the major hospitals but Liza's experience of shop-floor managing in mills and factories was in high demand in Melbourne's growing post-war industries and she was soon able to secure a well-paid supervisory position in a food processing factory with a large female workforce.

Alice and Charlie refused to accept rent from her and as Christmas approached she had accumulated a healthy bank balance. Dan had rented a quaint cottage in a suburb called Subiaco and she was so looking forward to joining him in the New Year.

Perth 1926

Western Australia's growing primary industries needed improved road and rail connections to the city markets and port and Dan's employment as an Operations manager with the road's board took him to all parts of Perth and out to the surrounding wheat belt and timber towns. He loved the work which made him feel like a pioneer. He got on well with his work crews, his savings were growing and with the rental of the Subiaco house, he was ready for the arrival of Liza and Daniel and looking forward to it.

On a typically hot January day he had finished supervising the blasting of a cutting through a difficult rock formation and returned to the shed that served as his office, to clean up ready for the journey back into town. After a quick wash, he changed from his dusty work clothes and was about to leave when he spotted a package on his desk. It was addressed to him but as he didn't want to miss a lift in the truck taking the men back into Perth, he decided to take it with him and open it when he got home.

Such was his popularity with his colleagues that he was unable to refuse their invitation to join them for a swift beer before closing time and soon found himself with glass in hand in the company of his surveyor, road engineer and supervisors. They were all ex-servicemen who were familiar with Dan's wartime service history.

The conversation turned to football and whilst his companions argued the merits of local rivalries, Dan took the opportunity to open the package. Inside was a small cardboard cylinder with a note rolled around it and secured with an elastic band. He opened the cylinder first, emptied out its contents and then read the note. The object in his hand was a live rifle bullet and the note said *'Remember Cork!'*

His immediate reaction was to close his hand to hide the round from the others and pocket the note. But he was not quick enough, as the men were more alert to his discovery than he had expected. He was so shocked by the warning and embarrassed at being caught in the attempt to deceive them that he couldn't respond to their expectant stares. The engineer took the initiative in breaking the silence.

"*Looks as though you are in a spot of bother, boss,*" he observed, with a note of concerned enquiry in his voice and before Dan could reply, he added,

"*Whilst it's none of our business, I'm sure I speak for all of us in asking if there is anything we could do to help?*" Their unanimous nods of agreement affirmed the support of the others.

Dan's hesitance about revealing his secret was more driven by his wish not to expose his men to danger and certainly not by any lack of trust in them. To have tried to exclude them after what they had seen would have been received as an irredeemable affront to their honour and so he resolved to tell his story.

They listened with rapt attention and without interruption. At the conclusion of his tale, their silent reception puzzled him until he guessed that it had not been entirely news to them. Before he could confirm this, the engineer confessed that, "*We have an affiliation with the secret army and we were asked to look out for and offer assistance should a certain English officer come our way.*"

It was clear they had known about him all along and that true to their code they had determined to keep his secret and respect his anonymity unless he might need their help.

"*We suggest you advise your own contacts of what has happened so that the Melbourne authorities are not alerted to your whereabouts.*"

"*Thanks for your loyalty and support. I really appreciate it, especially being a 'new chum' and I am sorry to have put you in danger.*"

"*No apology needed, Dan. It's no more than a man should expect from his mates. We will continue to watch out for suspicious strangers on the site and any threatening characters who might be staking out your house.*"

As he left the pub and despite his concern about involving them, he felt better for having shared his problem and drew some comfort from the thought that they were keeping an eye out for those who threatened his life. At the same time he suffered the sickening realisation that his hope for a settled future with Liza and his boy had been dashed by the repeated consequences of his violent past and despaired of ever escaping it.

He was in urgent need of a new plan of action and an easing of his growing anxiety. He was in no mood to return to the solitude of the cottage and set out for Cottesloe to share his concerns with Elspeth and Bill.

Before Dan had decided how best to get there, one of the departing drinkers stopped his car, asked him where he was headed and suggested that as he was driving home towards the coast, Dan was welcome to a lift. His companion had made the most of his drinking time and was happy to chat away without appearing to notice or care whether his passenger was listening and by the time they reached a junction, at which their roads diverged, he was feeling calmer and had started to get his turbulent thoughts under control. As it was not far to his destination, he decided to walk the rest of the way and was soon swinging along at his accustomed marching gait whilst, in his mind, he wrestled to calm a riot of worries and fears.

By the time he had begun to thread his way through the tree-lined suburban avenues that led to his friends' house, it was almost dusk but he was so wrapped up in his thoughts that he was oblivious to his surroundings. So much so that it almost cost him his life.

The crunch of footsteps on gravel in the driveway ahead alerted Dan to imminent danger and dropping into a defensive crouch he leaned back into the protection of a high garden fence. The powerful strike, intended for his head, collided with the top of the fence, sending such a violent vibration down the tall pickets that Dan was thrown off balance and in tumbling sideways was fortunate again to escape the follow up stroke, which crashed into the fence just where he had been crouching. His powerfully-built assailant, who had sprung from the shadow of a gateway, wielding a wicked length of fence post, was intent on delivering a lethal blow.

Dan was unarmed and totally defenceless against this unexpected attack and his only hope was to break away and outrun his attacker. In falling away from the fence he had rolled sideways, out of range of the deadly club and before the killer could regain his balance and strike again, Dan was up and running for his life. But, just when he thought he had got away, his path was blocked by two more men and a third emerged on his flank, boxing him in against the fence and exposing him to continued assault from the rear. All were brandishing clubs and one held the additional threat of a large hunting knife.

Dan had fought his way out of many dangerous encounters in the past but never against such unfavourable odds and without the means to fight back on at least even terms. He cursed his lack of caution and failure to arm himself despite the warning. His attackers began to taunt him and the accent of at least one of them betrayed his Irish origin and confirmed that their motive was reprisal for the killings in Cork.

He knew that he could neither escape nor win but tried to identify the weakest gang member to attack so that he could go down fighting rather than wait for their combined assault. Having picked out the most likely candidate, Dan was about to charge him when a gun-shot shattered the silence followed by the sound of running feet and a commanding voice shouted

"Hang on you blokes, let's even up the odds a bit!" This caused the encircling thugs to draw back and turn away to face the challenge from the advancing intruders.

But, before he could decide whether to fight or run, he heard from behind him the call, *"Quick Dan, climb over the fence"*. He needed no further urging and with two short strides and a frantic leap, he seized the top of the pickets and rolled over, head first, into the garden on the other side. Fortunately a soft flower bed cushioned his fall and on regaining his feet he was amazed to see Elspeth standing there with a lethal looking shot gun tucked under her arm.

Later, after a hot bath and a solid dinner, Dan found himself in Elspeth and Bill's lounge, surrounded by an exuberant group of revelers comprising, as well as his hosts, several of his workmates, all of whom were eager to share their versions of how they had thwarted the almost deadly attack.

Fortunately for Dan, his colleagues had readily appreciated the seriousness of the warning he had received and decided to follow him in case of attack, whereas Elspeth had responded to the noise of the encounter in the street and on seeing Dan's plight had rushed to get Bill's gun and had ably demonstrated her ability shoot. As for the attackers, they had fled taking advantage of nightfall, to escape through the maze of darkened streets. Clearly Dan's cover had been blown and there was general agreement that it would not be safe for him to remain in Perth even with the protection that the secret army men could provide.

After his mates had left, Dan, Bill and Elspeth talked late into the night about what he might do and where he might go. He was devastated by this reversal of fortune just as he was about to be reunited with Liza and his son.

26

Heading North

Dan's instinct was to stay and fight. In the years since the war, he had been constantly on the move seeking to find his real self and how he wanted to live.

Now, just as he had recognised and declared his love for Liza and was looking forward to their life together and becoming a father to his son, the Irish vendetta threatened, once more, to drive him on. He was sick of fighting and killing in other people's causes. It was time for him to defend himself and his own.

Over the next few days there was intense communication with Liza and his friends and supporters in both Melbourne and Perth. He was persuaded by the force of their arguments that to settle in Subiaco would expose not only himself but more importantly, his family, to the certain threat of reprisal. Reluctantly, he acceded to their collective urging that he should move to a place where he would be harder to track down and where, should the worst come to the worst, he would be better placed to detect his enemy's approach and defeat him. But where, Dan wondered, could they settle happily in peace and security.

It was Charlie who came up with the solution. For some years he had invested in anticipation of his retirement and amongst his interests was a controlling share in a cattle station in the remote far north-west region known as the Kimberley. He reasoned that Dan had gained a sufficient introduction to livestock management whilst crossing the Nullarbor, that he would soon learn what it took to run a top-end station and how better to protect his investment than to have a trusted friend in charge. Although the distant north west of the state was a remote and underdeveloped place, with an almost mystical reputation, Dan was aware of the achievements of the pioneering dynasties in establishing vast cattle rearing enterprises out of the tropical wilderness and that the state government was keen to encourage further investment and suitable settlers to further develop this land.

A cattle station in such a place certainly met the security criteria and with Liza's support and Charlie's assurance that there would be sufficient back up from experienced and reliable station hands to save him from making a hash of things until he had got the hang of it, Dan agreed to give it a go.

It was essential that his departure from Perth was as unobtrusive as possible and with Bill's help he was listed under an assumed name as a member of the flight crew on a scheduled WA Airlines service via Geraldton to Derby, with Bill in command.

Dan was sad to leave Perth but at the same time full of excitement in anticipation of what might await him in this remote land. The loss of the promised home in Subiaco had been a severe blow for Liza to bear but she too hoped, desperately, that Dan would succeed in developing a future for them in the north. The arrival of the weekly flight was a significant event in such a small settlement as Derby, so Bill ensured that Dan remained onboard until the alighting passengers and those who had come to greet them had dispersed. It was too dangerous to expose him to the inquisitive scrutiny that newcomers attracted and as soon as he had been smuggled into the freight storage shed and exchanged his uniform for riding clothes, he was on his way to a stockman's camp on the outskirts of town.

In the Kimberley 1926

Charlie had done a good job in stressing the need to make Dan's arrival as unobtrusive as possible and the small party that had come to meet and guide him to the station had spread the word that their unusual visit to town at the height of the wet season was caused by the need to collect some vital medical supplies.

The foreman, who came to greet him on arrival, looked every bit the part from his tall wiry build to his craggy weather beaten face. Dan had anticipated his finger crushing handshake but instead of the expected harsh Australian drawl he was greeted in a soft Scottish brogue.

But there was nothing soft about Archie McCann's attitude and approach to his job.

"G'day boss! I can't say that you are welcome, arriving at this time of year, dragging us out in the wet and making us neglect important station work. You had better prepare for a rough journey that you will never forget, that's if you make it and we don't have to send you back."

"Well, thanks for the warm welcome, Archie." Dan replied equally coolly. "I'll do my best not to live up to your worst expectations."

Although Dan made some allowance for the bushman's natural inclination to unnerve and put one over on the new arrival from the city by exaggerating the degree of hardship, he had a fair idea of what a long ride in the wet might demand of him. It would certainly be a stern test of his horsemanship and in the eyes of his companions a searching examination of his ability and right to be accepted as their leader.

Taking advantage of a lull after the heavy overnight rain, the small party left the camp early the next morning. Dan rode alongside Archie in the lead, followed by two white station hands and three aboriginal stockmen who had control of the pack animals and a string of six spare horses. They rode all day through recurring showers, on sodden tracks which weighed down the horses hooves as they gathered up ever larger clods of viscous red mud. He began to appreciate the need for the additional mounts. The constant drenching defeated even the protection of his oil-soaked, cotton riding-coat and had he not padded his inner thighs and backside with sheepskin strips, the chafing and bruising he suffered would have been unbearable. It would be some time before he regained the hardness in the saddle he had built up droving on the Nullarbor. He hoped his body would soon remember how to do it.

At nightfall, the rain came on even harder, defying even their combined fire-lighting skills. They made do with cold beef jerky washed down with rainwater for tea and suffered a humid night of intermittent sleep in damp swags with clouds of mosquitoes for company. Dan was happy to learn that the wretched mud had its uses by serving as a protective barrier against insect bites when smeared across the face.

For days they pushed on stolidly, their progress determined by the rough terrain and their horses' laborious gait. Although daunted by the seemingly endless carpet of red sludge, Dan had experienced worse on the Western Front, where wounded men had drowned in the quagmire, albeit not traveling on horseback and in such steamy hot conditions. The rain and heat had brought the land to life and they rode across a plain of Spinifex, taller than the horses' heads, which engulfed them like a great sea, whose grassy waves stretched into the far distance to break against the ochre cliffs of the rocky range stalking their flanks.

Apart from unavoidable curt answers to Dan's questions about the country, Archie maintained a taciturn silence and the other men followed his lead. Dan had met his like before in the Scottish regiments he had fought alongside and among the Black and Tan volunteers in Ireland. Even if his words could have breached the barrier of disregard that the bushman held for outsiders, especially pommies like him, he still faced the even more insurmountable obstacle of the Scot's historical disdain for the English. He knew it would take action rather than smooth talk to make his mark with these men. Despite their silence and seeming indifference, they watched closely how he was coping on the road, with the weather and in the saddle. It was on this performance that he would be judged.

But, although the country was testing him even more severely than his companions, it was soon to provide him with the opportunity to meet their challenge. As the mountainous ranges closed in on their path, the way began to rise, bringing them out onto a ridge from which they had a panoramic view of the country that lay ahead. The scale and emptiness of the outback was not new to him but he was amazed by the expanse of luxuriant country below. The lush green of the grassy plain reminded him of rich English parkland and the colour of the bordering mountains ranged from fiery ochre to gunmetal gray, as the clouds flirted with the sun. But what really held his awed attention was the mighty flood-swollen river which, like a great silver serpent whose sinuous coils roamed across the plain, dared those, either foolhardy or brave enough, to attempt a crossing. With a sense of both excitement and foreboding, Dan realised that to get to their destination they would have to overcome this obstacle.

Melbourne 1926

On hearing of Dan's narrow escape from his enemies Liza readily supported his decision to quit Perth and head for the north. But in the subsequent days she came to confront the harsh reality of what this meant for her and her hope of a life together with him and their son.

She had loved her husband and still treasured the memory of their time together, filled with gaiety, good deeds and their bond of youthful, innocent romance. But since his death, her experience of war service and its aftermath had hardened her outlook and strengthened her self-reliance. She had succeeded in male dominated professions, born and raised a son without needing a man to protect and provide for them. Many had offered her this security but she would not settle for safety at the expense of hard won personal freedom. But, then there was Dan.

She had to admit that their passionate encounter in Blackpool was largely due to the loneliness of her recent widowhood and uncontrollable lust. She had taken full responsibility for her actions by keeping the birth of their son from him and by forsaking his financial support. Throughout the war she had longed for news of his safety which came mostly at second hand from Arthur and Beattie and in the few letters she received from him. Whilst still grieving for her Ted, Liza could not have borne the additional loss of their closest friend.

When it was over and he had returned, sound in body but confused and tormented in mind and spirit, she felt for him and offered him support but never sought to repeat the intimacy of that passionate night. Since then, she had taken on the tough challenges of managing and trades union leadership. She served in France and had even gone to prison for a cause. But she had seen little of Dan although aware of what he was doing, even during his service in Ireland. It was not until after he had visited her in jail and, despite her ungracious treatment of him, his having organised her early release, that she began to focus more intently on what he might feel for her and to question what he meant to her.

Dan was intelligent, self-educated, had worked his way from coalface to management and won his officer's commission under fire. He was worldly wise but principled and offered all that a woman might seek in a conventional marriage. Yet despite his hard-headedness and determination to succeed, there was another more sensitive Dan, whose constant questioning and searching betrayed a streak of romanticism that favoured risk over safety, in pursuit of possibly unattainable dreams. It was this Dan that Liza was drawn to

She recalled seeing him, for what she feared might be the last time, on the night he left to go to war. Her heart leapt and she struggled to maintain her composure and not break down in front of Arthur and Beattie. She had cried all through that night overcome by intense feelings of loss, more powerful even than those she had suffered on news of Ted's execution.

But it was not until she saw her initial fascination with Bill for the mere flirtation that it was and accepted that she had used him as an excuse to hide her real reason for going to Australia, that she knew the cause of her emotional turmoil. She was deeply and desperately in love with Dan.

She had already risked following him to Melbourne and despite the danger and uncertainties of joining him in the tropical north, she wanted him and was not going to let him go.

Alice and Charlie supported her decision and he undertook to escort her and Daniel to the Kimberley cattle station when Dan had settled in and signaled that it was safe for them to come.

Kimberley river crossing

The party broke camp and reached the river bank just before noon. Flood water had drowned the dry season causeway. The only evidence of its location was the points at which the dirt road disappeared under the water and emerged about a half mile away on the other side. To Dan's relief, Archie judged it passable, although it was wider and flowing faster than when they had crossed it on the way to collect him. Had it not been, they would have needed to back track to Derby and wait out the wet. But on the previous night he had gathered from the men's campsite talk that the flood would be only part of their problem in getting across.

Dan knew the bushman's love of tall tales and that this mob would deliberately embellish any story of disaster and death, to make him even more afraid of the impending crossing than was warranted. But whilst he had discounted the truth of their wilder claims, he looked at the surging river with both respect and heightened apprehension about the threat that lay hidden below its murky surface. He recalled one drover's sardonic assertion that

"Jeeze! Us blokes should be safe crossing this time seeing as crocs prefer soft white pommie meat to our tough hides!"

Despite his humorous intent, there was more than a hint of truth about the danger from large, ferocious crocodiles which rode the floods to hunt far upstream from their usual saltwater haunts. This was confirmed by the length of time Archie spent in discussion with his men before starting to cross.

The chosen strategy was straightforward and one that Dan had seen the Light Horse execute to perfection when training in Egypt. The river was too wide for a rope line and a raft would have been unmanageable in the surging water, even if they could spare the time to scour the plain for suitable timber. The plan was to swim teams of horses on a diagonal course, using the current to carry them down stream to a break in the opposite bank where they could easily scramble ashore. Whilst simple in concept it was not easy to do, as it required the lead rider to match the angle of crossing with the speed of the flow and rely on others to ensure the horses did not panic.

The aboriginal stockmen were adept at this manoeuvre and succeeded in crossing with the first string without mishap. The second followed their proven trajectory and had just gone a few yards from the bank when the smooth surface erupted into a maelstrom of water and spray. Terrified horses tried to break loose and it took all the skill and nerve of the riders to turn them and bring them safely back to the bank. But once on land the men could not hold them and they bolted into the bush.

It was some time later, when the frightened beasts had been rounded up and calmed sufficiently to be returned to the river, that they became aware of the loss of a pack-mule. A salty had struck.

Now they were really in trouble. The supplies that had gone across with the first party were insufficient to last the journey to the station and in a few hours it would be too dark to complete the crossing, even if the men and horses were prepared to risk more crocodile attacks. After much vigorous debate, Archie and the men agreed that they should make another attempt, but they could not agree on the best way to do it. Frustrated by the delay and fearful of the crocodile menace their disagreement deteriorated into ever more aggressive argument and was at risk of becoming a fight, when Dan intervened and suggested an answer to their problem. They were uneasy about accepting a proposal from him but desperation overcame their scepticism and they agreed to give him a go.

Dan's plan allowed them only one chance to get across safely and he had the remaining horses taken far enough away from the river to reduce their likely alarm at what he intended, but held close enough to start the crossing as soon as he gave the go ahead. When this had been done he and a stockman took up positions on the river bank and on Dan's command, each of them hurled an object high in the air which dropped almost simultaneously into the river, close to a tangle of trees and driftwood on their nearside bank. Two muffled explosions threw up spouts of water and sent ripples racing across the river. A shoal of dead fish came to the surface followed by the mangled body of the dead pack-mule and then, to the amazement and horror of the men, three huge and very scared saltwater crocs shot up the bank and raced away from the river into the bush. With the temporary removal of the crocodile threat, they lost no time in entering the river and though the increasingly dangerous current threatened to sweep them past their landing point, the crossing was achieved within the hour and without further loss.

Heading North

In camp that night a fire was started using a trick Dan had learned in the flooded trenches in Flanders. A space was made for him in the circle of men around the blaze. He was served a billy of hot sweet tea and invited to join in the feast of grilled fish that his explosive angling technique had harvested from the river. Then it was time for him to tell his tale.

His comrades in Perth had not allowed him to leave without some means of protection and as well as a revolver, they had supplied him with a few Mills bombs and he and the stockman had thrown two of them into the river to disturb and frighten away the crocs.

"But your aim was spot on, right near where the crocs were. How did you know where to throw them?" asked Archie.

"Last night, whilst you were telling yarns to scare me, I took some tobacco to share with the aboriginal stockmen and listened attentively to what they knew about the habits of man eating crocs. They told me that crocs do not devour their prey at once but store their kills for later consumption in caches under the water in tangled tree roots and the like, near to the river banks. When we had reached the river and were planning for the first crossing, I took a stroll along the bank and spotted the tracks the crocs had left when leaving the river, which led back to their underwater lair. The rest was easy, apart from ensuring the bombs were close to exploding as they landed in the river and as long as big Jim, who I knew had been a sapper and survivor of Fromelles, remembered his bomb throwing technique, there was nothing to it."

Dan was no longer excluded from the evening fireside conversations which turned to informative stories about the history of the Kimberley, life on cattle stations and useful hints on living and surviving in the wet. The respectful attention they paid him was well short of deferential but it left no doubt about who was their boss from now on.

The rest of their journey to the station, though hard on both men and horses, was relatively uneventful and Dan took full advantage of Archie's greater willingness to share what he knew. He had wondered why all the men were armed.

"Archie, why are you all carrying guns?"

"There are still large numbers of blacks roaming the bush who resent our intrusion into their country and clashes between settlers and them have led to deaths on both sides."

It was not long before he saw for himself one of the reasons for this enmity.

Shortly before they reached their own station boundary they came upon a number of dead and dying cattle that had been partially butchered for their meat and the remains left to predators and to rot in the sun. The riders were angered at this evidence of wanton cruelty and waste of valuable beef but, although he kept his thoughts to himself, Dan could appreciate why the nomadic hunters saw these herds as fair game. On reaching the homestead he was relieved to get out of the saddle and though pleased that he had been able to win over the men he would rely on, he had learned that in this country, there was more to running a station than just managing cattle and coping with the rigours of this land.

27

At the Kimberley Station

The homestead stood on a plateau, high above a flood-swollen river, separated from the work sheds, mustering yards and the stockmen's quarters by a dense screen of towering gum trees. A mile further back was the aboriginal camp from which the station drew most of its labour.

At the end of a bewildering first day's introduction to the layout and working life of the property, Dan settled on the house's verandah, gazing out across a grassy plain to the distant ranges, until the failing light and evening downpour obscured the view. He had heard and seen almost too much for a newcomer to grasp at once, but he was pleased that nobody held back in telling him what he needed to hear. Above all it was clear to him how vital it was to gain the loyal support of the station's experienced and knowledgeable foreman

Since the river crossing incident, Archie's attitude towards Dan had changed dramatically. He was no longer taciturn and tight-lipped and seemed keen to ensure that Dan knew all that was necessary for him to succeed as manager of the station. He accepted Dan's invitation to join him in savouring a smooth peaty, malt and to continue passing on all that he knew.

"The biggest challenge is to find and keep enough manpower to run cattle in this country. Although plenty of motor vehicles have come into the Kimberley since the war, the few tracks that might pass as roads are mostly impassable to cars and so most of the station work has to be done on horseback, with camels doing the heavy haulage. So we need lots of skilled riders and as there are barely two thousand Europeans in the whole of the region we pastoralists rely on native and half-caste stockmen and rouseabouts to run the herds.

Some time ago, the local tribe suffered two really bad seasons and was being decimated by hunger and disease. They chose to settle in the camp you saw, close to the station, preferring the guarantee of regular tucker

and a tobacco supply to the uncertainties and hardships of living off the land. The elders struggle to balance the demands of station life with their deep attachment to their country and obligation to their kin who refuse to give up their nomadic freedom.

As a result, whilst we manage to get along, black and white relations are always delicate and as you saw from the men's reaction to the cattle poaching, they can easily become hostile."

Archie stressed that maintaining workable relations between the station and the camp was essential to the viability of the cattle business and that this was a most important responsibility of the station boss. This advice was not lost on Dan who had heard the stories of settlers being murdered and of the vengeful massacres of Aboriginals. On the next day he arranged a visit to the nearby camp to introduce himself to the tribal elders and to find out how he could prevent such tragedies happening on his station.

The meeting was formal and drawn out by the indirect nature of the conversation. Some English was spoken and understood but he was accompanied by a stockman from the tribe who translated when necessary. The Elders received Dan politely but with a sense of reservation and restraint that gave him no clue as to what they thought or felt about his arrival. When they finally got down to business, he confirmed his expectation that established practices and white man's law would continue to govern all aspects of station life and the running of the business. In return, the leaders asserted their traditional right to apply custom law to their affairs and to resolve issues that arose within their community and between their people and other tribes. Dan had been told, beforehand, what this entailed and whilst he was uncomfortable about some of the practices and punishments that had been described to him, he was even more concerned to avoid undermining tribal discipline and making enemies of these people. He assured them of his support for these rights as long as any penalties stopped short of death which would be sure to be investigated by the police and they had bitter memories of what that could lead to.

After the formalities and with the exchange of gifts, their mood lightened and as he left he detected a twinkle in the eyes of these previously unreadable men. Looking back, he could see that whatever they were saying to each other was the cause of increasing hilarity and he thought he heard shouts that sounded like "boom, boom", followed by almost hysterical laughter. When they were beyond ear-shot, Dan asked the stockman about their change of mood and why what sounded like '*boom*', was making them laugh. The stockman grinned and confided that the elders knew all about Dan's crocodile escapade which they thought was hilarious and that they had named him "Boom, Boom Boss". They respected this display of what they saw as white man's cunning and had formed a correspondingly favourable opinion of him before the meeting. Dan smiled ruefully and reflecting on how well they had hidden any hint of regard from him during their talks, resolved never again to underestimate their shrewdness.

As soon as they reached the station he ordered two prime steers sent to the camp, as a sign of his respect and that a periodic supply of beasts continued to be reserved for the hunters to reduce their temptation to poach.

The previous manager had neglected both the house and the business. The wet season was a good time for building repair and especially working indoors. The carpenter and his helpers were kept busy replacing stained and greasy wall coverings with fresh painted hessian linings and laying floorboards over the packed earth floors as well as replacing rotten boards and plugging the plentiful roof leaks. Dan had to make the place more habitable and especially a more comfortable home in time for the arrival of Liza and Daniel. Elspeth had dispatched a consignment of furniture from Perth to replace the rough cut benches, tables and bunks that had served the needs of the previously all-male residents and this was coming by sea to Wyndham and would arrive with other essentials on the dry season's first supply train of hardy camels.

The business was barely breaking even. It was almost entirely dependent on export opportunities and although the reopening of the Wyndham meat works gave them a small but regular outlet for canned beef to feed the Belgian Army, competition from the Argentine and other foreign beef suppliers denied them easy access to the British market. To make things worse, Dan's arrival at the station had coincided with a season of particularly severe flooding which greatly restricted movement. Although the rain ensured rich grazing for fattening the cattle they were often in danger of drowning and riders still had to brave the deluge to herd them safely to higher ground.

This was made even harder by the coincidence of the aboriginals customary walkabout time with the wet season, as this further depleted the number of stockmen he could call on. Such was the strain on his resources that on one occasion even the cook was required to saddle up and Dan was forced to do his share. But, despite this diversion from his management duties, it gave Dan valuable hands-on experience of the challenges his men faced in cattle mustering, under tough conditions, as well as the chance to get to know the country that surrounded the station.

Taking it over in the wet season, without the benefit of a handover from the outgoing manager, had been a severe test but it had hardened him and by the time the rains began to ease he was feeling on top of the job and completely in charge of the station and its people. They had been cut off from the main towns for longer than usual by the exceptional floods and he was just completing a check of their heavily diminished stores when a great hullabaloo broke out and there was a mad rush of people past the storeroom door. He wondered what the alarm could be and was about to race after them when Archie burst in and announced the arrival of the first dry season camel train.

Everyone was overjoyed at the prospect of fresh food supplies and Dan went out to join them in welcoming its arrival. He was so distracted by his relief that they had lasted out and his eagerness to catch up on the newspapers and mail, that he was slow to notice the three riders who were dismounting by the homestead door. A man, a woman and a young boy emerged from behind their mounts and a familiar voice called out,

"G'day! Dan. I know we're a bit late but what's a man got to do to get a drink round here?" It was Charlie and with him Liza and Daniel had come home to Dan at last.

28

Together at Last

Together in the Kimberley

Trembling with emotion and struggling to find his voice, Dan approached Liza with conflicting feelings of joyful anticipation and trepidation. He had long dreamed of this reunion and visualised how it would be, but although he had known she was on her way to him, her sudden appearance overcame his resolution. After all this time, the dream had become reality. She was here and he did not know what to do or say. All the well-rehearsed openings he had planned evaporated before he could give them voice and he was afraid that anything he might say could betray his inner turmoil and wavering resolve.

Liza smiled but showed equal reticence in her greeting and for a moment they approached each other tentatively, more in the manner of sparring cockerels seeking to anticipate each other's impending attack, than long separated lovers, united at last. Then they came together in a warm but wary embrace and greeted each other in typically dispassionate Mancunian monotones with,

"Hello, Liza love!" and *"Good to see you Dan!"*

Charlie looked on, at first concerned by their lukewarm exchange but then reassured when, in unison, they reached out and drew young Daniel into their embrace.

It wasn't until later that evening that Dan and Liza found themselves alone and free to talk. She was the first to speak and typical of her forthright style she raised the issue of their meeting.

"Dan, I'm sorry for greeting you so coolly, today. I could sense that you were finding it as difficult as I was and before I try to explain my feelings I want to reassure you that I have not changed my mind about wanting to live with you and that I have no regrets about coming to Australia and joining you here, that is, assuming you still want me to."

Before Dan could respond she held up her hand to stay his speech and continued to talk.

"You know how devoted I was to Ted and how happy we were together. So much so that when he died I thought that there could never be anyone who would replace him in my heart and certainly not you. You were always one of our dearest friends and when I have tried to understand why I made love to you, I put it down to my loneliness, a subconscious fear that the war might take you away and that like poor Ted, you would not come back."

Pausing for a moment, as if she were seeking just the right words, she lowered her eyes and blushing with embarrassment, she continued

"I must admit I was overcome with hunger for a man-it was wonderful and I have no regrets. Although I acted purely from passion and without heed of any consequences, later when I thought about that night and what I had done, at least I felt safe knowing that it had been you, a friend of Ted's that cared for me and that I could trust.

When you enlisted, I was devastated and because you had reacted to that wicked, bitch of a woman who gave you the white feather, I felt guilty that if you had not come to see me in Blackpool, it would not have happened and you might not have joined up. As the war went badly and the casualties grew and grew, I hungered for news of your survival and I was so relieved when you came home, unharmed.

But, because you were so lost and disturbed and although I had given birth to our son, my feelings for you were more of care and concern for your health and happiness and I certainly didn't want a husband to take away my freedom to live as I wanted. Nor did I want to stop you searching for meaning and direction in your life.

It was not until you left for Australia that I began to listen to my heart and knew that in denying my true feelings for you, I had been living a lie. I had reasoned that in going to France as an ambulance driver, I was as good as any man and would prove it by doing my bit. But whilst this was true, it was when I met Alice and heard her talk about wanting to be closer to Charlie that I knew that I had wanted to be nearer to you.

When you returned from Ireland, although you were disturbed by what you had experienced and done and your life was in danger from your enemies, you still found time to visit me in prison and used Elspeth's influence to get me out. This deepened my feeling for you and made me hope that you had done this because you felt more than just a brotherly sort of care for me.

When you had gone I met Bill and was attracted to his charm and energy. Our brief flirtation fooled me into thinking that I wanted to start a new life of adventure with him out here but dear wise and worldly Elspeth had seen through my self-deception and she knew truly what I wanted and needed.

Little did I know that she had him in her sights and that she was not going to lose him to me. She invited me to tea and told me that she was coming to Australia. She flaunted her intention to gad about with you and soon after our meeting she made sure that I found out about her relationship with Bill. I was embarrassed at having made a fool of myself over Bill, but to my surprise, I was even more disturbed about Elspeth's designs on you. I was jealous and that could mean only one thing."

Liza had spoken clearly and calmly up to this point and Dan had listened without interrupting her, increasingly moved by what she had to say. But now she was becoming more agitated, catching her breath and sobbing almost uncontrollably, as she gasped out,

"Oh Dan, I am such a fool for taking so long to tell you how much I love you, want you and need you in my life!"

Dan was so choked up he couldn't speak and dropping to his knees beside her chair he pulled Liza to him, wrapped his arms around her and shed tears partly of pain but mostly of joy. They clung together like this until their tears dried up and Dan could trust himself to speak.

"Liza, if not declaring love is foolish then I am a bigger fool than you. Sweetheart, you are so brave to have followed me here and opened up your heart, without really knowing whether I truly love you or just feel responsible for you. I am so very happy that you do love me and I want you to know that I am so much in love with you.

I too was blinded by my memories of Ted and so disturbed and guilty after our night together, that what I saw as a need to look after you was really driven by love. That I was brought up to hide my deeper feelings and not allow anyone to get too close has made it harder for me to know and reveal myself, even to you.

Of course you know that I had my moments with Elspeth but that was always more about lust than love and as you said she was too smart to see it as more than it was and to get in the way of you and me.

Since the war my searching and restless wandering had found me no answers until I came to Melbourne and heard that you were coming too. It was then I knew that what I really wanted was to make a new life with

you. But just when that seemed in reach, first in Melbourne and then in Perth, I found myself on the run again. I was beginning to believe that it was not to be when, suddenly, there you were.

So please believe that my cautious greeting was not the result of any doubt about my loving and wanting you but rather a sign of my fear that we might be denied the chance to live together. Now that you are here and I know that you want me as much as I want you, I promise that if my enemies find me again, I will stay to fight them and there will be no more running away."

Liza was no longer tearful and with a resolute look, she clasped his hands and said *"No, Dan. We will stay and fight together. You are no longer alone."*

The next few days were taken up with unloading supplies into storage and allowing the camels and their drivers to rest up for the next stage of their journey. Early, on the day of their departure, Dan was setting out on a tour of the station buildings to show Charlie the improvements he had made, when the camel train swung by. Most of the cameleers were Afghans but riding at the rear was a very fair-skinned white man with a strikingly red beard. As he passed, he greeted them with a cheery

"G'day!" and before passing out of earshot, turned in his saddle, looked back at Dan and with a wave of his hat added

"Top of the morning to you, boss!"

Charlie remarked that to be so cheerful when setting out on such a hard journey, was just like the Irish. Dan laughed, nodded in agreement and they continued their tour of inspection.

Station Life

The next few weeks were the happiest and most care-free that Dan had experienced since he had returned from the war. He delighted in the work of running the station and the love and support that Liza's presence brought into his life. She had readily and skillfully taken on a range of responsibilities which lightened his managerial load and both stockmen and domestic staff were in no doubt as to who was boss in matters of bed and board and the general health and welfare of all employees, including dependants living in the tribal encampment.

She proved so adept at mediating the rivalries and frequent squabbles between the domestic staff that her impartiality left none of the parties overly aggrieved and her judgments were readily accepted. As a result there was less need to call upon the tribal elders to intervene in these disputes which, rather than meeting their disapproval, was a secret source of satisfaction and relief. They wondered at her guile and some of the resolutions were both so creative and hilarious that they added welcome spice to their camp fire story-telling and earned a place in tribal folklore.

When two young women claimed ownership of the same, much sought after, position in the kitchen and rejected Liza's suggestion that they share it, because this would cause them to lose face in the eyes of the tribe, Liza said she understood their stance and publicly praised the principled nature of their respective positions. She assured them that under the circumstances and to preserve their honour she could not favour either of them in filling the job and instead would have to consider employing another woman in their place. Before this decision could be acted upon, both women underwent a remarkable change in attitude towards the possibility of working together and assured Liza that they were more than willing to share the job. News of this resolution was soon the talk of the station and everyone wondered whether Liza had known that her proposed replacement was a hated rival to the other two. But Dan, Charlie and the elders were more intrigued to know how she had found this out.

On the rare occasions that counseling and cajoling failed her, she demonstrated an awesome ability to separate brawling lubras and end the fights without disturbing her composure and the neatness of her dress.

Even the Chinese cook, who was a holy terror in the cookhouse and enforcer of formality in the dining room, refused to recognise her unmarried status and conceded her supremacy by deferring to her position as the 'Missus.'

She had colluded with Elspeth in selecting the new furniture and moved quickly to replace the hard masculine barrack-room style of the homestead with fittings and furnishings as comfortable and tasteful as those to be found in the better homes of Perth. In the absence of suitable fabrics, she showed great ingenuity and taste in using every day materials such as bleached hessian panels to line the rough timber walls and to make window blinds, dyed in delicate shades of colour.

Her experience as a factory supervisor served her well in identifying amongst the staff, those with the skills to assist her and others with the potential to learn and Dan soon accepted that he would have to revise his priorities because Liza had monopolised his best carpenters.

He was amazed at the extent of the medical expertise she had picked up as an ambulance driver on the western front. It went well beyond basic first-aid and her skill in setting broken bones, treating burns and suturing nasty wounds had eased pain and reduced the risk of infection until professional medical help was available. She had even dared to wield a scalpel to save the life of a very badly injured stockman.

Father and Son

Dan was happy and relieved to have settled his relationship with Liza, but he was at a loss as to how to get on with Daniel. As if it were not sufficient of a shock to discover that he was a father, to be confronted by a ten year old boy, about whom he knew so little, was a challenge he felt unprepared to take on. He had barely begun to accept the possibility of spending the rest of his life with Liza when the reality of fatherhood was thrust upon him.

Dan's first impression of his son was of a strong, bright but reticent boy whose lithe build favoured his mother, whereas his red hair and freckled skin resembled Dan's. When they got together for the first time without Liza's presence, their conversation was stilted and suggested considerable caution and reservation on both sides.

Children had never been part of Dan's plans or dreams. He had no idea how to speak to a young boy and his relationship with his own father gave him no clues.

Liza had told Daniel a great deal that cast his father in a positive and even heroic light, but he was tightly bonded to her alone. Apart from Arthur's grandfatherly affections, he had not experienced an adult male influence in his life and, at first, was more than a little intimidated by this stern, warrior of a man who was his father.

Dan started by asking the safest of questions.

"What are your favourite subjects at school? What are your hobbies? What do you like best about being in Australia, so far?"

To which Daniel answered respectfully and directly, but without much enthusiasm nor any sign of warmth. Charlie had been right when he advised Dan that he would have to win the boy's confidence but he wondered how best to do this.

Daniel was equally unsure of how to engage with his father. Even though he was impressed by Dan's manliness and favourably influenced by his mother's attachment to him and the respect that all at the station showed him, he was determined not to accept second place in his mother's affections. An innate stubbornness prevented his opening up to this stranger and whilst happy to respond forthrightly to Dan's questions, until he felt safe enough to trust him, he would not reveal his true feelings.

Liza had spoken of Daniel's practical bent and how he loved to tinker with mechanical things and work with his hands. He had even managed to take Arthur's pocket watch apart and reassemble it without reference to any instructions. At the same time she smiled, knowingly, when she revealed that, like his father, he possessed a stubborn streak and a tendency to follow flights of fancy which soared only to crash to earth when his interest moved on to new, equally short-lived interests.

Although Dan was inexperienced with boys, he was adept at observing interactions between men and it had not escaped his attention that Daniel was mightily impressed with his 'uncle' Charlie. So that when, with Dan and Liza's blessing, Charlie conspired in suggesting that Daniel might like to start working with the carpenters and farriers, from whom he could learn all about cattle station life, whilst helping them do something useful, he leapt at the chance. This proved to be a very effective strategy and within days Daniel's reserve had begun to thaw and he threw himself into the work and soon won the acceptance of the rough and ready Australian tradesmen. Gradually, his coolness towards Dan gave way to respectful acceptance and he joined his father on the morning rounds of the workshops, stores and stock yards.

Boy in the bush

Of all the new experiences and adventures a boy could find on a busy outback cattle station, what had impressed Daniel most was his visit with Dan to the aboriginal settlement to confer with the tribal elders. The grave old men treated the youngster with a respect that belied his tender years and on his return he was soon quizzing the aboriginal stockmen and station boys about the history and customs of their people.

It was a great surprise to Liza and Dan when Archie reported that Daniel had not turned up for work and as nobody had seen him that day, asked *"Is Daniel sick?*

"He was in good spirits and perfectly well when he turned in last night."

Dan confirmed. But when Liza returned from checking Daniel's room and reported that, *"His bed has not been slept in and his clothes and boots have gone."* They began to worry about his absence.

A search of the homestead and questioning of the hands revealed that he had begged rations from the cook, saying he was intending to ride out early to join the muster. His favourite mount had gone and, more ominously, a rifle was missing from the gun cabinet. Within the hour a mounted search party assembled, the tribe was alerted to the young master's absence and a tracker was assigned to accompany the riders.

For some time, Daniel had wanted to get to know the aboriginal boys better and he was particularly keen to learn about their hunting methods and skill in throwing spears and boomerangs to down 'roos and birds. He had set off at night to take up position along a trail that he knew the hunting party would follow in the morning. He intended to join them and hoped their acceptance of him around the homestead would enable him to join in the hunting trip.

He was not a natural horseman but he was no longer a novice and he had learned much about riding from the stockmen and especially his uncle Charlie who had ridden with the famous Light Horse. But whilst he had become more accustomed to riding along the rough and ill-defined trails, this was his first time out in the trackless bush at night.

When he set out on his nocturnal adventure, Daniel had been full of excitement and was confident he could find his way through the bush. But now, after riding for an hour through trees and featureless scrub, everything began to look disconcertingly similar and when he came upon a great cleft rock for the second time, he knew that he had been following a circular route and he was back where he had started. He cursed himself for not paying more attention to what the stockmen had told him about navigation in the bush. He knew that he should have set his course by the stars but whilst he could identify the Southern Cross, he had not taken a bearing when leaving the homestead and he had no idea at which point of the compass he should set his course.

He had completed a night walk in Derbyshire with the Boy Scouts and, even though they traversed some of the High Peak district trails his father had taken on his way north, he was reassured by the glow of city lights and the occasional rumble and whistle of freight trains from the plain below. But here the silence was so heavy in his ears that he felt it threatening him. Daniel was lost in the bush and he was very afraid.

Panic overcame reason as he spurred his horse on, seeking comfort in motion until he recalled some of the bush-craft the men of the station had tried to instill in him.

He reminded himself that there was nothing to be afraid of in the bush and even though he had taken the precaution of carrying a rifle, the only danger lay in being unprepared for survival in the outback. He had sufficient food and water to last several days and his thick Driza-Bone coat was proof against the night's chill and early morning dew. The only thing he had forgotten were matches for lighting a fire. Uncle Charlie had told him that when you are lost in the bush, it is best to stay put and resist the temptation to wander around getting more and more panicky, using up energy and depleting your resources. Then you should start to ration your supplies by eating and drinking sparingly and if safe to do so, light a fire and make smoke to signal where you are and hopefully, attract those out searching for you. The recollection of this advice calmed him and except for the fire-lighting, he followed the other precautionary steps, hobbled his horse and settled down for the night.

He had had sufficient to eat and drink and his horse blanket and coat kept him warm and dry. But he was still uneasy. A full moon shone with the intensity of stage-lights and completely banished the darkness. It was so bright that every feature stood out in the landscape more starkly than if it was daytime. He was particularly spooked by the ghostly grey and white trunks of the naked boabs and gum trees and though he couldn't hear a sound he could sense a lurking presence that knew he was there. The romantic adventurer in him had fled leaving behind a frightened boy who had never slept outdoors and who was lost in this ancient and timeless land.

Even if he could have slept he was afraid to close his eyes, but when he rolled onto his back and looked up he was entranced by the array of glittering stars that filled the whole of the sky. This wonderful display of natural gems calmed his troubled mind and when he spotted the Southern Cross formation, stationed directly above him, he believed it was keeping watch over him and he was no longer afraid. Fortunately his earlier panic had sapped his energy and he fell into a fitful sleep. At dawn he was awakened by the raucous squawks of crows, the twittering of flocks of small colourful birds and the welcoming *chortle! chortle!* of strutting magpies. He felt less alone and frightened, but he was still lost.

He luxuriated in the warmth of the early morning sun and all his night-time terrors had gone. He concentrated on thinking about what his father would do in this situation and like Dan he was determined not to give in to his doubts and fears. Gradually, he began to recall the bushmen's advice. It would be safe to explore further as long as he noted the position of the sun to maintain his bearing and marked trees with his knife at points where the terrain forced him to divert from a straight line. This would ensure he maintained a constant direction and a clear line of retreat to his starting point if the way ahead proved unpromising or impassable. Before leaving his campsite, he made a large arrow on the ground from stones and tree branches to show searchers the direction he was taking.

Daniel planned to travel until noon and then to turn back if he failed to contact any aboriginal hunters. The trail became steep and rocky and to avoid making his horse lame and to conserve the water he had to share with his mount, Daniel dismounted and led her up the slope on a loose rein. A combination of lack of sleep and the energy sapping climb, in the increasing tropical sun's glare, dulled his senses and slowed his reflexes, causing him to stumble and lose his balance.

At last the slope began to level off and he found himself on the edge of a narrow ravine that fell away steeply into a deep canyon, whose bottom was obscured by tree tops and dense shade. Daniel stopped for a welcome breather when a large and ferocious looking goanna shot between his mare's legs causing it to rear up and pivot on its hind legs, away from the ravine's rim. Daniel was caught napping. He had released his grip on the reins to mop the sweat from his brow when the horse's flank struck him a glancing blow, pitching him head first down the steep rocky slope towards the canyon's bottom, far below. Sliding and rolling downwards, he was unable to gain purchase on the unstable scree until he struck his head on a tree stump and lost consciousness.

Charlie, Dan and his mob of riders, led by Archie, had come across Daniel's directional arrow and guided by their tracker and the blaze marks on the trees they were able to trace the boy's progress until they arrived at the edge of the ravine.

There was no sign of Daniel or his mount but evidence of hoof marks and the traces of Daniel's precipitate slide down into the canyon confirmed their worst fear, that he had suffered a fatal fall. They lacked the ropes necessary for climbing down and heavy in heart they set out on the long detour to reach the canyon's floor.

On arrival they started an intensive search along the bottom of the canyon and the nimblest among them climbed the side up to the point where the marks of Daniel's passage ended, at the edge of the precipitate drop into the canyon. But they did not find his body. Dan drove the searchers on until frustration and exhaustion began to sap their resolve. They explored for two days, camping in the canyon, but without success. Finally, it was the dour and pragmatic Archie that dared to suggest that the search was pointless and that Daniel's body might never be found. Dan rounded on him furiously and swore that he would never give up searching and leave Daniel out there. If it had not been for Charlie's caring but firm intervention the altercation might have come to blows. But after another two days, as their supplies and stamina drained away, even Dan accepted that they should give up the search.

The ride back to the homestead was an almost unbearable torture for him as he blamed himself for not paying more attention to Daniel and owned how much his son had meant to him. As they approached the house Dan quailed at the sight of Liza running towards them. She was screaming and waving her arms wildly. He feared that he would be unable to cope with her frenzy and the grief that would overwhelm them both.

But as she came up to them he was amazed to see that she was crying and laughing at the same time. He leaped from the saddle and as she fell into his embrace, she gasped out that,

"Daniel's back, bloodied and bruised, but he's alive!"

Dan was so overcome that he could not speak and as he stood clinging to Liza, the riders galloped towards the homestead whooping and hallooing with joy.

Daniel was sitting up in bed. His head was swathed in bandages and numerous other scars and bruises on his body were covered in fresh dressings.

Dan joked, *"You remind me of a wounded soldier."*

Then he embraced his prodigal son and burst into tears of relief and joy. When he had recovered sufficiently to listen to Daniel he was amazed at his story of survival.

"My first memory, when I came to, was of bumping and bouncing along, slung over the back of my horse. I remembered nothing after that until I awoke in my bed with Mam tending my wounds."

Liza continued the story.

"Until the horse brought him, unconscious, to the homestead steps I didn't know he had been injured."

Her first-aid experience had kicked in immediately and she had tended to her son, leaving her no time to fret and worry.

"*We saw where he had fallen into the canyon,*" Dan interjected, "*so how did he get back having suffered such nasty cuts and bruises?*"

"*That's the strange part of the story.*" Liza replied. *When we got him into the bedroom and cut off his tattered clothes, instead of seeing horrible cuts and scrapes, all of his injuries were dressed with poultices made of leaves and foliage and the wounds had been treated with some strange smelling salve.*"

She went on to show her professional approval of what had been done to ease Daniel's pain and which, despite his clearly having spent several nights in the bush since his fall, had prevented any sign of infection.

On the next day both Dan and Liza rode out to visit the tribal elders, taking with them cattle, ample supplies of tobacco and other gifts that were highly prized by the wise old men and their people.

The following days were full of station action and at night during and after dinner, Dan, Liza and Charlie indulged in reminiscences about their wartime experiences and the tortuous road that had brought them together again in the Kimberley. Even more delightful was the addition to their company of Bill and Elspeth who had flown up from Perth to visit Bill's parents on their property and to see how Daniel was recovering. Young Daniel was particularly happy at their arrival, as he had become very attached to them during his stay in Perth, and it soon became apparent that he was both besotted with aircraft and that, even more than his father and uncle Charlie, Bill was Daniel's hero.

Together with Dan and Daniel, Bill and Charlie threw themselves into the mustering and readying of cattle for Market, whilst Elspeth focused her usual zest on helping Liza improve the homestead's comforts. In the evenings they played card games, sang around the piano and it was as well that the supply train had fully restocked the reserves of malt whisky. It was during one of these convivial evenings that Elspeth raised the issue of Daniel's isolation from boys of his own age, other than the black station youths with whom he had begun to ride and run wild in the bush, and the need for him to finish his education

Dan was grateful for her doing this as this sensitive issue was very much on his mind. But, in deference to Liza's feelings, because they had only recently been reunited as a family and Daniel's brush with death, he couldn't bring himself to speak about it. However, much as they wanted to keep Daniel with them, he could only get the kind of education he needed by going back to Perth.

When a private school was proposed, Dan's reservations about meeting the tuition and boarding fees were met by Bill's and Charlie's assurances that they could access a scholarship to Guildford Grammar School, especially considering their remote location and Dan's excellent war record. Elspeth anticipated Liza's concerns by offering to board him at weekends and keep a close eye out for his welfare.

Daniel's response to this proposal was typical of a boy of his age. He showed dutiful concern at being separated from his parents but once he learned that he would return to the station during the main holidays and that at weekends, when Bill was in town, he could go to the airport to learn about the flying business, he became a more than willing recruit. As the time for Bill, Elspeth and Charlie to depart came closer, Daniel's enthusiasm was almost uncontrollable and on the day he left with them, Liza cried, Dan did his best to hide his turbulent feelings but with a bare peck on his mother's cheek, a manly handshake with his father and the most perfunctory of waves, Daniel rode away full of the adventures that awaited him, back in Perth, both on the ground and especially in the air.

29

Duty Calls, Once More

The droving of the cattle for sale in Derby was relatively uneventful compared with the challenges of Dan's original journey out to the station. He rode with the assurance of much more practice, his hardened body coped without pain or protest and even more importantly his stockmen's ready acceptance that he was the boss, enabled him to relax and even enjoy the journey through the drying country.

Few cattle were lost and the sale prices were good. The men celebrated and spent their pay in the pubs and flesh pots of Derby and Dan ordered the supplies they would take back with them. When this was done he decided to treat himself to lunch at the best hotel in town and he was interested to hear from the inn keeper that he might enjoy the company of a gentleman newly arrived from Perth. Introductions were made and Dan was intrigued to find himself seated at a corner table with a large, tough looking man who wore the uniform of an officer in the Western Australian Mounted Police.

After they had exchanged the usual pleasantries they set to probing each other's backgrounds and soon unearthed their common experience in the Great War. Inspector George Wardle had served with the Light Horse at Gallipoli, Romani and Beersheba and Dan was delighted to hear that he was acquainted with Charlie. This discovery and several beers dissolved their formality and George began to explain what had brought him up from Perth.

"You will know that the police patrol, sent in pursuit of tribesmen suspected of the murder of a squatter, have been accused of the indiscriminate massacre of native men, women and children. A Royal Commission has been appointed to investigate these allegations and as the members of the suspect police contingent are refusing to testify against each other and the charges rely solely on the word of the tribes-people, supported by white missionaries, I have been sent north to lead a patrol that is to gather evidence about what really happened."

George was remarkably forthcoming about his assignment for a senior and usually much more tight-lipped Australian policeman and the fact that he had asked so little about Dan's background suggested that he had prior knowledge and that this meeting was more than just a happy coincidence. This suspicion was confirmed when George passed on greetings from his chief in Perth who had met Dan and tried to recruit him at Bill and Elspeth's Cottesloe party, and confessed that he had a request to make of Dan and that there was a member of his party whom Dan might remember and could be pleased to meet again.

George confided that the report of the massacre was a very hot political issue in Perth.

"I am under great pressure to conduct as impartial an investigation as possible into this incident. On one side is the silent collusion of the police brotherhood and the squattocracy and on the other the influential church groups which back the missionaries' reports. I have been instructed to enlist your help because you are a practical man of the world who has seen police service under even more trying circumstances than these and you have a reputation for sensitivity and even-handedness in dealing with your aboriginal employees and the local tribe. I hope you will agree to join our expedition and be a credible witness to the diligence and validity of our enquiries."

Dan was both flattered by the implied character reference and concerned that, once more, the call to duty entailed a return to the ranks of uniformed authority and his possible involvement in state-sponsored violence. Was this his destiny? Would he ever live a life of peace? Before he could raise the impediment of the outstanding criminal charge against him in Melbourne, the Inspector assured him that

"When you meet the man who is waiting to be reacquainted with you, your concerns about your Victorian difficulties will be answered."

So they really had done their homework about his background, thought Dan and it was clear to him that the WA authorities had been sufficiently unconcerned to keep his recent history under wraps. Having neither accepted nor rejected George's invitation, they rose from the table and Dan followed him out of the hotel and along to the nearby police barracks.

He did not recognise the tall, spare, dusky-skinned Sergeant who emerged from the horse stalls until he spoke in a familiar rasping tone.

"G'day! Lieutenant. Taken any good marks lately?"

"Good God!" gasped Dan. "Sergeant Grommet! What are you doing here?" and with a firm handshake added, more familiarly,

"It's good to see you again Alf."

Dan had not seen Alf Grommet since that fateful first encounter with him and Charlie in the hospital in Alexandria, but whilst he needed to catch up on what Alf had been doing since then it would have to wait. The Sergeant of police was well briefed on Dan's situation and he suspected the hand of Charlie in this.

His intuition was confirmed when Alf said, "Before I tell you about me, you'd better hear my news. I've got a message from the boss and he insisted I tell you straight away. There's been a change of government in Victoria and the charges pending against you have been dropped. So now you are no longer a wanted man."

Disbelief soon gave way to delight, closely followed by the realisation that the WA police and George had been aware of this before setting out to recruit him.

"Thanks Alf. That's good news and a great relief to me. Wait until Liza hears about this."

"Congratulations!" Boomed George, "This calls for a drink." and so they returned to the hotel bar to celebrate Dan's deliverance and where he could learn more about the expedition and why Alf was involved.

Alf was typically terse and laconic in telling his story.

"After discharge from the army I returned to my family in Victoria but when I was unable to make a go of it there, we headed west to the Kalgoorlie gold-fields. Like most, I failed to make a fortune, so then I went to work as a track maintenance supervisor on the Perth-Kalgoorlie railway. The money was good and they soon saw I knew how to organise men. Then the Police heard about me so, here I am, glad to be back in uniform and in secure employment."

He had soon earned his stripes and prior to coming north he had been a member of the team investigating the murder of an inspector and sergeant of the Gold Stealing Detective Squad whose bodies were discovered down a mineshaft near Boulder. He had been selected for this assignment both because of his police experience and his ability to command the respect of whites and blacks. Whilst not as adept as the full-blood trackers, his grandfather had taught him sufficiently well to be skilled enough to interpret their leads and to ensure there could be no biased misdirection. Also, his superiors judged, correctly, that his inclusion might be a significant factor in persuading Dan to say yes and join the expedition.

Dan had twenty-four hours to make his decision before the party set out for the East Kimberley scene of the alleged atrocities. He weighed the pros and cons with his painful memory of Irish policing much on his mind. Three considerations decided him. This was a mission of enquiry with no mandate to either hunt or punish suspects. He had a good reputation with the native people without being as closely involved as the missionaries and his presence as a well-regarded settler would act as a strong deterrent against any police attempts at revenge.

On the following day he joined the police column riding out of Derby, as his stockmen set out back to the station with their supplies and a letter of explanation for Liza. As they reached the outskirts of the town they passed the huge old boab prison tree that had been used as a police lock-up and which testified to the harsh treatment that had been meted out to bewildered aboriginal prisoners who had no conception of white-man's law. This sight steeled his resolve to ensure their enquiry would be as fair as possible and conducted strictly according to the law.

Their journey back past Halls Creek took them through fantastic country. Great red escarpments lined their route and stately boabs studded the slopes like sentries set to defend their ground. The eerie beehive domes of the Bungle Bungles fascinated Dan whilst some of these craggy mounds resembled great slumbering owls watching everything through their hooded eyes. But it was not just the spirit of the land that marked their passage and Alf pointed out to Dan the tell-tale signs that local tribesmen were watching and well aware of their purpose.

The first stage of their enquiries focused on meetings with the aggrieved natives and their missionary advisers. The meetings were long, drawn out sessions and the evidence often vague and sometimes contradictory. The claims regarding those said to have been massacred by the police patrol ranged from the tens to the hundreds. It was claimed that the bodies had been burnt and buried to hide evidence of the crimes and whilst some bone middens had been opened up, expert opinion was divided as to whether the bones were of human or animal origin. Some of the memories had already merged with local folklore memory and some old people confused the aboriginal killer of the stockman, whose action started the ill-fated police manhunt, with their revered champion, the warrior, Jandamarra, who led his people against white occupation of their land in the 1880s.

That the stockman had been murdered was undisputed but as to the incidence and extent of retaliatory violence by the police, the picture was far from clear. George and Alf kept a tight rein on the men of the expedition and Dan felt that his presence was contributing to the restraint shown by all parties. Whilst there was no incontrovertible evidence of a large scale massacre, Dan concluded that some degree of revenge had been taken by the arresting patrol but he was unable to get a firm grip on how many people had been killed and by whom.

Into the Bungle Bungles

After a month of touring the locality, visiting alleged massacre sites and questioning those with relevant information, George called a halt to proceedings and prepared his party for the return trip to Derby. On the way back, Dan was so taken with the wild beauty of the Bungle Bungle ranges that he decided to stay on and explore for a few days and he was delighted to get the Inspector's approval for Alf to accompany him.

The ancient landscape and strange terra cotta-like domes fascinated him and at times they followed the dry beds of rivers that would have been truly frightening in their ferocity when flooded by wet season rains. The volume and size of boulders paving these water courses testified to the power of the rivers when in spate and their unevenness and instability forced the riders to dismount and lead their horses across the rock strewn pavement. Dan was fortunate to have Alf as his guide and companion. His innate hunting skills supplemented their diet of jerky and canned beef with choice roasts of snake and goanna meat. He saved Dan and the horses from drinking from dangerously polluted pools and at night, by firelight under a vast canopy of stars, he recounted the aboriginal stories of the earth's creation as well as the known history of Jandamarra's rebellion. In return, Dan spoke freely for the first time about his wartime experience and Alf told of the Gallipoli landing which had cemented his close relationship with Charlie.

They had seen no obvious sign of other human presence in this vast lonely landscape but Alf assured Dan that they were being watched and one afternoon, as they picked their boulder-strewn way along Piccaninni Gorge, they encountered a small hunting party heading home with a substantial catch of wallabies and goannas. Alf could not speak their language but hand signals interspersed with a few mission-learned white fella words, enabled the hunters to communicate their friendly intent which was reinforced by a gift of tobacco that would enhance their prestige back at their camp.

After this meeting they rode on enjoying a few more days of solitude until they saw a lone figure up ahead, sitting on a rock whilst his horse grazed on the surrounding grasses. As they came closer Dan was surprised to recognise the drover from the station supply-train who again called out his customary

"*Top of the morning,*" greeting. He had set a small fire behind the rock on which he sat and a spurt of steam signaled that his billy was coming to the boil. They readily agreed to join him in a brew of strong black tea with the aromatic addition of selected gum leaves and in turn they contributed damper fresh from their breakfast fire and a tin of blackberry jam.

The man's name was Paddy Flynn and he explained that he was traveling with another stockman in search of stray steers which had wandered beyond the bounds of their home station. He was no lover of the blacks and swore that some of the missing cattle, by now, would have been speared and butchered by the local tribe. He claimed that only a few days back he and his mate had been forced to fire on a large hunting party that was dismembering a cow. Glancing at Alf's uniform and taking in his half-caste tan, the Irishman looked uneasy and answered reluctantly when Alf asked him whether their shots had hit any of the aboriginals.

"*I might have winged one or two of them*", he replied, "*but we couldn't be sure as it was near dusk and we didn't stay around in case they decided to ambush us after dark.*"

Alf passed no comment and draining his mug signaled to Dan that they should be on their way. They parted amicably with the stockman but when they had gone a mile along the trail, they stopped, looked quizzically at each other and Dan said, "*Are you thinking what I am?*"

On the previous night Dan had told Alf about his time with the Black and Tans in Ireland and the clash with the IRA flying column near Cork, which had led to the death of the rebel commander's brother.

"*A bit too much of a bloody coincidence for my liking*", agreed Alf, "*especially after what you told me last night and your brush with those Republicans in Melbourne and Perth.*"

"Yes!" Dan mused "*I should have been more alert to his being Irish when he cheerio'd Charlie and me at the station.*"

Before they could confer more, Alf cocked his head and said he could hear horses coming along the trail and that there were more than just two riders in the party. True to his Light Horse experience and greater riding skills, Alf took the lead and turning off the track, urged his horse up a steep stony slope that would reveal no obvious sign of their passing. On reaching the top they dismounted, hobbled their horses and crawled back to the crest to look down on their pursuers as they passed. There were six riders in all and Alf's choice of stony ground was vindicated by the presence of an aboriginal tracker amongst the group. Their ruse had succeeded but Alf predicted that the tracker would notice the lack of hoof marks on the track ahead and that the hunters would soon be back on their trail. He proposed that as he was the better rider and bushman, he would go on with both horses to lead off the chase, whilst Dan hid in the bush and then walked to an agreed rendezvous within a cluster of the beehive-like domes.

Alf was right and after the chasers had mounted the slope and set off after him, Dan emerged from the shelter of a fine young boab tree, took a swig from his water bag and set off towards the meeting place, taking his bearing from the sun. Even in winter time the tropical sun was a force to be reckoned with and radiation from the rocky surfaces pushed the temperature close to the hundred mark. The lengthening afternoon shadows across the floor of the gorge provided welcome shade but Dan became weary and increasingly light headed, despite taking regular swigs of his water.

The occasional stagnant pools were brackish and only fit for lying in to cool off.

As he walked on he was refreshed by the cooling effect of evaporation as his clothes dried on him. His drinking water was running low and he resorted to the desperate measure of sucking on a smooth river pebble to keep his mouth moist and reduce the temptation to drink more of his diminishing fresh water supply.

He was relieved when he reached the meeting point before dark but there was no sign of Alf. His safest option was to stay put until dawn, as he would surely get lost in the maze of look-alike canyons or risk a crippling fall in the intense darkness of a moonless tropical night. The parting from Alf and his horse had been so sudden that he had grabbed only a water bottle and his rifle. He was tempted to light a fire to make up for his lack of a swag but as he had no idea of how close his enemies might be he couldn't take the risk and so he faced a cold night without food or shelter.

Despite making up a bed of dried leaves and grass and piling on tree fronds for covering, he slept fitfully and woke stiff and chilled to the bone. He was happy to welcome the sun's warming rays as they cleared the gorge's rim and embraced him. Taking his bearings from the rising sun, he set out in the direction from which Alf should have come. It was mid-morning when he came upon his dead horse. She lay on her side with blood still seeping from numerous bullet holes in her chest, but there was no sign of Alf and his mount. Then he heard a volley of shots followed by the sharp crack of a police carbine. Alf was alive but in trouble.

Gunfire echoed off the canyon walls, making it hard to get a precise fix on the shooters. Using the cover of boulders stands of boabs and convenient patches of tall grass, Dan made his cautious approach towards the likely scene of the action. After covering half a mile or so at this snail's pace, he began to edge his way up the sloping canyon side to gain the advantage of looking down on the combatants whilst maintaining his concealment. At the mid point of the incline, he positioned himself behind the substantial bulk of a gnarled old boab and peering out from its shelter he could see the dangerous spot that Alf was in.

He was bailed-up in a mound of huge boulders and could only have been flushed out by a suicidal frontal assault. The dead bodies of two of the attackers, lying just short of this position, proved that this had already been tried with fatal consequences. Alf's vulnerability lay in his exposure to shots from the surrounding slopes and his limited supply of water and ammunition.

The tell-tale rattle of dislodged pebbles tumbling down the canyon side allowed Dan to spot one of the gunmen who was wedged between two rocks just below Dan's position and over to his left was the man called Flynn. Both had rifles and were taking turns in trying to hit Alf when he rose to change his position. Their deliberate and unhurried aim confirmed that they were no novices when it came to shooting and that they knew that time was on their side. Dan was eager to lessen the odds against them but fortunately his military training and experience was more of the sapper's plan-ahead school than that of the 'over the top and at 'em' style of the infantry.

He was a competent rifleman but not in the same league as mounted infantrymen, such as Alf, nor was he a match for the men below him. If he fired and missed he would expose himself to more accurate return fire and the men were sufficiently far apart that even if he achieved a first time hit on one, the other gunman would be alerted and able to shoot back before Dan could aim and get off a second round. But his experience as a 'tunnel rat' on the Western front and his trench and street-fighting skills gave him a chance of creeping up and disabling them, without using his firearm. Fortunately, whilst the men were only a few hundred feet apart, an intervening outcrop of rock and trees put them out of sight of each other and if he could descend silently, he would be able to take them out in turn without being detected.

His approach to the first of his targets was painstakingly slow. He had discarded his boots to avoid the sound of leather grating on rock and by crawling and slithering most of the way down the intervening slope he was unseen, but always in danger of dislodging a noisy slide of pebbles and stones. The nearest shooter was so intent on his target that he did not look back until the rattle of falling debris alerted him to Dan's desperate lunge. A sharp jab to his forehead with Dan's rifle butt felled him before he could make a sound and having checked that he was unconscious but still alive, Dan relieved him of his weapon.

He was elated by the easy success of his plan but then chastened by his failure to consider how he would keep his man captive without any means of securing him. Then he recalled the technique employed by Gurkha soldiers in disabling German sentries, when their English officers forbade them to take off their heads. With one stroke of his cattleman's skinning knife he rendered his unconscious victim immobile by severing an Achilles tendon.

Dan's blood was up. He was no longer the easy going station boss. Adrenalin flooded his body and he was back in that desperate mood of kill or be killed that had saved his life on so many past occasions. His approach to the second marksman was just as careful but even more determined and ruthless than his attack on his first victim. Flynn had no chance to resist and was knocked out, disarmed and hamstrung like his mate

When his heart had returned to a normal beat, Dan turned to deal with the two remaining assailants. They had stopped shooting and so he had no idea where they were hidden. If he waited long enough they might come to see why their comrades weren't firing but he preferred to take the initiative by luring them out of cover. Also, he needed to let Alf know he was there so that he avoided the risk of being shot by mistake and to assure his mate that he was no longer alone.

By now the sun was beating down on his side of the gorge and this gave Dan the means of contacting Alf without giving his position away. He still had the tin from which he had supplied the aboriginal hunters with tobacco and turning the shiny base to the sun he began signaling to Alf, knowing that he would have become familiar with the use of the heliograph during his desert campaigning. As Alf's position was in shadow, he could not respond in kind but his loud call of *"Cooey!"* confirmed that Dan's message had been received and understood. The flashing light might have exposed Dan's position to the two remaining opponents and so he moved further along the slope and took shelter in a dense patch of scrub.

Now that he no longer had to hide his presence he could light a fire and use it to his advantage in flushing out his prey. Striking a match, he set fire to a small pile of leaves and dried grass which soon spread along the canyon side. A slight breeze was blowing away from his position and so there was no danger of the fire getting out of hand and turning back to threaten him. The dried grass covering and foliage burnt slowly with sporadic bursts of flame and an expanding pall of smoke.

Soon, this had the desired effect as one of the men was panicked into breaking cover and fell victim to Alf's deadly marksmanship. A crashing noise from the bush, the whinny of a horse and thud of receding hoof beats confirmed that the last one had abandoned the fight.

Alf and Dan celebrated their victory with a billy of tea laced with a generous dash of Irish whiskey found in the supplies of their former foes and toasted their good fortune in overcoming such odds. The dead men's belongings confirmed their Irish origins and the one who got away proved to be the aboriginal tracker. The prisoners were too focused on their wounds to be communicative but they said enough to confirm that this had been an IRA inspired assassination attempt in revenge for what they called Dan's Cork atrocity.

Both men felt in need of a good night's rest before heading back out of the bush and were so confident that the captives were unable to get far with their leg wounds, they settled down to sleep in what was referred to as 'Alf's redoubt'. In the morning their confidence had proved to be misplaced as Flynn was missing. He had overcome his pain and handicap sufficiently to make his escape on horseback and there was no point in tracking him as he was long gone. Dan commandeered one of the dead men's horses and the hobbling captive was employed in wrapping the dead riders in their swags and securing them on the spare mounts. Then the party set out for Hall's Creek where the surviving gunman and the corpses could be handed over to the local police.

The journey was slow and uneventful allowing Dan further chance to marvel at this magical country. But then as they emerged from a long winding gorge they saw flocks of birds descending, rising and circling. As they drew closer it was easy to detect magnificent eagles amongst the mass of crows engaged in disposing of some dead carrion. Dan dismounted to get a closer look at this primal act of nature when the birds scattered to reveal the naked, headless remains of what had been a man. A few feet further away, his missing head, minus its eyes, was impaled on a tall stake. What was left of its bright red hair and beard proved that it was Flynn who had suffered this terrible fate. The shock and horror was enough to relieve Dan of his breakfast and it was some time before he regained his composure and accepted the cup of water handed to him by a grim-faced Alf.

They waited long enough for the Irishman to bury his mutilated comrade under a pile of stones, sufficient to protect his body from further scavengers and resumed their journey in silent and somber mood. Alf believed that the fugitive had died by native hands but added that this was in no way related to any customary practice. It was most likely that the man had fired on and inflicted harm, if not death, on the hunting party and that this was a case of angry reprisal. The fate of the aboriginal tracker was unclear but Alf said that he would have been punished according to traditional law and that this might have involved being speared through the leg and suffering exile to a remote bush location. The surviving prisoner was in a state of holy terror and was more than relieved to be handed over to the Halls Creek constables and housed safely within the thick walls of the police lock up.

It took most of the afternoon to tell their story to the Police sergeant. The prisoner was only too willing to corroborate their account and due deference was paid to Alf's status as a fellow WA police Sergeant. Dan enjoyed a long hot soak in a hotel bath and then met Alf for a welcome beer in the bar. It was only then that the shock associated with the violent encounters caught up with him and his hand shook so much that he spilled his beer onto the bar counter. Alf was quick to see the sign and both experienced and wise enough not to pass comment. Instead he encouraged Dan to talk by asking questions that allowed the story to unfold at a pace comfortable to the teller. Alf had seen many men's reactions to violent death-some froze, some ran away screaming and worst of all some remained as calm as though nothing had happened only to lapse later into mania and even go on to shoot themselves.

Dan's account was lucid and detailed and as he spoke, the shakes began to subside and tears began to flow, especially when he came to the discovery of the mutilated body and blamed his self for maiming the man so that he was less able to make good his escape. Alf just listened and nodded assent but did not respond to Dan's plaintive questions

"Why can't I just live in peace? Will the violence and killing never end? Perhaps that poor bastard wouldn't have met such an awful fate if I hadn't hamstrung him and reduced his chance of outrunning the hunters?"

Then when he had said all that he could, Dan closed his eyes, slumped in his seat and sobbed until he could cry no more. When he was spent, the sympathetic barman, who had heard about their ordeal, topped up his beer adding a double whisky chaser on the house. When he was done, Alf took him by the arm, led him back to his room and saw him safely into bed. He had already taken the precaution of removing Dan's rifle and knife from the room on the pretext that the police needed them as evidence. Leaving the hotel, Alf walked to the edge of the town and out into the moonlit bush to deal with his own demons in his own time-honoured way. The trees stood out starkly in the ghostly light and he could feel the age and powerful spirit of the land but for him this was a comfort rather than a threat and he was not afraid.

They stayed in Halls Creek until all formalities were completed to the police's satisfaction. Messages had been sent to Inspector Wardle at Derby and in return the Inspector congratulated Alf and Dan on surviving the ambush and assured them there would be no adverse legal repercussions, especially in respect of the atrocity committed on the hapless Flynn, by persons unknown. A returning patrol, that had gone out to examine the ambush scene and retrieve the dead body, reported that all was in accord with Alf and Dan's account, but that the cairn of stones had been scattered and that there was no sign of the corpse nor its head. It was clear that this would end the police interest and that there could be no case against the alleged killers without there being a corpse.

Dan's secondment to the Police expedition was ended and the message from Derby thanked him and released him from this duty. When his inland route to the station diverged from the main road to Derby, he and

Alf said their goodbyes and turning for home, Dan wondered whether they would meet again. He rode on steadily looking forward to being with Liza and getting back to station life. After a mile he turned a bend and to his surprise and delight he came upon Archie and a party of his stockmen whom Liza had sent to ensure he got home unscathed.

30

The Peace of Home

The reunion of Dan and Liza was much happier and less reserved than their meeting on her arrival from Perth. They had so much news to share that they were unusually late to bed and yet they still found time and energy to make love with the abandon and passion of their Blackpool coupling but with the added tenderness and bond of commitment that came from more than just friendship and caring.

Within the month, they were married at the station. Elspeth and Bill flew Daniel up from Perth and telegraphed congratulations and love came from Charlie and Alice in Melbourne. The celebrations and feasting lasted several days and the tribesmen put on a special corroboree to honour the union of the Boss and his Missus.

Station life soon returned to its normal rhythm and all were focused on ensuring the new born calves were safely delivered and recorded as members of the herd. At last Dan felt that he was free from danger and that he could shake off his curse and live the life of peace he so dearly wished for. The station was very quiet when the stockmen were away and Dan was so confident of his men's ability to do the job without his constant oversight, he had agreed to Liza's urging that he stay back and spend some time with her. She craved for his company and also, suspected that he had not fully recovered from the shock of his recent ordeal and hoped he would rest for a while longer. After all, there hadn't been time for a proper honeymoon.

The days grew hotter and the land more parched as the dry season approached its end. Dan suggested that they make the most of the opportunity to camp out before the rains and swollen rivers restricted their freedom of movement. He felt the need for an energetic ride to shake up his sluggish system and as he wanted to check the level of water remaining in a nearby billabong he agreed to meet Liza at the mouth of a picturesque gorge where she would join him with a cart-load of supplies and camp gear.

Dan set out early intending to reach his destination before the full heat of the afternoon, when riding became too taxing for both horse and rider. To his satisfaction the billabong still held sufficient water to meet the needs of the cattle in that locality and just after noon he stopped for lunch and brewed a refreshing billy of tea. He was less troubled by flies and mosquitoes at this time of year and he settled so comfortably in the shade of an old guardian boab that he was soon fast asleep.

It had taken some time for him to accept that although he was alone in this vast wilderness, there was no threat of major predators and so long as he had sufficient food and water he was safe. But now he could relax and give in to his tiredness as readily as if he had been at home in his favourite chair. The sun was losing its heat and the shadows lengthening when he was jolted from the depths of a very pleasant dream, by the repetitive dripping of water onto his forehead. He knew it couldn't be rain and through his sleep rhymed eyes he could see the outline of someone standing between him and the sun. At first he thought Liza had come to play a trick on him but when he had brushed some of the moisture across his face to clear the stickiness from his eyes he saw that it was a man and that the drops had come from the canteen that the stranger was holding above Dan's head. He was slow to regain his wits and was not concerned until the man spoke.

"Top of the evening to you, Lieutenant Bevan, at last we meet face to face." The Irish accent caused his body to tense and his face gave way his alarm. *"Yes!"* The stranger drawled. *"You thought you had seen us all off but as you can see, they were the foot soldiers and you failed to kill their commander."*

Dan needed no introduction. At last his nemesis, the commander of the IRA unit in Cork had caught up with him and now he was at the Irishman's mercy.

"We should've done for you in Melbourne or Perth and but for that half-breed peeler and those heathen blacks we'd have topped you in the gorge. You've led me a merry dance and caused the death of some fine men. But now you're all mine and I am going to make you pay for that and especially for blowing up my brother. The question is should I kill you as slowly and painfully as I can or should I treat you as an officer and a gentleman by killing you cleanly with one shot between the eyes?"

Dan was in shock and very much afraid. In just a few minutes the peace that came from the belief that his trials had ended with the shoot-out in the gorge, was shattered by the realisation that the game was not over and that soon he could be on the losing side. Fear flooded his muscles with adrenalin but he was too stunned to move. He had no weapon close to hand. His rifle was in its holster on his horse and even if he could have palmed his knife, the Irishman's Luger pistol hovered just inches from his forehead. There was nothing he could do but try to hold off the indignity of wetting his pants and summon up sufficient courage to pretend he was not afraid to die. But stubbornness was in his nature and a show of defiance was his last resort.

"So, you cowardly bastard, after hiding behind your men for so long you have finally dared to face me and only then by creeping up on me when I was asleep, and unarmed. But then what could one expect from a murderer of innocent, unarmed men, women and even children!"

Dan could see that his thrust had hit home and punctured the Irishman's bravado.

"You should talk of murder." The gunman spat back. "You, who ambushed and blew up such a fine bunch of boys without warning or chance of escape."

Even in this perilous situation, Dan's conscience was pricked and he knew that the commander had a point but he was not going to admit it.

"That's rich." He retorted. "If they hadn't been so eager to rush and gloat over the carnage that our men would've suffered, had your culvert bomb not been detected and turned against yours, they wouldn't have been killed by their own trap."

This was too much for the man's pride. His face flushed and he lost all control. The crack of the pistol was deafening at such close quarters and Dan felt a searing pain in his left leg. The intended knee-capping shot, the IRA's trademark punishment, had missed its mark and gone through the fleshy part of his thigh. Dan's act of defiance had succeeded in destroying the gunman's composure but also, it had deprived him of any vestige of self-control.

"I was going to finish you quick and clean", he roared, "but now you'll get what you deserve – a slow, lingering end, shot by shot through your legs, arms and then your head."

Dan was writhing with pain and could barely hear what his tormentor was saying but he knew that even more agony was to come before the release of the final shot. When it came, the final shot was even more deafening and it reverberated off the canyon walls. Blood, bone splinters and slimy brain matter splattered across Dan's face and chest and the smell of cordite was his last sensation before he fell back and his mind collapsed into oblivion.

A group of riders, returning to the station, heard the shots and when they came on the scene they found Liza with a band of aboriginal hunters, keeping watch over the body, whose blood was still seeping from the huge hole that the point blank shot had blown in the victim's head. He was dead and with due care, but without ceremony, the stockmen wrapped the corpse in a horse blanket, tied it onto a pack mule and set off in solemn procession back to the station. The blacks stayed back a while before loping away into the bush, as suddenly as they had arrived at the scene of the shooting.

Dan had been brought back, washed clean of brain fluid and gore. He was laid out on the marital bed and Liza sat beside him keeping vigil. The foreman and others assured her there was nothing to be gained by sitting there so long and urged her to go and catch up on much needed sleep. She ignored them and such was her authority and their respect for the missus, they slipped away and left her to her lonely watch. Tough as she was, she lacked the youthful stamina of her war service days and whilst still holding Dan's cold hand, she fell asleep.

It was dark when she woke. The silent room was bathed in the soft light of a kerosene lamp which cast Liza's shadow over the bed and across Dan's face. She was cramped and aching from the uncomfortable position she had adopted on the hard wooden chair and was starting to stretch when she realised that pressure on her fingers had woken her up. She was no longer holding Dan's hand. His enclosed hers and was gently squeezing her fingers. Dan was back and very much alive.

She jumped up, shouted out the good news and seeing that his eyes were open, leaned across and kissed him tenderly on his forehead.

"Liza is that you"? He murmured, "Where am I? What happened?

"Welcome back my love, you've suffered a terrible shock and been unconscious for hours. But don't worry you're safe at home with me and nobody can hurt you anymore." She replied.

This seemed to calm him and closing his eyes he drifted back into a deep peaceful sleep.

Liza gets her man

Some hours later Dan awoke again. He was stiff and sore and when he tried to stir he felt the agonising pain of the gunshot wound in his leg.

The Peace of Home

Liza still sat by his bed as though she had never gone away, although the persistent ministrations of the station staff had finally prevailed and she had retreated to catch up on some sleep. They greeted each other tenderly before Dan asked her again what had happened and how had he been saved from torture and certain death.

Liza plumped his pillow, took his hand and began the tale of his deliverance.

"I decided to surprise you by arriving early at the meeting place and having a comfortable camp and welcoming fire ready for you. But when I heard the first shot, I unhitched one of the carriage horses and rode towards its source. I heard the shouting as the Irishman raved at you and tethering my horse, I crept up as close to you as I could. Then when he raised his pistol to shoot you again, I rushed forward, pressed a revolver to the back of his neck and blew a hole in his head."

The dying man had fallen forward onto Dan and when she saw his closed eyes and the blood on his face she feared that her shot had gone through the assassin and killed Dan. She was horrified and began to shake with fear and panic and it wasn't until a passing mob of hunters arrived, checked on Dan and assured her he was unconscious but alive, that she began to calm down and knelt to tend his wound and staunch the flow of blood from his leg.

"My God!" Dan gasped. *"Liza, it was you who saved me. But where did you get that gun and learn to shoot?"*

She laughed at his surprise and told him that wounded officers recuperating at field hospitals in France passed the time by shooting at bottles and cans and that some of the nurses and ambulance crews had joined in. The pistol she had used was Charlie's father's Colt which he had carried through the war and which he had entrusted to Liza when he brought her to the Kimberley to rejoin Dan. It was too powerful for her to shoot accurately at a distance but close up behind her unsuspecting target and using both hands she was able to fire the deadly shot.

She assured him that his troubles really were over. The killer was dead and his body on the way to the police at Derby. Dan's leg would be painful for a while but as the bullet had gone straight through the soft tissue, missing muscles and sinews, he would suffer no loss of mobility.

Dan was overwhelmed and could only voice his heart felt thanks and wonder at Liza's ruthless courage.

31

No More War

When word came from Perth that the Government in Canberra had called in the Irish ambassador and received his assurance that there would be no more trouble from IRA elements on Australian soil, Dan and Liza truly believed that they could now live in peace and focus on the normal challenges of running cattle in the top end.

Western Australia had been a late and reluctant member of the Australian federation and for a while, in the '30s, there was a concerted push for secession by the Dominion League and two thirds of WA voters said they preferred to leave the Commonwealth. Dan was pressed to run for state parliament but he had enough to do in keeping his business afloat, as the global financial depression caused mass unemployment in Australia's major cities and shrank international meat markets.

He was firmly planted in Kimberley soil and over the years he and Liza had developed equity in the station and by the late thirties they were equal partners with Charlie and Alice and had increased the size of their holding by acquiring stations from their less fortunate neighbours, who had not come through the tough times.

Alf Grommet had tired of police work and at Charlie's invitation and to Dan's delight he had come north to manage one of their outstations. He and Dan were able to get together to chat about old times over a malt or two when he came in on business.

Dan's war was finally over and although the civil strife in Spain and the rise of Hitler to Chancellor in Germany warned of European unrest, it all seemed so far away and no longer his concern. Daniel had qualified as a commercial pilot and having flown for several years with Bill's airline he was now one of its chief officers.

In 1938, despite the protests of his parents, he chose to head for England where to everyone's delight he called on the now ageing but still active Beattie and Arthur in Manchester. They were so happy that Dan and Liza had tied the knot and succeeded down under. They welcomed Daniel as though he were their grandson and whenever he flew into Ringway aerodrome he made a point of visiting them to indulge in one of Beattie's legendary steak and kidney puddings and listen to Arthur's tales of campaigning on the North West frontier.

Through his work in aviation Daniel had befriended some RAF pilots and on a balmy September day in 1939 he was invited to visit their squadron at its Biggin Hill base, where he hoped to get a glimpse of the revolutionary new fighter plane, the Spitfire. On this warm late summer's day he was crossing the tarmac apron outside the maintenance hangers when a ball plummeted towards him out of the sun. Although his game was Australian football, his father had ensured he had developed an appreciation for soccer and its skills. Positioning himself under the ball he trapped it with his foot and brought it under control, ready to pass to one of the surrounding pilots and ground crew who were playing a scratch game between their duties.

A round of applause and ribald calls of *"Good on yer cobber!"* confirmed that his effort had met the English airmen's approval and he was urged to join in. After the game he was invited for a drink in the pilots mess and when it came his turn to shout a round, a keenly awaited radio broadcast came over the amplified Tannoy system and reduced the noisy bar to silence.

Prime Minister Chamberlain came on the air to speak to the British people about his negotiations with Herr Hitler. In somber tones he announced that *"I am speaking to you from the Cabinet Room at 10 Downing Street. This morning the British Ambassador in Berlin handed the German Government a final note stating that, unless we hear from them by 11 o'clock that they were prepared at once to withdraw their troops from Poland, a state of war would exist between us. I have to tell you now that no such undertaking has been received, and that consequently this country is at war with Germany."*

Uproar broke out in the bar. Hats flew in the air, pilots cheered, embraced and one slapped Daniel on the back and shouted, *"Jolly good show. We're in it at last!"*

Despite their infectious enthusiasm and his sympathy with their cause, Daniel was not one of them. Slipping out of the building, he wandered away to the strains of 'land of hope and glory' wafting on the breeze and walked slowly towards his car and passing the hangers he was almost deafened by the roar of a Spitfire's Merlin engine revving at full throttle on its test bed.

All through his adolescent years, he had thrilled to the war stories of Bill and Charlie but his father had said nothing of those days and stressed only that peace and liberty were all that really mattered. He wondered what Dan and Liza would make of this declaration of war, the certainty that Australia would join in and his intention to join up to fight for freedom's cause.

The Kimberley Trilogy
Book 2

BATTLE FOR THE NORTH

Battle for the North reunites the heroes and heroines of *For Freedom's Cause* – Dan, Charlie, Elspeth Liza and Alice, in frustrating Japanese espionage plots and raids into northern Australia during World War II. The action takes place in the Kimberley wilderness and celebrates the daring and heroism of mounted North Australia Observer Unit patrols, nicknamed the 'Nackeroos' or 'Curtin's Cowboys'.

Following the bombing of Darwin and Broome, Japanese marine commandos land on the Kimberley coast to establish a foothold and deny the US and Australian navies a secure re-fuelling and supply base. With Australia's regular forces deployed in the Middle East and Singapore, all that stands between them and success is Dan Bevan's and Charlie Elliott's part-time observer patrols, which battle a Japanese special forces unit from Broome to their Kalumburu base and join the fight to push the enemy back into the sea.

Flight Captain Daniel Bevan returns from the Battle of Britain to join the air war over northern Australia and whilst Dan and Charlie conduct their guerrilla campaign in the bush, their wives and Lady Elspeth interrupt their war work in Darwin to thwart black market thugs and hunt down a murderous spy.

The Kimberley Trilogy
Book 3

KIMBERLEY KILL

Frustrated by its inability to acquire sufficient energy to power its ever expanding economy, China has invaded Russia, annexing the Siberian oil and gas fields and precipitating World War Three.

A key satellite communication base in the Kimberley is threatened by invading Indonesian special forces. All that stands in their way is a small Norforce patrol backed by an Aboriginal tribe, whose female leader is intent on avenging the murder of her father, their Elder, and the desecration of their Wandjina guardian.

Three strong-minded and determined people—the devout Muslim leader of the Indonesian Kopassus force, the MIT-trained daughter of an assassinated Aboriginal elder and the middle-aged, former SAS Anglo, gas platform engineer and part-time leader of the Norforce patrol—strive to assert and impose their conflicting beliefs and loyalties when they clash in a chase across the Kimberley wilderness.

VICTORIA'S TWINS

I am busy researching background for a book about two of the most significant cities of Queen Victoria's Empire as they emerged from modest beginnings and flourished during the turbulent years of the 19th century.

Gritty Manchester and Marvellous Melbourne experienced the growth in their economies, politics, societies, cultures, infrastructure, media and sport that led to their becoming today's large, influential, internationally famous and vibrant metropolises. As well as one being my birthplace and the other my home, they have much in common and are surprisingly complementary.

Both are home to world famous liberal leaning newspapers and their cities stories are told through the eyes of two of their most illustrious and campaigning editors.

This book will be available in late 2016.

About the Author

BARRY SMITH
Was born in England and educated in Manchester and at Cambridge University, where he read history. Australia has been home for over fifty years and he lives in marvellous Melbourne, where he is now living his dream of being a published writer.

Most of Barry's career has been in HR management and for 20 years before retirement he ran his own consulting business, focusing on turning around toxic management teams. Since retiring he has completed a doctorate focused on *"How I want to live and work in what's left of my life"* and over the past 10 years he has pursued dreams emanating from that – such as, crossing Siberia, touring Moorish Spain, finding his Manchester Regiment, Grandad's grave at Gallipoli, crossing USA by train and camp touring around Australia, carrying out research for and selling his Kimberley Trilogy of historical novels, in pubs and on outdoor markets from Cooktown to Broome and back.

Books about his travels – *Wordspinner's Way*, *My Russian Dreamroad*, *My Spanish Dreamroad* and *My American Dreamrailroad* – recount and illustrate with photographs and 'Brysonesque' commentary, Barry's travels around Australia, selling books in pubs and on markets, living in St Petersburg and crossing Siberia, touring Moorish Andalusia and railroading across the USA from sea to shining sea and back. These can be ordered from Blurb at au.blurb.com.

You can follow Barry's further musings and adventures on Facebook at www.facebook.com/BarrySmithWordSpinner.

www.ingramcontent.com/pod-product-compliance
Ingram Content Group UK Ltd.
Pitfield, Milton Keynes, MK11 3LW, UK
UKHW021329180426
11947UKWH00017B/1530